NO JOKE

NO JOKE

BILL NOEL

ISBN: **978-1-937979-57-7**

Enigma House Press
Goshen, Kentucky
www.enigmahousepress.com

Chapter One

Have you ever seen a stranger and knew, at first glance, that something was wrong? Could it have been the vacant look in his eyes? Or was it the long, wool coat he was wearing over red swim trunks and black patent leather shoes? Maybe it was the seven-foot-long fishing rod he was flinging around over his head like a drum major's baton. And, oh yeah, did I mention he was standing in heavy traffic in the middle of Center Street?

I hadn't noticed any of this until squealing tires and honking horns drew my attention away from gazing in the window of Avocet Properties to the man weaving around the stopped cars while their drivers hurled profanities at him as they came inches from running him down.

He swung the fishing rod at the closest vehicle, encouraging the exasperated driver to maneuver around the gentleman to escape the wrath of the weapon.

I looked around and didn't see anyone moving to save the confused fisherman.

I stepped off the curb, waved for two oncoming vehicles to

stop, then sidled up to the stranger. I ducked away from the flailing rod that seemed to have a mind of its own and said, "Could I be of assistance?"

A pickup truck going the other direction zoomed past. The truck's horn blasted; the driver gave us a one-finger wave. At least he hadn't hit us.

The five-foot six-inch tall, thin, mid-seventies rod waver looked at me, blinked twice, and lowered the weapon.

I put my arm around his bony shoulder. Instead of waiting for him to answer, I nudged him to the curb and pointed for him to sit on a rocking chair under the awning of the real estate office.

"Nice fishing rod. Could I see it?" I asked, hoping to get it out of his trembling hand.

He looked at his hand like he was seeing the piece of sporting equipment for the first time. He handed it to me and looked at the street where he'd come so close to being roadkill.

I took the rod and leaned it against the chair on the other side of the stranger.

He shook his head like he was shaking cobwebs out. "Thank you, kind sir, for retrieving me from yon street. May I have your moniker?"

During my sixty-nine years, I'd never been asked that question, yet I assumed he wanted my name.

"Chris Landrum," I said. "And you are?"

He leaned forward then glanced at his fishing rod. "I'm Wallace, umm, Wallace Bentley." He reached to shake my hand.

"Pleased to meet you, Mr. Bentley."

"Call me Wallace." He chuckled. "All my friends, and strangers who save me from getting squashed, call me that."

"Do you live on Folly?"

The temperature was in the mid-seventies, but he pulled

his heavy coat around him like he was freezing. He closed his eyes. For a moment, I thought he'd fallen asleep, until his eyes shot open. "Folly … Folly Beach." He rubbed his tongue along his front teeth. "Can't say that I do, Mr. Landrum, Chris. I'm here with friends."

I waited for him to continue. He didn't, so I said, "Friends?"

He looked toward the beach. "Didn't know ocean water was so cold this time of year."

"Sure is. You say you're here with friends. Who are they?"

"Guess that's why surfers wear those skin-tight, black trash bags."

Okay, forget the friends' names. How to reunite him with them was becoming more important. "Wallace, where're your friends?"

"Marvin, he goes by Pete; Salvador, who prefers Sal; Raymond, who prefers Ray. My departed wife, God rest her soul, and I call him Son."

I was beginning to have second thoughts about having rescued the irrational, deranged, or nutty gentleman sharing the rocking chairs with me. I took a deep breath and pretended like we were having a sane conversation.

"Are those your friends?"

"There's one more. I have trouble remembering his name. He's not a friend. He's Sal's brother. That's where we're staying."

I looked around, hoping someone would arrive to collect Wallace.

Several people walked past; none appeared interested.

I didn't blame them, but I couldn't leave him here in his confused state.

He snapped his finger and brought me out of my wish to

beam myself anywhere but on this bench. "Got it." He sat back and smiled.

"Got what?"

"Sal's brother's name. Something like Humidor or Thermador." He smiled like that explained everything.

"Like the thing you keep tobacco in, or like the kitchen appliances?"

"Chris, it is Chris, right?"

I nodded.

"You're not making a lick of sense."

Pot calling the kettle black popped into my head. I'd run out of words to share with my new acquaintance.

Wallace said, "Sal's brother, he's a guy who lives down that street that has the river in its back yard."

"Theodore Stull?"

I had retired to Folly Beach, a small, quirky, South Carolina barrier island ten years ago, where I'd received numerous lessons from my equally quirky friends on how one plus one seldom equals two.

"Bingo."

I'd met Theodore Stull a couple of years ago when I joined his walking group. For those who think walking is healthy, I'd respond with five words: It nearly got me killed. Theo, as he preferred to be called, came closer than I had to meeting his Maker because of the group. But that's a story for another time.

"Are your friends at Theo's house?"

Please, please say yes, I thought so I could deliver him to them. Theo lived a short walk from where we were sitting.

"Hear about the dead body?"

Not the answer I was looking for. "What dead body?"

"The one at the beach."

"Tell me about it."

"Sal's seventy-nine, that's years younger than Theo. Do you know Theo?"

I wondered if anyone would notice if I smacked him with a fishing rod.

"Yes, I know Theo. What about a body at the beach?"

"Dead body."

"Did you see a body?"

"That's what I'm trying to tell you, young man."

"Where was it?" Folly Beach had six miles of ocean beachfront, so I hoped he would narrow it down.

"Hard to tell. I don't know much about your island. Just got here a few days ago. Seeing a dead body had a distracting impression on me."

He could say that again.

"When did you see it?"

"Sal thought Theo was losing his mind. He wanted to be here for his brother. That's why we're staying with him."

One more time. "When did you see the body?"

"Must've been today."

"What time did—"

"Could've been yesterday."

I was ready to pull my hair out although, since I was a few hairs shy of bald, I would have to do it figuratively.

"So, you're not certain—"

"I know." He snapped his fingers. "It was January 20, four years ago. Remember it well. That guy, what's-his-name, was sworn in as president. I'll never understand why. Yes, sir, that was the day."

Chapter Two

Seconds before I started screaming, a City of Folly Beach patrol car cruised past, and I recognized the driver. Allen Spencer was new on the force the year I'd moved from Middle America. We had numerous conversations over the years. I watched him grow from a young, green beat cop to one of Folly's most experienced law enforcement officials.

He looked my way and nodded.

I waved for him to stop, and he pulled around the corner of the real estate building.

"Hey, Chris, wonderful day, isn't it?" Allen said as he approached the chairs and looked at my new acquaintance.

"Great day, Officer Spencer. Have you met Wallace Bentley?"

Allen moved in front of Wallace and held out his hand. "Don't believe I have. I'm Allen Spencer."

Wallace didn't make eye contact but shook Allen's hand.

The officer focused on the fishing rod. "Going fishing, Wallace?"

Wallace looked over at the pole. "I'm a friend of Sal."

I interrupted their disjointed conversation before it went further off the rails. "Officer Spencer, have a second? I've got a question about the new parking rules on East Arctic."

He looked at me like he had no idea what I was talking about, a look well-founded. I'd made it up. Regardless, he said, "Sure."

I stood. "Wallace, wait here. I'll be back."

I took Allen by the elbow and walked around the corner.

"What stray have you picked up now?"

"Allen, I didn't want to say anything in front of him. Let me tell you what I know."

I proceeded to tell Allen about escorting the oddly-attired man from the center of the street and who he'd said he was visiting. I shared Wallace's story about seeing a dead body at the beach. I'd learned, over the years, that Allen listened to what I had to say, regardless how strange or farfetched it may sound.

I asked if there'd been a report of a death or missing person.

He said there was none he was aware of. Although, it didn't mean much, since there were so many visitors to the island it could be days before someone would've been reported missing.

Allen fiddled with his black leather duty belt then took a deep breath. "Do you put credence in his story?"

"Hard to tell. He had me convinced until he couldn't remember if he'd seen the body today, yesterday, or four years ago. He slipped in and out of reality."

"Sounds like he may need a transport to the psych ward."

"Not yet. He appears harmless. If it's okay, I'll walk him to Theo's to see if his brother's there."

"First, let me see if I can do any better with him."

I smiled. "Have at it."

We returned to Wallace and to a continuation of his story which was as odd as his attire.

I told Wallace I'd shared what he'd said about seeing a body.

Wallace told Allen he had but was confused about when.

I thought it was a major understatement, since his time of the sighting ranged from three hours to the lifespan of a hedgehog.

Wallace seemed to return to the real world when he started describing where he was staying and who he was with. He laughed when Allen said something about Theo being part of a walking group started by another of my friends, Chester Carr. Members of the group called Theo ET which, instead of a comparison to the cute alien from another planet in the old movie by the same name, it meant Energizer Turtle because of Theo's slow pace.

Wallace responded by saying, "That boy's as slow as a turkey trottin' to Thanksgiving dinner."

Allen tried once more to pin down a more accurate time on when Wallace had allegedly seen a body. He was no more successful than I'd been. He looked at me and shrugged.

"Tell you what, Officer Spencer, why don't I walk Wallace to Theo's house? If we can get a better fix on when he saw the body, I'll give you a call?"

Allen turned to Wallace. "That okay with you?"

It was better than him saying, "Is that okay?" or "Would you rather I take you to a padded room in nearby Charleston?"

Wallace agreed with the plan.

Before Allen headed to his patrol car, he said, "You will call me if you learn anything about a body." It wasn't a question.

We started the three-block walk to Theo's. Wallace's gait was quicker than his host, although not much.

Theo owned a large, two-story, elevated home that overlooked the marsh and the Folly River. His two-year old Mercedes was in the drive, so I assumed he was home, or hoped so. My luck continued when Theo opened the mahogany front door. He'd made a fortune after inventing a replacement-window system filled with an exotic energy-saving gas. He'd sold the business to a national window replacement company for several million dollars then moved to Folly. Instead of appearing like a multi-millionaire, most of the time Theo looked homeless. At five-foot-eight, he was a couple of inches shorter than me, had an equal amount of exposed scalp, and looked older than his mid-eighties. He wore a USS Yorktown ball cap, black knee-high support socks and blue jogging shorts. One vestige of his earlier success was his white, button-down dress shirt. The collar and cuffs were frayed, but the shirt had been custom made to fit his trim frame.

Theo looked at Wallace then at me. "Chris, good to see you. I see you met Wallace. What brings you out?"

I started to answer when he added, "Sorry, I'm being rude. Come in."

Theo said it like there was nothing unusual about seeing Wallace standing at the door, sweat running down his cheeks from wearing a wool topcoat in seventy-degree weather, while carrying a fishing rod. We followed Theo to the great room where he had a panoramic view of the Folly River from floor to ceiling windows.

Theo looked up like he was speaking to the heavens, and yelled, "Hey, Sal. Wallace is here."

Theo motioned for us to sit on his oversized latte-colored couch. I heard someone coming down the stairs.

"Well, well, well," boomed the loud voice of the newcomer to the room. "My good friend, Wallace, returns."

Theo said, "Chris, meet my brother, Salvador."

"Call me Sal," said the man whom Theo claimed to be his brother. I say claimed because Sal didn't look or sound anything like Theo. The man who walked over and shook my hand was several years younger and at least five inches taller than Theo. He had long, gray hair, wore black, wide-rimmed glasses that looked like they came off the pages of a style magazine—a magazine from the 1950s. In contrast to Theo's dress shirt, Sal had on an open collar, red and blue striped shirt that would have been at home in a lounge singer's closet, and like the glasses, a closet in the '50s.

"Chris," boomed Sal, "see you met my good buddy, Wallace." He hesitated then chuckled. "You don't have to make a fool out of Wallace. He does it all by himself."

That was a line I didn't want to touch. I didn't have to.

"Chris," Theo said, "Salvador is a stand-up comedian. Done it most of his adult life."

"Adult, huh," Wallace said.

"And so is Wallace," Theo added. "In fact, I have four house guests. All of them make a living in the world of comedy. Wallace's son, Raymond, and another of their friends, Marvin Peters, are somewhere on the island having—"

"Having too many beers," Sal interrupted, "hittin' on some of your charming Southern belle barmaids."

"Now, Sal," Theo said, "you don't know that."

Wallace looked at me. "See why I had to get out of the house?"

That was the sanest thing he'd said since I herded him out of the street.

I looked at Wallace and Sal. "How long will you be visiting?"

"A while," Sal said, clarifying nothing.

Theo elaborated. "They're taking a respite from touring. They've been on the road for a long time."

"How long you ask?" Sal asked and answered, "We started traveling around the country with Daniel Boone. That coon-skinned cap guy couldn't tell a joke if his life depended on it but was a hell of an injun fighter."

If that was as funny as his show, a respite was long overdue.

"We started doing comedy in 1965," Wallace said.

Since he'd said he saw a body either today or four years ago, I wasn't ready to put faith in the year they started.

Theo said, "I believe that is correct, isn't it, Sal?"

Sal must have been running low on jokes. He nodded.

"Nap time," Wallace said, related to nothing.

I took the hint. "Guys, it was nice meeting you. I'd better be running."

Sal said, "Likewise." Wallace yawned.

Theo said he'd walk me out.

I nudged Theo to the front porch, closed the door so Wallace and Sal couldn't hear, then told Theo what'd happened.

He shook his head. "Remember when we first met?"

"Sure."

"Some of my, our, friends thought I was getting Alzheimer's because I seemed to forget things."

I said I remembered.

"Truth be known, it was because I couldn't hear. I was too stubborn to get hearing aids."

When I met Theo, if anyone wanted him to hear what they were saying, they had to speak in a voice the decibel level of Niagara Falls. After two harrowing experiences where he nearly got killed, he decided the electronic aid to his hearing might be a good idea.

"Yes."

"After I almost got killed then got off my high, stubborn, horse and got these, everything changed." He pointed to his hearing aids.

Interesting, but nothing I didn't know.

"There are two reasons I'm telling you this. First, Sal thinks I'm losing my mind. All he remembered before showing up at my door last week was the phone conversations we had before I got the aids. I couldn't hear him. I had to guess what he was talking about. That's not easy to do because he tends to talk comedy, jokes, weird things.

"Anyway, he has a bigger heart than he shows, and came to make sure I was okay. That's the reason he gave. It may be true, although I'm guessing it's more than that. I don't think they've worked in years, except maybe Wallace's son. He makes regular appearances at clubs and on TV. They came bumming free rooms. They don't think I know. Understand?"

I did, but suspected there was more. "You said two things."

"They're worried about Wallace. As you can tell, his mind wanders from sharp to *huh?* They believe that if he can get settled somewhere for more than a few days, he may not have as many distractions. He can concentrate on seeing things better."

That didn't make much sense. "Do you think it'll work?"

"Probably not."

I shared what Wallace told me about a body, then asked if Theo thought Wallace actually saw one.

"In his mind, he did. In reality, who knows."

I didn't want to call Allen with that analysis, yet knew I'd better. I owed him that much for letting me take Wallace to

Theo's. I called when I got home to share what little I'd learned after returning Wallace to his temporary residence.

Allen said it sounded like Wallace might need more psychological help than the others with him could provide. If I thought he didn't appear to be harmful to himself or others, it was okay to let Wallace stay. I thanked him for caring.

"Chris, I told Chief LaMond what your new acquaintance said about a body."

Chief Cindy LaMond and I had been friends since she arrived nine years ago from East Tennessee. She was promoted two years back to chief, or Director of Public Safety, of the Folly Beach Department of Public Safety. For reasons that defied explanation and beat all odds, I'd been involved in several murder investigations since arriving on the island. That would've made sense if my career was in law enforcement.

I'd spent a better—some might say best—part of my life being a tiny cog in the bureaucratic wheel of a large, health-care company in Kentucky. After moving to Folly, I'd owned a modest photo gallery, which didn't defy the odds and, like eighty-percent of small businesses, went belly-up a year ago. I had no business being involved in crimes, much less murder, but when my friends were touched by evil, I felt the need to get involved. Cindy was a part of some of the cases and had proclaimed me as being a murder-magnet; not the legacy I desired to perpetuate.

I sighed. "What did she say?"

Allen chuckled. "I won't tell you what the chief said. It was laced with four letter words."

"Don't suppose love was one of them?"

"She mumbled so many so fast, I could've missed it but I don't think so."

"Figures."

"Tell you what she did do. She said while she didn't think

there was a speck of truth to what the delusional fishing-rod waver told us, to be safe, she sent a couple of our guys to walk the dunes. Unless a body is out in the open, I doubt they'll find anything. We're short-handed, so they only had a short time to check."

"Good," I said. "It's an effort. Thanks for following up."

Chapter Three

The following morning, I walked next door to Bert's Market for a danish and a cup of complimentary coffee. It wasn't the breakfast of champions, but my chances of becoming the champion of anything were long gone. Bert's was a must-visit location for locals and vacationers in need of food, drink, and the necessities of island life, such as toilet paper, beer, and gossip. The grocery prided itself on never closing. To me, it met the meaning of *if they don't have it, you don't need it.*

I was sipping coffee and talking to a couple of employees who always had a smile plus an occasional bit of information about what was happening to share with customers on the six-mile long, half-mile wide island. Our conversation was interrupted by Charles Fowler.

"Chris, see you're bummin' coffee," Charles said as he winked at the employees.

His use of the word bummin' fell under the definition of irony when spoken by Charles. I met the long-time resident my first week on Folly. For reasons I couldn't articulate, we became best friends. He *retired* to the island at the age of thirty-four, after a less-than-illustrious career on the line at Ford in Detroit, and a few years working for a landscape company where he'd proudly bragged that he'd been a hoer.

He was a couple of years younger than I, more than a few pounds lighter. While I'd been spending thousands of hours a year working, he'd spent an equal number of hours perfecting unemployment. When I opened the photo gallery, Charles appointed himself executive sales manager. Since I'd never paid him, I was glad to let him wear the inflated title.

Bert's employees said they needed to get to work and left Charles and me to do whatever.

He watched them go behind the deli counter. "Rumor is that you've been playing school crossing guard on Center Street."

"Where'd you hear that?"

"Tell you one thing, I didn't hear it from you."

Charles was one of the island's repositories of rumor, fact, and trivia. Two things irritated him more than should bother a rational person. Unless you wanted to hear an earful of nasty, don't call him Chuck, Charlie, or any derivative of Charles, and if you know something that he would deem important, you'd better not dally telling him. I often practiced that second irritant.

"Who told you?"

He huffed. "Amber. She heard it from Marc Salmon, who heard it from—"

Amber was a waitress at the Lost Dog Cafe who knew as much as or more than Charles about the goings-on on the island. Marc was a long-term city councilmember who was in the Dog nearly as often as Amber.

"Got it, that's enough. Did you know Theo Stoll has a brother?"

Charles pulled his shoulders back. "Sure, Salvador. Theo told me a while back that his younger brother was a stand-up comic, had been big back in the heyday of stand up. Why?"

"Did you know Salvador is staying with Theo?"

Charles tilted his head like he was thinking about it. "Is that who was fishing in the street?"

Finally, I knew something that Charles didn't know. "No, it was Wallace Bentley. He—"

"What's that got to do with Theo and Sal?"

Several customers converged on the area where we were standing.

"Grab coffee and let's walk."

Charles got a cup.

I refilled mine and led him up the long block to Center Street then right toward the Folly River.

We'd walked a block before Charles began to pester me about what I knew about Theo and his brother. He would've started the questions sooner but had been distracted by a couple walking two Labs. Four-legged creatures were one of the few things that could distract my friend from zeroing in on whatever he wanted to know.

We crossed Center Street and were standing in front of City Hall when Charles pointed at the sidewalk. "Park it, and tell me what herding a fisherman out of the street has to do with Theo and Sal."

The Devil was not in the details to Charles, although he'll bestow the wrath of the Devil on anyone who didn't share all the details. I began with finding Wallace in the street then, after a couple of dozen questions, managed to finish by telling him I escorted Wallace to Theo's house. He wouldn't be satisfied until he knew the color of Wallace's bathing suit, if his shoes were slip on or lace up, and if I knew the brand of fishing rod.

I tried to explain how Wallace seemed to confuse reality with fantasy.

"Don't we all?" Charles asked.

No, I thought and shrugged.

I saved the part about Wallace seeing a body for last. If I'd mentioned it earlier, the conversation would've gone in a different direction. I never would've finished the story.

Charles's eyes bulged. He put his hands on his hips and glared at me. "He said what?"

I repeated what Wallace had said, emphasizing the part about Wallace not knowing if he'd seen it yesterday, the day before, or four years ago.

"How're we going to find it?"

Years ago, Charles decided he was a private detective. He had no formal training, had never been a police officer, yet figured that since he'd been a lifelong reader of detective novels, he knew everything there was to know about the profession. The scary thing was that, over the last decade, he, a cadre of our pals, and I had solved several crimes that had stumped the police.

"You mean the alleged body that had been somewhere along some beach between one day to four years ago?"

"That's the one."

I rolled my eyes.

He looked at his phone. "Whoops. I'm supposed to deliver something for Dude."

Dude Sloan owned the surf shop and had Charles deliver packages to local customers. That, along with helping restaurants clean during busy spells, and providing an extra set of hands for local contractors, provided Charles with enough income to afford his tiny apartment and minimal living expenses.

He turned and started to walk to the surf shop when my

phone rang. Charles's nosy factor kicked in. He stopped, then reversed direction.

"Hi, Theo," I said.

Charles leaned closer.

"Sure, what time?"

Charles had no idea what I was talking about but pointed to his chest.

I took the hint. "Can Charles come?"

Charles smiled and nodded.

Theo said, "Could I stop him?"

"No."

I looked at Charles. "Theo's house, noon, tomorrow."

Charles gave a bigger nod as he headed to the surf shop.

Chapter Four

I was in front of Theo's a half hour before the time he asked us over. Charles considered on-time thirty minutes before those of us who pay attention to watches define as on-time. My friend is not constrained by owning a watch, seldom checks the time on his cell phone, yet his altered reality prevails. And, no, it does no good to argue with him. It's easier to adjust to his time.

An older model, silver Lincoln Town Car land yacht was parked behind Theo's Mercedes. Charles jogged up the street, stopped in front of me, panted, and put his hands on his knees.

"You're almost late," I said.

"Nope. Didn't want to keep Theo waiting."

Theo wasn't as familiar with Charles's time-altered universe; he acted surprised to see us on the porch.

"Oh," he said and looked at his watch. "I didn't expect you this early."

Charles said, "We're not ear——"

"Got here quicker than I thought we would," I interrupted

before Charles got into a time-wasting discussion about time. "We can come back later."

Theo stepped back, waved us in. "No, no, that's fine. Not sure the others are up."

I didn't see anyone else on the first floor but heard sounds from a television coming from upstairs.

Theo motioned for us sit on the couch in the great room then asked if we wanted coffee. We declined.

He looked at the stairs, joined us on the couch, and whispered, "It's good that I caught you alone. The whole crew will be here this morning. They said they wanted to meet you."

That seemed strange since I'd already met Sal and Wallace.

Charles said, "I'd like to meet your brother and his friends."

That was no surprise since one of Charles's unmet needs was to meet each living soul on earth, plus visitors from other planets who might stumble on earth during their space travels.

Theo bit his upper lip and glanced at the stairs. "Also, wanted to tell you something about Wallace. Chris got a hint when he brought him back yesterday. Charles, Wallace sort of loses touch with reality." Theo shook his head.

Sort of loses touch, I thought. Delusional would better describe him.

Charles said, "Oh."

"Sal told me it's been coming on for years. Said, at first, it was funny. His friends thought it was part of Wallace's act, except it kept getting worse; he did it all the time, not just on stage."

I said, "Has he seen anyone about it?"

"Chris, he's seventy-five. Men his age," Theo tilted his head. "Umm, men his age, and my age, think it's a sign of weakness to get head-doc help. He hasn't and flat out won't. Sal says Wallace is harmless, the group keeps an eye on him."

Keeps an eye on him like when he was nearly run down in the street. "I hope they're right. He could've been killed yesterday."

"I know. I wanted to ask you to be patient with him. He might not remember what happened. He might not recognize you."

I nodded.

"Think he saw a body?" Charles asked.

Theo looked at the stairs again. "Depends on how close he was to reality at the time. You understand, I barely know him. From what I've seen, I'd give it a fifty-fifty chance. There's something else you need to know. Wallace's son, Raymond is, how shall I say it, he's not personable."

Charles leaned close to Theo. "Meaning?"

Theo lowered his voice so low that I hardly heard him. "He's rude, obnoxious."

"Meaning?" Charles repeated.

"Didn't rude and obnoxious cover it?"

The sound of someone coming down the stairs kept Theo from elaborating.

Sal hit the bottom step, turned toward the couch, and smiled. He wore another colorful, open-collar shirt, black slacks, with untied boat shoes on sockless feet. "Well, if it isn't one of my old brother's only friends. I bet you're Chucky, the bum-looking buddy."

I took a step toward Sal, ostensibly, to shake his hand, but more to be between Charles—Chucky—and Sal so my friend couldn't attack.

"Good to see you again, Carl," Sal said as he grabbed my hand.

I faked a smile. "It's Chris. Good to see you."

Charles moved beside me and reached out for Sal's hand. "And I'm *Charles*."

"Whatever. Glad to see you. Theo says you're a crime-fighting duo. Something about you catch killers before the police figure it out."

"I wouldn't say that. We're—"

Charles interrupted. "Yes, we are."

"You helped save my bro's life a while back," Sal said.

"Theo was the real hero," I said. "He figured out who the killer was and—"

"And was seconds from an untimely trip to meet my Maker," Theo interrupted. "Enough ancient history. I told the guys you'd be stopping by."

"Yeah," Sal said. "He wants you to meet the rest of his houseguests. Don't know why, the rest of them are pretty unlikable."

After Sal's underwhelming greeting, and him thinking that the rest of the crew was unlikable, I wondered how we could get out of the house. The sounds of someone clomping down the steps stopped Sal before he could insult us further.

"Good morning, Wallace," Theo said, as the latest arrival made his way over. He had on a light-blue nurses' scrub top over red and white checkered pajama pants.

Wallace said, "We have visitors?" He wiped his eyes before glancing from Charles to me.

"You remember Chris," Theo said as he patted me on the shoulder. "You met him yesterday. And this is my friend, Charles." He put his other hand on Charles's arm.

Wallace blinked in the direction of Charles, then turned to me. "Can't say I remember. Were you at my show?"

Theo saved me. "Chris met you in town. He brought you to the house."

"Oh," Wallace said, apparently not convinced.

Two more men had made their way down the stairs while Wallace shared his confusion.

Theo said, "Here's the rest of the crew."

"Hi, gentlemen. I'm Marvin Peters, but prefer Pete Marvin."

He, like Sal and Wallace, was in his mid to late seventies, average height, bald, and unlike the others, chubby. From the muscle turned to flab in his forearms, he could've been a weightlifter in earlier times.

Charles and I introduced ourselves as the person we hadn't yet met walked past us on his way to the kitchen.

"That's Ray," Theo said and gave me a sideways look like he was reminding me about the rude, obnoxious one.

Pete started to say something when Ray returned carrying a cup of coffee. He looked to be about fifty, five-foot eleven, and movie-star handsome. It was clear that he got his looks from his mother.

"Who are you again?" he asked, not caring that he interrupted Pete.

We hadn't said who we were in the first place. I let it go and told him our names.

"Why are you disturbing our peaceful morning?"

"They're friends," Theo said. "Remember when we were talking yesterday? You said you would like to meet them since you weren't here when they brought Wallace back? I asked them to stop by this morning."

"Must have been Pete. I wasn't paying attention to what you were yakking about."

Wallace said, "Theo was telling us that they had a friend who owns a country music bar who may let us do our act there."

Wallace had been closer to reality than last night, yet he didn't remember me bringing him back. Strange.

"Sorry, Chris and Charles," Theo said, and waved for us to return to the couch. "That wasn't the reason I wanted you to meet the group. You've been nice to me from the day we met, can't say the same for everyone. I wanted my new acquaintances to meet you. Sure you don't want coffee?"

The phone in the kitchen rang, and Theo left to answer it.

Sal watched him go and leaned closer to Charles and me. "Glad we have a few seconds without." He nodded toward the kitchen. "The reason I'm here is I've been worried about Theo. We haven't talked often. The last couple of years when I called, he sounded out of it. He couldn't remember much of anything." He waved his hand toward his friends. "We had a break from touring, so I wanted to get over and help. Theo has money. I didn't want anyone taking advantage of him."

"How's he been since you've been here?" I asked.

Ray interrupted, "Old and stuffy."

"A gentleman, a true gentleman," Pete said, as he gave Ray a dirty look.

Sal flipped the back of his hand at Ray like he was flicking away a mosquito. "I don't understand it. He seems fine. Don't know what's going on."

Theo returned. "You talking about me again?"

"Nah. We were saying that since Chris and Charles are here, we'd ask if their friend, Hal, would hire us to do our act in his bar." He turned to me. "Of course, we've performed in large venues all over the country, entertained thousands. We'd like to get back to our roots, you know, intimate venues, closer to our adoring fans. We have all the money we need, so Hal wouldn't have to pay the fees we're accustomed to. Of course, we couldn't work for free. You understand, don't you?"

I glanced at Charles, who leaned back on the couch and folded his arms. Thanks, friend.

"It's Cal, not Hal," I said. "I don't know if he'd be interested. We'll ask."

"I can still picture that SRO crowd in Chicago, Sal," Wallace said. "Tuesday, wasn't it?"

Charles leaned my direction. "SRO means standing room only."

I whispered, "I know."

Sal patted Wallace's back. "Wallace, I believe that was a couple of years back."

Ray blurted, "Dammit, stupid. Join us on planet earth."

Wallace turned to me. "That's my charming son."

I nodded.

Theo said, "I know you two must run, so we won't keep you. I wanted you to meet my guests."

I didn't know we had to run but understood why. Theo was giving us an out. We apologized for having to leave so quickly and said it was nice meeting Theo's friends—Ray excluded. That remained unsaid.

Theo and, for some reason, Wallace walked us to the door.

I took the opportunity to ask, "Have you thought more about the body you saw on the beach?"

Wallace rubbed his chin. "Body?"

I reminded him what he'd said about seeing a dead body. I omitted the multi-year window.

"I said that?"

"Yes."

"Sorry, fine sir. I don't recall that."

Charles looked down as I said goodbye to Wallace and Theo.

As we walked away, Charles said, "Wow, let's do that again. I didn't know comedians could be so funny."

Right, I thought, along with, *Did Wallace see a body?*

Chapter Five

I was to meet Barb Deanelli for supper at Loggerhead's Beach Grill, located across the street from her oceanfront condo. She owned Barb's Books, a used bookstore located on Center Street in the space that had housed my unsuccessful photo gallery. We'd been dating for less than a year.

It was warm for April, so I took a seat on the restaurant's elevated deck and watched for her crossing West Arctic Avenue. I had acquired some of Charles's habits through osmosis. While not a full half-hour early, I arrived at the restaurant before the time we were to meet, enjoyed the warm breeze pushing in from the ocean less than a half block away, and talked to Becca, one of Loggerhead's servers.

Within a minute of the appointed time, Barb gracefully walked across the street. She was my height, much thinner, with short, black hair, and wore linen slacks and one of her several red blouses. She saw me leaning against the railing, waved and, seconds later, arrived at the table and gifted me a smile and a peck on the cheek. She asked if I'd been waiting long.

Not wanting to be accused of being Charles-in-waiting, I stretched the truth, saying that I'd just arrived.

Becca returned, and we each ordered a glass of wine. Barb added a conch fritters appetizer.

Barb watched the server leave, shrugged, and said, "What can I say? I'm starved."

She was four years younger than I, yet her metabolism was that of a twenty-year-old marathon runner. She never gained weight. I hated her for it.

After the traditional winter lull that affected most businesses on the island, vacationers had begun arriving, and Barb's Books reaped the benefits. The downside was that I hadn't seen her as often as I would've liked. I wish I could've said that about business when I owned the gallery.

Our drinks arrived.

Barb took a sip and said, "I hear that a, and I quote, 'stupid ass local' ran in the middle of traffic on the busiest street in town to escort a 'funny looking guy flailing a fishing pole' to the sidewalk." She took another sip.

Barb had moved here from Pennsylvania a little over a year ago, and had already learned how to accumulate gossip and an occasional fact with some of Folly's better practitioners of the art.

I grinned. "Where'd you hear that?"

"Sorry, bookstore owner, book-buyer privilege."

I reminded her that she was no longer practicing law, and that I doubted that there was any such privilege.

"Maybe not. The more important question, was it true?"

Becca delivered the conch fritters.

Barb stuffed one in her mouth, gracefully, of course, and I proceeded to share the entire Theo, Wallace et al. story.

Barb didn't interrupt, something I wasn't accustomed to from my other friends. When I finished, she asked, "Is Sal anything like his brother?"

It wasn't what I'd expected her to say, although it made sense. Barb was my friend, Dude Sloan's half-sister, and they were less alike than a turnip to a trampoline. Dude was an aging hippie stuck in the 1960s, had never met a sentence that he couldn't mangle, while Barb had been a successful attorney with the ability to use the English language as it was intended. I shared that Sal was different than his brother, although not as different as Barb was from Dude.

"Think he saw a dead body?"

"Good question. He could have, although his credibility tanked when he couldn't decide when he'd seen it. He also said that he performed in Chicago last week, when he was reminded by one of his friends that it'd been two years ago. It seems more fantasy than fact."

"That doesn't mean it couldn't be true."

"I agree. That's why I told Officer Allen Spencer, who shared it with Chief LaMond. Allen said that the chief had a couple of her guys walk part of the beach. I don't know what else to do."

There was little I could add about Theo's friends and the alleged sighting of a body, so I asked if she'd seen Dude lately.

She chuckled and said that he'd stopped in the bookstore to see if she wanted a surfing lesson. I remembered the one and only lesson I'd had with Dude. It was terrible. Wipeout was the one surfing phrase I could identify with. I swore I'd never get on another surfboard, more accurately, never attempt to get on another surfboard.

"What'd you say?"

Barb took a sip, looked in the glass, then at me. "I told the dear, sweet man that there was a better chance of getting me to go shark fishing barehanded." She chuckled. "Dude said, 'Okeydokey, you be sorry.'" Her smile turned serious. "I figured something out. Dude didn't think I'd go surfing. He was using what he knew to reach out to me."

Barb and Dude, other than sharing a father, had little in common. They hadn't lived near each other after high school and had only reconnected a year ago, the result of a horrific event that involved a hired killer who'd been sent to eliminate Barb. One of Dude's loyal employees had given his life to save Dude's half-sister. It wasn't the Hallmark Channel way of bringing estranged siblings together.

"What made you decide that?"

Her smile returned. "Suppose it was because after I said that a surfing lesson was off the table, he plopped down on the floor, crossed his legs yogi style, and said, 'Me be glad you here.' He pointed a finger at me then at his head, before saying, 'Maybe break pumpkin bread together.'"

That be Dude, I thought. "I hope you can spend time together. Dude's one of the good guys. From what I can tell, doesn't have many true friends."

"We're having supper next week. Maybe you can join us. I'll need someone to translate Dudespeak."

I laughed. "That would take someone with a greater Dudespeak vocabulary than I have. Charles often translates it for me. When are you meeting?"

"Don't know. It has something to do with a phase of the moon. I'll get back with him after the weekend to narrow it down."

Dude, in addition to being Folly's leading expert on surfing, and an expert on and still residing in the 1960s, is a worshiper of the sun god, and a student of astronomy. He speaks in solar terms rather than what the rest of us call days, hours, minutes. I find it endearing, and equally confusing. *That be Dude.*

I agreed to join them when Barb figured out when they were breaking pumpkin bread.

She gave a sigh of relief and changed the subject. "Karl and I attended a few comedy clubs in Pennsylvania. I wasn't, and guess I'm still not, big on jokes and many of the stand-up comics we saw felt that, unless their act was filled with profanities and sex jokes, they weren't funny."

Karl was Barb's ex-husband, who had been arrested and disbarred after bribing state legislators and governmental officials. Their breakup was the primary reason that Barb had moved to Folly.

"I went to a comedy club decades ago," I said. "You're right about the subject matter."

Our entrees arrived.

Barb had ordered broiled flounder and in a feeble attempt to eat better I'd selected the fried flounder; it beat a half-pound cheeseburger.

Barb took a bite then turned toward the beach. "The reason I brought it up was, didn't you say Theo's brother and his friends were in their seventies?"

"Three are. Wallace's son is younger, of course. He's probably fifty."

"I thought being a stand-up comic was a young person's game. The ones I saw were in their twenties and thirties."

"I suppose most are, although there've been several famous older comics."

Rodney Dangerfield, George Carlin, and George Burns came to mind.

"I'm sure there are, though it seems rare. My point being, I wonder how long ago it's been since Theo's group performed."

"Sal mentioned that they had a break in their touring. I suppose a break could be a few years. Why?"

"It's the lawyer in me being suspicious. From my experience, things seldom are what they appear. Your friend, Theo, is wealthy and in his eighties. That's an inviting combination for con artists."

"Sal said the reason for being here was to make sure Theo was okay. I know what he'd meant about Theo seeming forgetful, possibly suffering from early onset Alzheimer's. I also know that Theo's smart and, since he got his hearing aids, he's better. I doubt Sal and his buddies will be here long."

Barb shook her head. "Don't forget, you told me a couple of years ago that Theo came close to giving that con man in his walking group a million dollars."

Point taken. "I'll keep an eye on him."

Barb took another bite, washed it down with water, and patted my hand. "Good. He seems like a nice man who could use a friend like you."

We spent the rest of the meal talking about mundane items, like the unseasonably warm weather and the larger than normal numbers of early vacationers on the island.

She also reminded me that, unlike someone at the table, she had to be at work in the morning. Subtle, it wasn't. I walked her to her condo.

Instead of going home, I headed up Center Street and listened to the live music coming from St. James Gate and Snapper Jack's. I leaned against a wall near where I'd parked Wallace in a rocking chair after helping him out of the street and smiled when I thought of how he'd been dressed. I also remembered that his dress shoes looked like they'd recently been polished.

If he'd seen a body that day, he couldn't have walked far along the beach, or his shoes would've been sand covered. That could mean that the body was in the dunes close to the center of town. I also realized that since he couldn't narrow down when he'd seen the body, if, in fact, he had seen one, his shiny shoes could've meant nothing. If there had been a body and it hasn't been found, it must be back off the beach, probably behind the dunes' line.

Barb was right. While she had to go to work tomorrow, I had little, if anything, to do, so why not spend some of that useless time checking out the dunes closest to where I met Wallace?

Chapter Six

I called Charles at 7:00 the next morning. He'd never resisted waking me when he wanted to share something, or simply to pester me. It was payback time.

He answered with a yawn followed by, "My apartment better be on fire."

I was no fan of caller ID. "I thought you'd be up and hankering for a walk on the beach."

"Only if my apartment's on fire. What's so important to interrupt my beauty sleep?"

"The sun's up, it's a nice day, and I doubt extra sleep will help your beauty. How about meeting me at the Tides in a half hour?"

"Sure," he mumbled before hanging up.

That was the kind of wake-up call I'd received from him more times than I could count. It felt good returning the favor. Besides, I'd spent the last hour thinking about Wallace's claim about seeing a body. I'd feel terrible if there was one out there and I hadn't tried to find it. If Wallace was delusional, or if he'd stumbled on a body in his more distant past, a walk on the beach with a good friend was still a great way to spend the morning.

I was in the lobby of the hotel talking to Jay, a Tides employee and a friend, when Charles stumbled through the front door. He wore cut-off shorts, a Tilley hat that matched mine, and a long-sleeve, white T-shirt with *ASU* in green on the front. Charles has the largest collection of college logoed T-shirts and sweatshirts this side of the Mississippi River—possibly on both sides. I'd given up asking about them; a fact that I knew irritated him, which was more reason not to ask.

Jay hadn't learned. "What's ASU?"

Charles puffed out his chest and grinned. "Adams State University. You know, the one in Alamosa, Colorado."

Jay rubbed his chin. "Oh, that Adams State University."

"Yep, the Grizzlies."

"Interesting," Jay said, before excusing himself. I suspected he'd heard all he wanted to about Adams State.

Charles watched Jay leave, before saying, "Okay, what's up?"

"Couldn't I want to walk on the beach with a friend?"

"That's a remote possibility. Remote if this wasn't the beach where Theo's houseguest said that he'd seen a body. Seems to my sleepy brain that we might be here to gander at more than sun, surf, and sand."

"That'd entered my mind. A couple of Chief LaMond's officers looked to no avail. Besides, Wallace could've been off a few years on when he allegedly saw what he may or may not have seen."

"Those would have been cops who ran down here, ogled college coeds, peeked at a couple of spots along the beach, got tired of getting sand in their shoes, and headed back to their fun job of writing parking tickets." Charles pointed to his chest. "You've realized, after all these years, how outstanding a detective that yours truly is, and you called me to find the dead John or Jane Doe."

"Wow, you got me," I said, not hiding my sarcasm, although he was righter than I'd admit.

"So, what are we waiting for, Beachcomber Chris?"

We walked down the steps from the outside bar to the beach then headed left under the Folly Beach Fishing Pier. If a body had been this close to the pier, it would've already been discovered, so I didn't pay much attention to the dunes until we passed East Second Street where single-family residences dominated the beachfront and fewer people frequented the area.

Charles had brought his Nikon and started snapping photos of yellow flowers snaking through the sand, and shots of one of his favorite subjects, a discarded Doritos package. If I had to describe his photo style, I'd call it eclectic. Others less generous have said he was a trash photographer. Regardless, he loved snapping photos, so I waited while he composed his latest masterpiece. He hated trash on his island as much as he loved photographing it. He picked up the empty package and stuffed it in his pocket.

A couple hundred yards later, I figured, if Wallace had come this far, his shoes would've shown evidence of the walk. "Let's head the other way."

"You're the tour guide, lead on."

We returned to the pier quicker than it had taken us to get to our turn-around spot. It took little time passing the Tides and on the far side of the hotel's parking lot, the long, four-story Charleston Oceanfront Villas condo complex.

Along the next few blocks past the condos, houses were set farther back from the beach than in the direction we had first canvassed, so we spent more time looking at the dunes and the overgrown foliage on the street side of the barrier. Charles seemed less intent on taking photos and spent more time looking for signs of something that shouldn't be there.

I was a couple of strides ahead of my friend and was the first to see an object seriously out of place. Unless someone was looking for it, the body would've gone undetected. Wallace was right.

I stuck my arm out for Charles to stop then grabbed a three-foot long piece of driftwood. I stayed a couple of feet from the partially covered body and used the stick to move underbrush and sea oats away from the head. I was thankful that I hadn't had much breakfast. The face was covered with flies. Charles leaned closer but, from where he was standing, he could only see part of the corpse.

This was a crime scene, so I didn't want to disturb it more than I already had. I took several steps back, motioned Charles to do the same, and punched 911 on my phone.

"Did you recognize him?" Charles asked after I'd told the dispatcher where we were and what we'd found.

"His face was in the shadows. I couldn't see much. Don't think I recognized him."

I heard the siren from a Folly Beach patrol car as it pulled in the parking area adjacent to a path to the beach.

Seconds later, an officer I didn't recognize approached. He had his hand on the butt of his weapon as he glanced around like he expected an armed maniac to jump out at him. "Step back. Keep your hands where I can see them," he barked.

We did as directed while he stepped closer to the body and squinted at it.

He moved to the beach and keyed his mike. "Call the Sheriff's Office. We have a possible 187. Yes, umm, yes."

He keyed off his mike and asked us for identification.

I took out my wallet, and Charles said he didn't have any

ID on him. He didn't have credit cards and drove so seldom that he kept his driver's license in his car.

Officer Fisk, according to his name badge, jotted down the information from my license then stared at Charles like he wanted to frisk him to prove that he'd lied about no ID.

"Officer Fisk, my friend and I were walking down the beach when we saw the body." I pointed toward the dunes. "I'm the one who called 911." I hoped that would alleviate thoughts that we had something to do with the death.

Fisk pointed to the shoreline. "Most people walk out there. It's illegal to walk on the dunes, so what were you doing up here?"

I wasn't ready to get into a discussion about Wallace's comments. I pointed to Charles's camera. "My friend takes photos of the flora and fauna along the beach, especially in the area separating those houses and yards from the beach." I pointed at a pre-Hurricane Hugo cottage close to where we were standing.

Charles looked at me like, "I do?"

I heard a second patrol car approach plus the distinct siren from one of the city's fire trucks. I was relieved to see Allen Spencer scampering down the path to the beach. He was followed by two firefighters who doubled as EMTs.

Officer Fisk pointed toward the body as Allen and the EMTs moved toward the person who had no need for assistance from the medical techs.

The EMTs stayed near the body, and Allen joined the three of us closer to the water. "What do we have?" Allen asked, although I suspected he knew.

Fisk gave a facts-only rundown while glaring at Charles and me like he had caught us, red-handed, killing the guy.

Allen thanked Fisk and told him to get the crime scene

tape from his car to mark off the area. Allen was the senior officer on the scene, and he let Fisk know it.

"Who's Officer Friendly?" I asked. "Thought he was going to shoot us for finding a body."

Allen watched Fisk return with the tape. "He's new. He was over in Columbia and worked for the University of South Carolina's Division of Law Enforcement and Safety, or something like that."

Charles said, "Why the piss-poor attitude?"

"He's trying to prove that he's up to the job. He's also pissed because he was one of the guys the chief asked to scout the beach the other day." Allen looked toward the gathered EMTs and Officer Fisk. "The body's well-hidden, so I can see how he missed it. That doesn't mean that he won't catch an earful if the chief finds out that it's the same body the guy with you was talking about."

True, I thought.

Allen, once again, glanced toward the body then turned to me. "I suppose it is the one?"

"Appears to be," I said.

"Crap," Allen said, not an official police code.

No joke, I thought, but remained silent.

Chapter Seven

A series of ominous-looking clouds rolled in while Charles and I were waiting to give a statement to the detective from the Charleston County Sheriff's Office. The Folly Beach Police Department provides the public safety needs of the community, which include both police and fire protection. The department is outstanding, yet relies on the Sheriff's Office when it comes to investigating major crimes. Today's find qualified.

Officer Fisk and an officer who arrived on a black ATV erected a ten-by-ten-foot canopy over the body to protect the scene from the rain that appeared moments from soaking the site.

Detective Callahan from the Sheriff's Office arrived the same time as the rain. He wore a navy sport coat and gray slacks, hardly appropriate beachwear.

Charles and I followed Allen and Callahan to the detective's unmarked vehicle, where the police officials took the front seats. I'd met Callahan three years ago, when he was assigned a murder case involving members of a film crew that had descended like locusts on the island to shoot a movie. A swarm of locusts would've been more welcomed after the filming wreaked havoc on the island and exposed residents to corpses. Callahan had struck me, at the time, as being too young for his position. Nevertheless, he proved to be competent. I was glad to see that he'd caught this case.

The detective wiped the raindrops off his coat sleeves before twisting around in the driver's seat and facing me.

"Mr. Landrum, here we are again. Please don't tell me that you've stumbled on another murder."

Allen answered for me. "I'm afraid he has."

Callahan sighed then took a notebook out of his coat pocket. "Start from the beginning."

I thought about starting from our walk on the beach today, but decided Callahan needed to hear it all. I had to stop several times so he could write down the cast of characters and tidbits from the bio on each of them. The list included Theo, his brother, and the other three stand-up comics.

Allen Spencer chimed in a couple of times to tell the detective that he had met one of Theo's guests and that Chief LaMond had heard most of the story and had dispatched two officers to canvas the area for a body.

"See if I have this right," Callahan said and closed the notebook. "The Folly Beach Police Department heard about the possibility of a body along here three days ago, sent officers to scour the area, they found nothing, yet Mr. Landrum and his friend, Mr. Fowler, have no trouble finding it. Is that correct?"

"Mostly," Allen said.

"Mostly?" Callahan asked.

"Wallace, the gentleman that Chris introduced me to, seemed confused. Remember, he said he could have seen the body that day, or years ago. Even then, all he said was that it was in the dunes. You know how many miles of dunes there are around here?"

Instead of guessing, Callahan glared at Allen. "Yet the two guys in the back seat walked four blocks from the hotel and found it."

Charles and I were asked by Callahan to tell our story again, plus repeat the names of the people visiting Theo. He gave us his card and asked that we call if we remembered anything else.

We said we would and were dismissed. It was still raining, although not as hard, as we walked back to the hotel and waited for it to end so we could continue home.

Charles slipped his camera under his shirt, pulled his soaked hat down as far as he could on his head, then reminded me that I'd said it was going to be a nice day.

———

The rain moved out overnight, and Folly Beach was rewarded with a stunning sunrise. The full spectrum of reds reflected off a layer of low clouds closer to the horizon while soothing oranges filtered through the higher clouds closer to the beach. It was the kind of morning that drew me to the island a decade ago. I no longer had the photo gallery, yet I hadn't stopped practicing my lifelong hobby of photography. I grabbed my camera, a light jacket, my Tilley, and headed out to capture images of the early April morning.

My first stop was at the coffee urn near the back of Bert's Market, an activity that I did so often that I could do it blind-folded. With coffee in hand and a camera strap over my shoulder, I walked a block to Center Street, the epicenter of commerce on the island. My first reaction was to turn toward the beach but, after what'd happened yesterday, I headed in the opposite direction.

My quest for the perfect photo, a quest I'd had since I'd taken up photography decades before the word digital had been used to describe a method of making photo images, was put on hold when the sinewy, sixty-six-year-old body of Dude Sloan nearly ran into me.

"Whoops, me be distracted," Dude said as he stopped inches from my feet.

He wore one of his many tie-dyed, psychedelic-colored shirts with a large peace symbol on the front. With his thinning, curly, long gray hair, Dude could be mistaken for Arlo Guthrie, the folk singer.

The surf shop, with all letters lower case for reasons known only to the owner, was a couple of blocks behind me, so I assumed he was headed to work. "Morning, Dude," I said and stepped aside so he could pass. "Heading to work?"

He shook his head. "No, be walking to Portugal."

"Have a safe trip," I said with a straight face.

"Boss," he said with an equally, although more straggly, straight face.

We were in front of the Folly Beach Crab Shack, where one of its employees was sweeping the sidewalk.

Dude moved closer to the road and leaned against a Palmetto tree at the edge of the sidewalk. He appeared to have postponed his walk across the Atlantic.

I said, "I hear you offered Barb surfing lessons."

He rubbed his hand through his week-old beard. "She as stoked about lesson as you were."

I didn't need to be reminded of my ill-fated surfing lesson from years gone by. "She enjoys spending time with you."

"Not as much as she enjoyin' with you." Dude hesitated

and slapped his knee. "Aha, me remember news flash." He tilted his head in my direction. "Hear you do it again."

Not having Charles, my Dude translator, with me, I had to ask more questions than I normally would. "What am I doing again?"

"Findin' bod in brambles."

I didn't need a translator for that. "Yes. Where'd you hear it?"

"Folly rumor mill be runnin' three shifts. Like, he told her, her told her, her told he, he told me."

I doubted any of the he's or she's who transported the story to Dude was the person who put the body where I'd found it, so it would be a waste of time to get names. "Did you hear who the man was?"

"*Affirimente.*"

"Who?"

"He be called murder vic."

I sighed. "What about his name?"

"Clueless."

A condition many who didn't know Dude well might agree with. They *be* wrong. While my friend's speech pattern bore a distant resemblance to proper English, his mind was sharp, his sense of humor keen, his concern for others touching.

I nodded like he'd told me something profound.

Dude snapped his fingers. "Speakin' of fractional sis, we be breakin' bread together. You hang with us? Need help understandin' lawyer talk."

I didn't want to tell him that Barb had already invited me. "Love to. When?"

"Soon." He pantomimed talking on a phone. "Let you know."

On any other sidewalk in the universe, our conversation would be considered strange or downright stupid. From my experience, it made perfect sense on Folly Beach, South Carolina. It ended abruptly when two of my most recent acquaintances, Wallace and Marvin, appeared beside us.

Wallace smiled, looked at the woman sweeping the sidewalk, at the light green doors leading to the Crab Shack, and back to Dude and me. "Mushroom walks into a bar. The bartender yells at him to leave, saying 'We don't serve your kind here.' The mushroom says, 'Why not? I'm a fun guy.'"

Marvin laughed, Dude looked at Wallace and blinked, and I wondered why I hadn't walked in the other direction when I reached Center Street.

After the hilarity died down, Marvin said, "Wallace closes his act with that. Audiences love it." He stopped as if that said it all.

I tried to bring a touch of sanity to the conversation and introduced Dude to the comedians, told him that Marvin Peters preferred to be called Pete, and said that Dude was a good friend who owned the surf shop a couple of blocks from where we stood. I shared that the comedians were visiting Theo.

Dude smiled. "Theo be cool geezer. Be hangin' long?"

Great question. I looked forward to their answer.

"Maybe," Pete said.

I'd waited for that?

"Hear about dead bod Christer found?" Dude asked.

"I found it first," Wallace said.

"Me be confused," Dude said.

I explained to my confused friend that Wallace had told me about seeing a body along the dune line, then I'd shared that information with the police. I didn't think it would be helpful to share when he claimed to have seen it.

"That's right," Wallace said. "I saw the poor soul yesterday afternoon. Tragic, so tragic."

"Why be hangin' with Theo?" Dude asked, oblivious to the fact that Charles and I had discovered the body before Wallace had claimed to have seen it. I wrote the contradiction off to Wallace's escapes from reality.

Pete put his arm around Wallace's shoulder, and said, "Theo's brother, Sal, had several conversations with his brother in recent years and felt Theo may have memory issues. He wanted to be close and asked the rest of us if we wanted to take a break from our grueling touring schedule to spend time here."

"That be kind."

"We've been friends for a long time. It's the least we could do for Sal."

That reminded me of Barb's question about how long it had been since the comics had worked. "Where was your last gig?"

"Up north," Pete said.

"Cool, For Santa at North Pole?" Dude asked.

Pete and Wallace had never been exposed to Dude's sense of humor and didn't respond.

Dude smiled. "Be kiddin'."

"Oh," Pete said. "Good one."

"Santa not alone. Mrs. C plus elves be with him."

Wallace said, "Want to go on the road with us? We could use some new jokes."

Dude nodded. "Me ponder it."

Enough, I thought, and said, "I think Dude has a full-time gig here. When did you perform last?"

Wallace glanced skyward. "Don't recall."

That was no surprise.

Pete added, "It's been a while. Tell us about finding a body. Who was it?"

Wallace jerked his head toward Pete. "Body. What about a body?"

Dude said, "The bod you said you saw other side of last sunset."

Wallace looked at Dude and at me. "I don't understand what he's talking about."

I wondered if it was how Dude said it, or if Wallace had already forgotten what he told us about seeing the body.

"I'll tell you later," Pete said and turned to me. "The last time we talked, you said a good friend of yours owned Cal's Bar. You were going to talk to him about getting us a gig."

That wasn't how I remembered it, but reinforced that I knew Cal, that I'd mention it to him.

"When?" Pete asked.

I avoided the question. "I'll get back with you or Sal after I talk to Cal."

"Good, guess we'd better leave you to your conversation. Sorry to interrupt."

Dude said, "*Adios.*"

I said, "Talk to you later."

Wallace said, "What body?"

Chapter Eight

C al's Country Bar and Burgers, better known as Cal's to everyone, except the IRS, was located a block off Center Street in a building that had seen its better days a decade ago. The interior's condition matched the exterior. The bar hadn't opened for the early drinkers.

Its front door was locked, so I went in the side entrance. Overhead, fluorescent lights, not illuminated when the bar was open, cast a cold, depressing image. The walls were painted dark green with patches of the previous brown paint showing through areas chipped away from contact with tables, chairs, and an occasional inebriated customer taking out his frustration over lost love, lost fortune, or lost keys. The ever-present smell of stale beer and long-ago fried burgers rose from the shredding indoor-outdoor carpet. According to owner, Cal Ballew, those "unique" features made Cal's the perfect country music bar.

Cal was on his knees, fiddling with something behind the ancient Wurlitzer jukebox parked on the edge of the wooden, elevated bandstand sandwiched between the restrooms in back of the room. He heard the door slam behind me and twisted around to see who'd entered.

"Good afternoon, Cal. Need help?"

Cal groaned as he maneuvered his seventy-four-year-old body from kneeling to standing. He reached his six-foot-three-inch, slim frame's full height, and wiped his hands together like he was knocking the dust off. "Not unless you're an electrician. This dang music machine keeps shorting itself out. Know how hard it is to get someone to fix this antique?"

"Not easy?"

"About as rare as plutonium in the parking lot."

I was impressed that the country crooner knew what plutonium was and agreed that there wasn't much of it in the lot.

"I doubt I can help." Far from profound, but true.

"One thing this old bartender can do is get you a drink. What's your pleasure?"

It was still early, so I said Diet Pepsi.

Cal said he thought he could rustle one up, as I followed him to the beat-up, dark, wooden bar along the side of the room. He massaged his lower back as he bent his curved-from-age spine over the cooler. His long, gray hair covered one of his eyes. His signature sweat-stained Stetson, which normally held his hair in place and had traversed most of the South with him for forty plus years, was parked at the other end of the bar.

Cal grabbed a beer then I followed him to one of the dozen tables where he flopped down in a chair. He pointed to the side door. "Since you came in that way instead of the front, I'm guessing you ain't here for alcohol, music, or chillin'."

"Can't slip anything by you, can I?" I didn't remind him another reason for my side door entrance was that the front one was locked.

He smiled. "Truth be told, I reckon you could slip something by me if you were hankerin' to." He pointed his index finger at his head. "Think after four decades on the road sleeping in my car, now seven years trying to keep this place off life support, my brain's as shorted out as that old jukebox."

I had never seen my friend this down, and I'd seen him in a few bad situations, including nearly getting killed. I was also struck by how different the bar and its owner were when illuminated by unforgiving fluorescent lights. When Cal's was lit with a couple of dim lights over the bar, plus neon beer promotional signs, with traditional country music blaring from a healthy jukebox, Cal's came alive and was a popular hangout for locals and vacationers who were fortunate enough to stumble in.

The man who could pass for one of the area's homeless and, who happened to be sitting across from me, would walk on the stage wearing his Stetson, a white rhinestone coat that had travelled as many miles with him as had his hat, and an endearing smile. He'd lean close to an old silver microphone and sing a country classic. I can't guess the number of nights, Cal's voice, image, and sad songs would transport me back to my early years listening to the country greats of the time. A night at Cal's was magical.

I considered it an honor to be his friend, but it was difficult at times to step behind the magical stage and see the realities of his world, and I suppose the real world of most who appear bigger than life when they're on stage.

I told Cal about Theo's houseguests. Cal was a member of the walking group that Theo was a part of, so he knew Theo's experiences on Folly. They weren't close, yet Cal felt a kinship to Theo.

I finished, and Cal asked if I wanted another drink. I declined, and he went for another beer, returned, looked around the empty room, then lowered himself in the chair. He looked at the ceiling, and said, "Stand-up comics and country crooners from my era have a passel of things in common. In the '60s, before comedy clubs began to spring up like rabbits, there weren't many places for comics to perform, so many of them travelled around the country the same way I did. I'd grab a gig wherever I could find one and, occasionally, there were comics sharing the stage. We led nomadic lives." He grinned. "Hell's bells, I've got a couple of ex-wives to prove it. Anyway, we hit tiny towns, tinier towns, towns that weren't even towns."

"That had to be rough."

"If I made enough money to pay for a couple of meals and gas to get to the next town; it was a good gig. I heard that many of the funny guys who were making the rounds were about as successful as I was. Once a few comedy clubs opened, mostly along the left and right coast, some of the guys, or an occasional gal, made it big. Comedy clubs were the thing in the 1970s. One old-timer told me there were more than three hundred of them in the '80s. People laughed more back then."

I was surprised that Cal knew that much about the history of stand-up comedy, and I told him so.

"Chris, if I hadn't taken the road to poverty by being a country singer, I dreamed about being a funny guy."

Cal could be funny but had never struck me as being a comedian. "Did you try?"

He wiggled his hand. "Could have made it big, yes, I sure could have."

"What stopped you?"

"Couple of things. I had a piss-poor memory. Couldn't remember a routine." He shook his head and closed his eyes.

I wondered if he was reliving a time on stage. "The other thing?"

"Couldn't tell jokes."

That'd be an impediment. "I'm glad you couldn't. I can't picture you being anything but a country singer."

"Enough about my past. Why are you telling me about Theo's jokesters?"

"They were wondering if you'd let them do their thing from up there." I pointed to the stage.

"Are they any good?"

"Never heard them."

Cal looked at the stage and at me. "They can't be as bad as some of the singers, and I use that term loosely, that show up open-mic night."

Cal's had open-mic night every Tuesday. The level of talent ranged *from I wonder why they don't have a record deal*, to *I wonder why anyone ever told them that they could sing worth a darn.*

"That's great. I'm sure they'll be thrilled."

"They don't expect to be paid, do they?"

"Afraid so."

"If they think that, they are funny. Pard, I can't afford to pay me. I care a lot more about myself than I do them."

"How about me telling them that they can perform for tips. If they show that they can bring in a big crowd, you'll consider paying them."

Cal rubbed his chin. "That'll work. See if they can do their thing on Sunday night. That's my slowest time. They can't run off too many customers."

On that ringing endorsement, I left Cal, so he could get back to playing electrician.

Chapter Nine

I wondered why I hadn't told Cal about one of the comedians claiming to have seen the body and decided it may've changed his mind about letting the group perform. My mind wandered back to thinking about what Wallace had said and his state of mind when he said it. I didn't wonder long. My phone rang.

"Good afternoon, chief."

"If you think it's a good afternoon, you're in a time zone other than mine. Give me a hint about what's good about it?"

"Well—"

"Never mind," she interrupted. "That's not why I called. Are you roaming around my fair city?"

"If you mean roaming like walking aimlessly, of course not. I am out, was at Cal's, now heading home."

"Crap, if I wanted a definition of roaming, I would've grabbed a dictionary instead of a phone."

"Why did you call stupid, old me?"

"Don't put yourself down. You ain't that stupid. Now old, well."

"Cindy, why'd you call?"

"I learned a couple of things about the body that my crack force couldn't find, yet some senior citizen had no problem stumbling across."

"What?"

"It'll cost you."

I sighed louder than I'd intended.

"No need to get huffy," the chief said. "I'll let you off easy. Meet me at the Surf Bar in five. All I need is an order of fries. Since the head of local law enforcement is supposed to be sober most of the time, you'll get off cheap buying me a Coke."

She hung up before I could say that I'd be delighted to buy her fries and a Coke. She was right, it often cost much more to get information out of her.

The Surf Bar is across the street from the section of City Hall housing the Department of Public Safety. When I arrived, Cindy was at a table near the front door of the rustic bar. The interior was small, and most of the tables were occupied by customers ranging from college students getting an early start on happy hour, a couple of construction workers, whose clothes looked like they had been down-and-dirty in dirt, and a lone middle-aged man, gripping a beer bottle while staring at a surfer video on the monitor in the center of the back bar.

Cindy waved a greeting. She's in her early-fifties, five-foot three, with curly dark hair and a quick smile. Today, it wasn't at full wattage.

"Rough day," I said as I sat opposite her.

She looked at the table, at the dollar bills attached to most every surface, and shook her head. "Do you know how many moving violations my guys handed out yesterday?"

"How many?"

She gave me a tight grin. "Hell if I know. Halfway through the pile of paperwork, I hurled it at the wall. I lied about wanting a Coke. Would you mind going over to the bar to grab me a Blue Moon on tap while I sit here feeling sorry for myself?"

"With fries?"

"If you insist."

I told the bartender what I wanted.

She pulled a Blue Moon for Cindy, handed me a Coke, and said she'd bring the fries to the table when they were ready.

Cindy took two gulps of beer before I settled in the chair. I didn't figure that a pile of moving violations would've put her in the sour mood. We've been friends for years, so I felt comfortable pushing.

"What's bothering you?"

She took another gulp and tapped her fingers on the table. "Nothing."

I stared at her.

She sighed. "Okay, you beat it out of me. The little squirt's beginning to piss me off."

The *little squirt* was how she occasionally described Larry, her husband, although for obvious reasons, never to his face. Larry, who owns Folly's hardware store, had been married to Cindy for seven years. He was a decade older than his wife, at five-foot-one, was a couple of inches shorter, and way more pounds lighter than his spouse would admit to being. I'd known each of them before they met. They were the happiest couple I knew.

"What's he doing?"

"He's beginning to piss and moan about me having to work so much. He forgets that, during the holiday season, he handcuffs himself to the store, and the only time I see him is if

I go there to buy a set of Allen wrenches, whatever the hell they are."

Cindy and Larry had gone through a horrific time a couple of years back when he'd been accused of murdering a friend who'd tried to blackmail the hardware-store owner about something from his past. They had weathered the storm and, from what I could tell, were still madly in love.

"Have you talked to him about it?"

"We talking about the same Larry?"

I didn't answer.

"Talking to that squirt about feelings is like talking to a cockroach about its family tree."

The fries arrived, and she asked the server if she could find another beer hanging out somewhere in the bar.

The server said she thought she knew where one was and went in search of it.

Cindy shook her head. "How'd you manage to shanghai the reason for me wanting to talk to you? You want to hear what I know about the body, or not?"

"Yes, although I'm more concerned about you."

She patted my hand. "You're so freakin' sweet. Downright sickening."

"Thanks, I think."

"Don't let it go to your balding head. I spend most of my time dealing with the dregs of society, slobbering drunks, and arrogant vacationers. Compared to what I have to deal with, you're not so bad." She smiled. "Thanks for caring. We'll be okay."

The server had been successful in her search for another beer.

Cindy took a drink, a sip instead of the gulps she'd chugged earlier. A good sign.

"Okay, here's the skinny. The body that my entire police

force couldn't find, but you managed to trip over without breaking a sweat, was Michael Hardin. Name ring a bell?"

"No."

"Hmm," she said. "Anyway, he celebrated his forty-seventh, and last, birthday, a couple of months ago. He was well-known by the Charleston Police Department, although not because of his benevolent donations to their orphans' fund. He had a rap sheet the length of a roll of toilet paper. To sum it up, he'd been a drug dealer. It gets sketchy at that point. According to Detective Callahan, the late Michael Hardin, may've been a confidential informant for their drug unit."

"May have been?"

"He thought it was more than *may have been* but couldn't confirm it. If Hardin had been a CI, that role ended a while back. Hardin made a career change three years ago."

"Became a cop?"

"Funny. He turned to bookmaking, not the kind you read."

"A bookie?"

"Yes, the ancient art of taking bets ain't kosher although, if caught, you don't get thrown in the hoosegow for as long as you do for selling drugs."

"Did he live over here?"

"No, he had an apartment in downtown Charleston although, according to a couple of my guys, he spent quite a bit of time hanging out in some of our restaurants, as well as the Pier."

"Plying his trade?"

"No doubt." Cindy chuckled. "One of my guys said he wasn't too hard to recognize. He wore a straw hat with a feather sticking out the top."

"That rings a bell. I think I saw him a few times. Average size, good tan, well-dressed. I remember the feather. I thought it was strange." I shrugged. "Over here, who knows?"

"That's the one."

"What killed him?"

"Unless he had a massive heart attack while strolling through the dunes, it was blunt force trauma caused by something hard smacking him in the head."

"Has anyone talked to Wallace Bentley since the body's been identified?"

"Callahan did last night. Wallace swore that he'd never seen anyone dead, or alive, at the beach. The police must've been smoking pot to think that he had."

"Yet Wallace told Allen Spencer and me that he'd seen a body. He'd been confused about how long ago it was."

"Welcome to my world," Cindy said before taking another sip.

"What's next?"

"Let's see. I'm going to wolf down the rest of these fries, finish this beer, head home, see if I can communicate with the cockroach, and—"

"About the murder," I interrupted.

For the second time in an equal number of beers, she said, "Hell if I know."

Chapter Ten

I left Cindy attacking the rest of the fries and stopped at Barb's Books. I could've called, but it was easier to visit. Besides I'd rather see Barb than talk to her on the phone.

A woman was buying four used books, and a man was browsing a shelf of mystery novels when I entered.

Barb saw me at the door and held up one finger, indicating that I should wait.

The customer finished her purchase and nodded to me as she left.

The man continued browsing without paying attention to us.

"Good," Barb said as I approached the counter. "I was getting ready to call. Dude asked if we could move supper to tonight instead of some future moon phase."

I peeked at my watch. "I think I can work it in my busy schedule. Where and when?"

Barb smiled. "Busy schedule?"

"Retirement's a full-time job."

She rolled her eyes. "6:00, the Crab Shack. Think you can

take a break from your full-time job to help me understand what Dude's talking about?"

"For you, anything," I said, as the former browser became a book purchaser. I stepped aside so Barb could take the man's money. On my way out I said I'd see her at 6:00.

I had a couple of hours to kill before I was to begin my translator duties, so I walked to the end of the Folly Beach Fishing Pier. Along the way, I passed a dozen or so men and women watching over fishing rods, hoping to land the catch of the day. Several vacationers strolled along the walkway, hoping to get a glimpse of the dolphins that frolicked nearby, competing with the fishermen for food. At the Atlantic Ocean end of the Pier, I climbed to the second level of the diamond-shaped structure and gazed back at the beach.

The outdoor bar at the Tides was packed, and a rousing volleyball game was in progress at the court between the hotel and the pier. I smiled, thinking about the many hours I'd spent over the years at this spot, reveling in how fortunate I was to live on the Edge of America, as Folly was called, being lucky enough to have a full-time job being retired, and having more friends that I'd accumulated during my life in Kentucky. I thought about how different some of my friends were to the others, to the point that I was asked by both Dude and Barb to serve as a translator. I chuckled when I reminded myself that they were related.

My mood changed as my eyes shifted from the Tides, past the Charleston Oceanfront Villas, to the spot where I discovered the late Michael Hardin. It was ironic how a matter of a few feet can separate the gaiety of the vacationers romping in the surf, soaking up the sun's rays, while the lifeless corpse of someone who would never laugh again had been so close. As much as we would like to think that we are in control of our lives, the reality is that, often, we aren't, and how we erroneously think we know what's happening nearby.

That depressing thought brought me back to what I remembered about Michael Hardin, not finding his lifeless body, but recalling I'd seen him around town. If it wasn't for his straw hat with the feather, I never would've noticed him. The more I thought about it, I realized that I'd seen him on the Pier. He had been talking to two men dressed like they were going to a business meeting rather than taking in the sights.

The three were in animated conversation, their body language hinted that they were arguing. It didn't strike me as unusual at the time, since conventions were often held at the Tides with participants taking breaks at the bar or on the Pier. Now that I knew one was the dead bookie, I wondered if their disagreement was related to betting. Could the two men have had something to do with his death? It was possible, although the incident took place a week or so before Hardin had been killed. I wouldn't be able to identify the men, nor had any idea what they were talking about. I shook the memory out of my head as I watched a young boy squeal when his dad caught a two-foot-long shark and dropped it on the deck in front of his son.

———

I arrived at the Folly Beach Crab Shack, where Barb and Dude were seated on the outside deck.

Dude waved. "Yo, Chris, hang with us?" Dude was on his best behavior since he called me Chris, not Chrisster, his usual permutation.

I didn't know if they knew that each other had asked me to

be part of their breaking pumpkin bread, so I smiled and said that I would.

Neither acted surprised to see me.

Barb scooted over, and I joined her on the bench seat. She kissed my cheek.

Dude said, "Ewe, mushy."

A server arrived, handed Dude a martini, a beer to Barb, then asked if I wanted anything.

I said I would have a white wine.

Dude took a sip and said, "Bc bod searchin' again?"

Not how I'd hoped our pleasant evening breaking bread, pumpkin or otherwise, would begin.

"Nope. Been a busy week at the surf shop?" I asked to change the subject.

"Nope."

"I've had more customers than most any week since I opened," Barb said, either understanding my desire to change the subject, or feeling left out of the conversation.

Dude nodded and turned back to me. "Hear who bod was?"

The death was on Dude's mind, and he wasn't to be deterred. "Yes, Michael Hardin."

"Be kiddin'."

"That's what Chief LaMond said."

Barb leaned closer. "Do they know what happened?"

"Nothing, other than someone hit him in the head. No suspects."

Dude closed his eyes and said, "Michael Hardin, Michael Hardin, me know him."

That got my attention. "You do?"

"He be bet taker. Me not above laying down lucre on soccer. Nice chap, pays bets *rapido*."

The server returned with my drink and took our orders.

Barb waited for him to go before saying, "You bet with a bookie?"

Dude shrugged. "Preachers no take bets."

"Do you know if he had enemies?" I asked.

Dude held up his forefinger. "One."

"Who?" I asked.

"Person thought he be baseball," Dude said as he rotated his arms like he was swinging a bat. He grinned and took a sip of martini.

"You don't know who?" I said.

"No. He, me, no best buds."

Barb waved her hand between Dude and me. "Might I suggest we move to a more pleasant topic?"

"You might," Dude said. "What?"

Barb smiled. "Dude, remember when you told me I needed to move here after my divorce?"

He nodded.

"After I was here a week, I thought you were crazy."

Dude said, "Why?"

"Everybody was so nice. I wasn't accustomed to it. They wanted to know all about me, why I was here, what I was doing, suggesting where I should eat. To be honest, it was off-putting."

Dude rubbed his chin. "Like chocolate pudding?"

Barb tilted her head. "No, I mean disconcerting, unpleasant."

Now I knew what Dude had meant about me translating.

Dude smiled. "You be on-putting now?"

"Chris told me that most newcomers either hated or loved Folly. I thought I was one of the former yet, the more I relaxed, the more I realized that the people were sincere and cared about me, a stranger; I began to look at things differently." She laughed. "So, yes, I suppose I've come to realize that most of the people here are on-putting."

"Cool," Dude said. "Talking newcomers, Sal's pals be strange."

Coming from one of the strangest, that was saying something. "What do you mean?"

"Sal and *moi* had confab. He no be surfer. Be fan of canines. Stopped Pluto and me in middle of sidewalk to say Pluto cute. I say he be. He, Sal, not Pluto, like to confab with Pluto." Dude stopped and waited for a comment.

Pluto was Dude's Australian terrier.

I waited for Barb to say something.

Instead, she looked at me with a glazed look in her eyes.

I took the hint. "Dude, have you met Sal's buddies?"

"Not that know of. Heard."

"What've you heard about them?" Barb asked. She was catching on.

"They be funny men. They be helpin' Theo. They be busted."

The last part got my attention. "Did Sal say that they didn't have any money?"

"No, he say they be stayin' in Theo's *casa*, eatin' Theo's food. Dude knows bummin' when sees it. They be busted."

"Oh," I said.

Dude took that as the end of the discussion about Sal and his friends and started talking about astronomy, one of his favorite subjects.

Barb knew as much about astronomy as I did, which could be summed up in one word: zilch. She moved the conversation back to how well she was doing with her bookstore and how much she liked her condo.

The conversation rambled for the next half hour while food and additional drinks were consumed.

Dude said he needed to get home to let Pluto out.

Barb said she needed to get home to rest up for another busy day in the store.

I said I didn't need to get anywhere and said I would walk Barb home.

To both Barb and my surprise, Dude picked-up the check, and thanked us for "hangin'" with him. He hugged Barb, and said, "Me no be huggin' Chrisster."

Chapter Eleven

I was curious about what Dude shared about Theo's guests being broke, which reminded me that the comedians wanted to meet Cal to talk about performing at his bar. I called Theo's at a reasonable hour the next morning. Apparently, 10:00 fell outside the definition of reasonable for people who'd spent their careers with their work day starting after 9:00 p.m.

Theo was awake and told me that he hadn't heard a mouse stirring upstairs. That wouldn't have surprised me, considering Theo's hearing problem, but he assured me he was wearing his hearing aids and would've heard his guests moving around. I told him why I was calling, and he said he'd have Sal call once he had his first cup of coffee. He added that I wouldn't want to hear from his brother before he had his coffee.

I was pondering whether to have a peanut butter sandwich or a four-day-old muffin for lunch when Sal called. I said good morning.

He mumbled, "What's good about it?"

"It's a lovely day."

"Maybe through your eyes."

He made up for his surliness when he said, "Sorry I'm cranky, mornings aren't my best time of day."

I resisted reminding him it was noon. I asked if his group still wanted to meet Cal.

He said, "Definitely."

I suggested that I could meet them at Cal's tonight and introduce them to the owner.

He said that was great and suggested 9:00.

I swallowed hard, as I knew that was pushing against my bedtime. As a concession to Theo, I agreed.

I wanted to remind—warn—Cal about his visitors, so I stepped into the bar an hour before the comedians were to arrive. There was a decent crowd for a weeknight. From the jukebox, Merle Haggard was telling us he was proud to be from Muskogee, a couple seated by the door were arguing about whether Roger Miller was a better songwriter than Kris Kristofferson, and Cal was tending bar while wearing his Stetson, a fire-engine red T-shirt with the Budweiser logo, and black jogging shorts.

I waved but, before I could say anything, he opened the cooler, grabbed a bottle of Chardonnay, and poured me a glass.

I moved to the bar, thanked him for the drink, and said something about him having a nice crowd.

Cal tipped his hat in the direction of two tables, with five customers at each. "This old cowboy loves conventions at the Tides, especially conventions where the meetings are as dull as a marshmallow in a briar patch."

Cal was from Texas, so I excused some of his sayings. "Great."

The jukebox played Cal Smith's version of "Country Bumpkin," one of the tables of conventioneers sang along, and I reminded Cal about Sal and his crew wanting to talk with him about performing. I told him they were coming tonight.

He pointed to the only empty, large table and said for me to grab it so we could talk when the funny men arrived.

Nine o'clock came and went, as did 9:15. Many customers had departed, leaving the conventioneers and the couple who continued to debate the pluses and minuses of country song-writers.

I was ten minutes from calling it a night when the door opened and Sal entered, followed by Wallace and Pete. Jerry Lee Lewis screaming "Great Balls of Fire" from the jukebox couldn't come close to holding the remaining customers' atten-tion compared to the sight of three seventy-something-year-olds strutting in.

One wore a robin-egg blue three-piece suit, one had on a red sport coat, a white open-collar dress shirt, and a black ascot with white polka dots, and the third gentleman was doing a Johnny Cash imitation, wearing all black. I didn't know how funny their act was, but they looked hilarious.

I peeked at Cal.

His eyes widened; his next move was a combination of head shake plus shoulders slump.

Everyone in the bar was staring at the three men who must've parked their time machine out front.

I was the only person who knew who they were, so I greeted them and led them to the table I'd been saving.

"Sorry we're a tad late," Sal said as he led the group to the table. "Pete couldn't find his ascot."

The Johnny Cash look-alike Wallace chimed in, "I thought I'd burned it. No such luck."

The three took seats around the table.

Sal said, "We wanted Cal to see us at our best. This is our stage wear. I say look professional, be professional."

"What're the chances of us getting beer?" Pete asked.

"Pretty good, pard," Cal said. He was standing behind Sal and looking down at the comedians. Three Buds?"

"That'd be a good start, barkeep. Cool hat."

I moved closer to Cal and introduced the group. I stuck with first names since I wasn't sure I remembered their last names.

Wallace tipped an imaginary hat to Cal and said, "A dyslexic walks into a bra."

Sal laughed, patted Wallace on the shoulder, and said, "Good one, Wallace." He turned to Cal. "We're comedians. Can't help being funny."

Cal looked at Wallace, without breaking a smile, even after Wallace couldn't help being funny. "I'll grab the drinks."

"Where're Ray and Theo?" I asked the group.

Wallace said, "Theo said it was too late to be running around. Ray, umm, Ray. Oh yeah, my son. He stayed at the house. He was talking to his agent about starring in a TV sitcom."

"Yeah, right," Pete said, "and I'm king of Kansas."

"He may join us later," Sal said, probably to prevent a battle between Wallace and Pete.

Cal returned, set a bottle of Budweiser in front of each comedian, and Pete pulled a pack of Marlboros from his coat pocket.

Cal slipped his hand between Pete and the cigarettes. "Whoa, pard. No smoking in here."

Pete's jaw dropped. "You're joking."

"Nope," Cal said. "You're the comedian. I'm an old country crooner."

Sal leaned toward Cal. "How can you have a country bar without cigarette smoke sucking out oxygen?"

"Well, turtle turd," Pete said poetically. "First, we can't light up at Theo's, now not here. What happened to freedom? I thought one of the Constitution's amendment things gave us the right to smoke in bars."

Wallace nodded, "Sir, we're comedians. Research has found that joke and smoke go together like pigs and pork chops."

Cal pulled his Stetson down lower on his forehead. "Gentlemen, I'm no expert in research and haven't read the Constitution since I was in high school, about the time it was written. In my book, smoke, choke, and croak go together." He pulled a chair from the empty table next to us, turned it around and straddled the back. "Let me tell you something. I spent more nights on the road than there are grains of sand out there on the beach singing in bars, restaurants, on bales of hay on pickup trucks, hell, even highway rest stops. Cigarette smoke was everywhere. I hated it, but it was part of where I performed; probably the same for you guys."

Wallace nodded again.

Sal started to say something, but Cal wasn't done.

"Two of my best buds from yesteryear; danged good singers in their day, died of lung cancer. One smoked like a forest fire. My other friend never stuck a cigarette in his mouth. Hell, he got lung cancer from secondhand smoke, was in hillbilly heaven before the term secondhand smoke was invented."

Sal said, "Sorry."

Cal was on a roll. "I can't stop people from doing stupid things. What I can do is slow them down when they're in here. Like my good buddy, great songwriter, and performer Roger Miller once penned, 'Don't we all have the right to be wrong now and then.'" Cal lowered his head, "Roger died of lung cancer."

That silenced the group.

Pete broke the uneasy silence. "Cal, speaking of dead, did you know the bookie that was dead on the beach?"

"Don't think so. What was his name?"

Wallace stood, smiled at Cal, and said, "What did the fish say when he ran into the wall?"

"Huh?" Cal said.

"Dam," Wallace said, then laughed at his joke.

Pete chuckled, and Sal shook his head.

It was past my bedtime. I began wondering if I was having a bad dream.

The comedians' beers were gone before two more songs finished on the jukebox, and Cal headed to the bar for refills. He returned, and the comedians greeted the bottles like they were their first drinks after being stranded on a desert island.

Cal turned his chair around and scooted up to the table. "Chris, you're always sticking your nose into everything. Do you know who the dead guy was? Ascot man there said he was a bookie." Cal pointed his beer bottle at Pete.

I said, "Name was Michael Hardin. He was——"

"Damn," Cal muttered. "I know him."

Cal's revelation quieted the group. I wanted to hug him for that welcomed event. Instead, I asked how he knew Michael.

"Hard to miss," Cal said, not answering my question. "The boy wore that stupid hat with the bird feather sticking out of it. He was in here all the time."

"I know who you're talking about," I said, "I don't remember seeing him here."

Cal removed his Stetson and ran his hand through his long, gray hair. "He mostly showed up late, probably past your bedtime."

"Was he here with the same people each time?" I asked.

"Nah, most nights he came in by himself. Sat at that table over there." Cal pointed to a table on the far side of the room.

I looked at the table then turned back to Cal. "Did that seem strange?"

"Chris, you know I don't like butting in anyone's business. I never asked him, and couldn't swear to it on a stack of Bibles. If I was a wagering man, I'd put a good helping of greenbacks on Michael taking bets."

Sal chuckled. "If he wasn't dead, you could place your bet with him."

Cal sighed, shook his head, turned away from Sal, and said, "Chris, I've seen a fair amount of betting in my day. Michael would park his rear end at that table, buy a drink or two, and, all casual like, some of my regulars would saunter up to his table, take a seat, lean over, and whisper something. Yes, they would."

Cal stopped and looked around the table like that had explained everything.

"What else happened, Cal?" I asked, hoping for more.

He rubbed his chin. "Let's see. Michael would take one of those flip notepads. You know, like cops carry."

I said I knew.

"He'd open it, write something and, after he finished scribing, the person with him would take cash out of his, occasionally her, pocket and give it to Michael."

Cindy said that Michael had dealt drugs before turning to bookmaking.

"Cal, could he have been dealing drugs instead of taking bets?"

"Suppose so, although I never saw him giving his visitors anything except cash. From what I know about some of his customers, umm, visitors, taking drugs would be a big stretch."

Cal looked at the table where he had remembered seeing Michael. "I'll miss him."

Sal leaned closer to the table. "That reminds me. A man goes into a Hallmark Store. He says to the clerk, 'Do you sell sympathy cards?' Clerk said, 'We do.' The man says, 'Could I exchange this Get Well Soon card I bought yesterday?'"

Now I knew I was dreaming.

Sal added, "Get it? It's a dead joke, like that bookie."

Cal and I stared at him.

Pete slapped him on arm. "That joke was funny when Ray told it, remember? That was, before you stole it from him."

Sal said, "Picky, picky. Ray ain't here. It seemed appropriate in light of the gruesome conversation those guys are having." Sal turned to Cal. "While we're talking about jokes, Chris said you were anxious to talk to us about bringing our Comedy Legends World Tour to your fine establishment."

Cal turned to me and mouthed, "Legends. World Tour. Anxious?"

"Sal, I said I'd introduce you to Cal and let him decide if he wanted to add comedy to his nightly offerings."

"Tomato, tomahto," Sal said as he waved his hand in my face. He turned to Cal. "What do you think, Cal, old buddy?"

Cal pushed his Stetson back on his head. "Tell you what, pard. Back when I was making numerous appearances on the Grand Ole Opry, I got to know Sarah Ophelia Colley Cannon and Louis Jones pretty good."

"Who?" interrupted Sal.

Cal grinned. "Sorry, only their good friends called them their real names. You might know them as Minnie Pearl and Grandpa Jones."

"Yes, sir," Sal said. "I didn't know them as well as you did, of course. Everyone in this business knew about those famous country comics. I saw Minnie Pearl in a show once in Birmingham."

Cal looked at Sal and at the other two comics with him. "The point I was going to make is I have a soft spot in my heart for joke tellers. I think, if we can come to terms, I could spare the stage for your show. A Sunday night would work."

Sal took off his glasses and rubbed the bridge of his nose. "Cal, our group has a limited number of open dates on the schedule. I was checking before we came over, and it looks like sometime in the next couple of weeks might work. Let's talk about our fee."

Cal leaned back in the chair and nodded. "Okay, let's. Here's the deal. As an advance, I'll pay you nothing. After you finish, I'll double it."

Sal started to stand.

Cal waved at him to remain seated. "Whoa, pard. I'll tell you what. Before you start, I'll introduce one of you as MC, and I'll tell everyone that tips will be appreciated. During your set, umm, acts, you can plug the tips."

Sal nodded at the other two stand-up comics. "That's several Franklins below our minimum. We're already on Folly, and some of our expenses are being covered by my brother, so we'll do you a favor and give it a go."

"Mighty fine of you, sir," Cal said.

I knew he was being sarcastic, but Sal smiled like he'd negotiated a multi-million-dollar tour.

They agreed to perform Sunday and said they better get back to the house to see how Ray was coming with his TV deal.

I stood, and Cal asked me to hang around. I stayed at the table, and Cal got more drinks for the table of conventioneers who were still enjoying their time away from the hotel.

He returned and scooted his chair closer to mine. "Didn't

want to mention it in front of Larry, Curly, and Moe. I figured, since you were nosing into the death of Michael, you need to hear about what happened two nights before he turned up deceased."

I started to deny that I was doing any nosing. Instead, I asked, "What happened?"

"You know Neil Wilson?"

The name sounded familiar, but I wasn't sure. "Tell me about him."

"Big guy, muscle turned to fat. I hear he played football at South Carolina."

"I know who you mean. Looks like a tall fire hydrant on steroids."

"That's him," Cal said. "He works security at a couple of places in Charleston. A few months ago, he asked if I needed a bouncer. He said he lived in an apartment on Ashley Avenue and was trying to find extra work close to home. I told him that I couldn't afford my part-time cook and me."

"I've seen him in Bert's. What about him?"

"He sashayed in, lumbered in, and made a beeline toward Michael Hardin. It was the last night I saw Michael at his office table. It was crowded, so I didn't hear what they were talking about. A few minutes later, I heard Neil bellow something like, 'Over my dead body.' He smacked the door so hard on the way out I thought the hinges were going to pop off."

"Any idea what it was about?"

"You're the detective. Knowing what I know about Michael, it must've had to do with money. If I had to guess, I'd say Neil owed Michael a piss-pot full of it."

"Enough to kill him over?"

Cal nodded. "You bet."

Chapter Twelve

I got up later and hungrier than usual. Last night at Cal's had pushed me past my normal bedtime, so I walked to Bert's for coffee and a two-pack of donuts, where I saw Chester Carr talking to Denise, one of the clerks. I had known Chester for several years, first when he worked at Bert's, much better two years ago, when he formed a senior-citizen walking group that I had joined to learn more about an alleged blackmailer among the walkers. That experience nearly got Theo and Chester killed, not to mention me almost losing my life.

"Morning, Chris," Denise said, interrupting her conversation with Chester.

I returned her greeting, acknowledged Chester. With the late Michael Hardin fresh on my mind, I asked Chester if he could spare a few minutes when he was finished talking to Denise.

He nodded.

I continued to the coffee urn.

Before I took my first sip, Chester was beside me. "Been missing you and Charles walking with us."

Chester was approaching ninety, stood five-foot six and, in the words of Charles's late Aunt Melinda, was "a spittin' image of Mr. Magoo."

"Sorry, Chester. I need to start back."

"I've heard that before. What's up?"

"Do you know Michael Hardin?"

Chester took his Coke-bottle-thick glasses off to rub his left eye. He returned the glasses to their rightful place. "Would that be the Michael Hardin you and Charles found out past the Oceanfront Villas?"

I smiled. "The same."

"Yeah, I knew him. Nice guy. I hated to hear what happened, although, I'm not surprised."

"Why?"

"I heard he was pushing drugs a few years back. Seldom anything good comes from that. After he got in deep doo-doo with the cops, he switched directions to become a bookie." Chester looked around and whispered, "I heard that he'd spent time in prison. That's a rumor; he didn't tell me. I'd guess that participants in both of those careers have shorter life spans than the average clerk in here."

That was hard to argue with. I asked if he knew anything more specific.

"Mind you, I never placed a bet with Michael," he said. "Don't suppose I ever will now. I know a few who did."

The store was crowded, and we were in the line of traffic to the coffee. If I'd learned anything from years of frequenting Bert's, it's not to stand between morning customers and their caffeine.

"Let's step outside."

It was in the low seventies and pleasant, so Chester followed me to the tree-shaded, parking area between the store and my house.

Chester took a sip of coffee and said, "You trying to catch whoever killed Michael?"

"Not really. I'd seen him a few times, was trying to learn more about him."

"That sounds like yes to me."

I shrugged. "Know if he had enemies?"

Chester watched a rusting, classic Fiat carrying a surfboard drive past then turned to me. "I didn't know him well. He was always pleasant. It seems he had a booming bookmaking business from the number of people I saw him huddled with. Betters lose more often than they win, so I reckon some of them could've been mad, but heck, it wasn't Michael's fault they lost."

"You weren't aware of anyone angry with him?"

"Not off the top of my head."

"Do you know Neil Wilson?"

"Doesn't ring a bell. Who's he?"

"Someone I hear had a beef with Michael."

"Describe him."

"Big guy," I said. "Played college football, works security in Charleston. I don't know him. I've seen him in Bert's a couple of times, but never talked to him."

"Still doesn't ring a bell. What was his problem with Michael?"

"Not sure. I heard they had an argument in Cal's."

Chester shuffled his feet in the sandy parking lot. "Now that you mention an argument, I do recall something. Don't know why I didn't think of it earlier. It was, oh, a couple of weeks back, when I saw Michael on the sidewalk in front of Snapper Jack's. He was puffin' on a cigarette and waving his arm around like he was being attacked by a swarm of bees." Chester hesitated and smiled. "I can picture it now. Sort of funny." He hesitated again and watched another vehicle drive by.

"And?" I said, channeling Charles's lack of patience.

"Sorry, my train of thought ran off the tracks."

"Michael fighting off a swarm of bees."

"Oh, yeah. Weren't bees. I was coming up from behind him, didn't see the other person until I got beside Michael."

"Other person?"

"Yeah, Michael was blocking my view. He was in a heated discussion with Janice."

"Janice?"

"Yeah, you may know her, Janice Raque. Nice little lady. She's in her late fifties, about five-foot three, short brown hair with bunches of gray sneaking in. She spends a lot of time walking the beach, hunting shark teeth."

That described several people. I didn't know if I knew her or not. "What about her?"

"She's usually chirpy, big smile, easy laugh. Not that day. She looked like she was ready to knee Michael in the, umm, well, somewhere that'd get his attention."

Chester stopped talking. I was beginning to wonder if I'd have to knee him to get him to finish whatever he was trying to tell me. "What was she upset about?"

"Couldn't tell you. I didn't want to stop and get in the middle of it. I did hear her say something about him not doing what he was supposed to do, how it cost her big bucks."

"Any idea what?"

"Nope, but I can tell you that dear, sweet Janice was royally freakin' out."

He didn't think about that when I asked if he knew someone who might have been angry at Michael?

"Do me a favor. Let me know if you hear anything else

about Janice and Michael, or if you hear anything about anyone else mad at him."

Chester laughed. "So, you want to know because you're *not* trying to figure out who killed him?"

"Correct," I said, wondering if it sounded as insincere to Chester as it had to me.

"If you say so."

That answered the question.

Chapter Thirteen

According to Chester and Cal, Neil Wilson and Janice Raque had issues with Michael Hardin. Could their anger have escalated to murder? I had a nodding relationship with Neil, but didn't know Janice. If anyone knew more about them, it would be Charles. It was a gorgeous day, so I walked eight blocks to his Sandbar Lane apartment.

He gave me a less-than-welcoming reception, as he motioned me in. He looked like he hadn't shaved for a week. His long-sleeved Virginia Commonwealth University T-shirt had a mustard stain between the m's in Commonwealth. His hair was a mess, matching the rest of him.

Charles was one of the most positive people I knew. He could find good in the most obnoxious people, liked most everyone, and was a walking, talking ambassador for Folly Beach.

A year ago, his long-term significant other, Heather Lee, an aspiring country music singer, had decided at the urging of a Tennessee music agent to move to Nashville to seek fame. To no one's surprise, Charles moved with her. To no one's surprise, Heather was a failure in Music City. She had been a regular performer at Cal's open-mic nights, entertaining the audience with her enthusiasm and positive stage presence. Her singing sucked. That wasn't enough to stop her from following her dream; a dream that became a nightmare when her agent was murdered. She skyrocketed to the top of the suspect chart with a bullet.

I helped prove her innocent through luck and with assistance from friends. The experience convinced her to lower her expectations and remain a big fish in the small pond in the country music world on Folly.

Charles and Heather returned to the beachside community, yet Heather never returned to her former, cheerful self. She slipped out of town, leaving Charles a note, asking that he not try to find her.

He was devastated. While he's shown glimmers of his former self, there've been bouts of despair. It seems I caught him in the middle of one of those downs.

"Up for a walk?" I asked as he looked around the room for somewhere for me to sit.

Charles had one of the largest collections of books outside the Library of Congress. Floor to ceiling bookshelves covered three walls in the living room, nearly as many in the other rooms, including the bathroom. Plus, each horizontal surface, including the two chairs in the living room, held stacks of reading material.

He muttered, "I guess."

That was the right answer, since it would've taken a forklift to clear a spot for me to sit. Some of my fondest memories had been when we walked agenda-free around the island. We were photographers, and the island was a photo-rich environment, so we'd spent hours taking photos, although that was a good excuse to talk about whatever came to mind.

We left the large, gravel and shell parking lot when Charles said, "What direction?"

I was more interested in helping my friend than where we walked. "Your call."

"I'm not in the mood to find more bodies, so let's not go to the beach."

I turned right on West Indian Avenue then walked a couple of blocks before he spoke again.

Charles kicked a rock out of the road and mumbled, "The only two women I've loved. One dead, one gone."

Four years ago, Charles's Aunt Melinda, whom he hadn't seen for many years, moved to Folly from Detroit, Charles's hometown. She had brought her boundless enthusiasm, friendliness, and endearing charm with her. She also brought a diagnosis of terminal cancer and died less than a year after arriving. Charles was still not over her passing. Now with Heather gone, he was struggling to return to the man I'd known for years.

"Charles, there's nothing I can say to lessen the pain, but there're many people here who think the world of you. They'd do anything to help."

He kicked another rock. "That's what's keeping me sane."

I started to joke about his sanity, something I could've done before all of this happened. He would've responded to my insult with a smart aleck remark, and we would have continued our walk. After Heather moved, his friends were on thinner ice, weighing their words carefully. His sense of humor had been a casualty of the loss of his two loves.

We walked another block before he said, "Learn anything new about Michael Hardin?"

I took that as a sign of hope that he was looking past his problems. I told him what Cal said about Michael Hardin's argument with Neil Wilson.

Charles stopped. "Big guy, six-foot two or three, lives out East Ashley?"

"That's the one. How well do you know him?"

"I don't. He was in Bert's talking to Norman. When he left, I asked Norman who he was, and he said his first name was Neil, but forgot the last name. He told me where the guy lived and said he was asking if the store wanted to hire him to provide overnight security when foot traffic was low and alcohol levels high. Neil told the clerk that they could pay him anything. He was desperate for work. It seems that Neil had two part-time jobs in Charleston."

"What did Norman tell him?"

"They didn't need help."

"It sounds like he could've owed Michael Hardin money."

"Hmm," Charles said. He bobbed his head up and down. "A good way to wipe out a loan is to wipe out the loaner. Think he killed him?"

"Don't know. I was going to tell Cindy."

Charles stopped in the middle of the street and pointed to the pocket holding my phone. "What're you waiting for?"

I started to say that I thought there was a better place than in the middle of the street to make the call. My argument against calling the chief would have fallen on deaf ears, so I moved to the sandy berm. I tapped her number, thinking there's something unsettling about having the chief on speed dial.

She answered with a growl. "What trouble are you going to cause me now?"

I smiled. "Afternoon, Cindy. Pleasant day, isn't it. I'm with Charles. "We—"

"Crap, double trouble. Want to know what's been so strange about today? Until now, that is."

"What?" I said, as Charles waved his hand at the phone, which was his signal for me to put it on speaker. I did.

"Glad you asked. Today has been peaceful. My competent police and fire departments haven't brought me any impossible situations, and not a single house has burned down. So I wait on the edge of my chair to hear how you plan to ruin it."

I assured her I didn't plan to and then told her about my conversations with Cal and Chester. I made the mistake of asking if she'd learned anything about people who'd been betting with Michael Hardin and might have reason to do him in.

"Gee, Chris, why hadn't I thought of that? I sleep better at night knowing that some of my citizens, you know, those without any law enforcement training, are always thinking of things that we, the dumb cops, would never think of on our own."

I stifled a smart remark for the same reason that I'd withheld one from Charles earlier. Cindy had been in a bad mood the last two times we'd talked. Today's disposition wasn't an improvement.

"I know you and your folks are doing what you can. I was curious if anyone had looked closer at Neil Wilson and Janice Raque."

"Hang on a sec," she said. I heard papers rustling in the background. She returned to the phone. "I was looking through the reports of interviews my guys conducted. I know who Janice is. Let's see, yes, Officer Fisk interviewed her yesterday. She claims to have been visiting friends in Charleston around the time that Michael lost his last bet. Neil Wilson hasn't been interviewed by my folks."

Charles leaned closer to the phone. "Cindy, he'd be a good one to talk to."

"Chris, you sound like Charles, your worthless friend."

"Cute," Charles said. "What about it? Neil had a reason to make the bookie disappear."

"We haven't talked to him, Chris," Cindy said with an emphasis on Chris. "That doesn't mean the Sheriff's Office hasn't. I've told you before, their folks often treat us local yokels like we're a few thousand cells short of having half a brain. To keep you from pestering me more than you already have, I'll share what you learned with Detective Callahan."

"Thank you," I said. "Who else is on the list?"

I didn't think Cindy had heard my question. She hesitated, then said, "NOYFB."

She had me on that one. "What?"

"It's police code for none of your, umm, freakin' business," she said and hung up.

Charles stared at the silent phone. "Chris, I think she made that up."

We started walking toward the center of town, with a rejuvenated bounce in Charles's step. He had something to think about that didn't involve Melinda or Heather.

I was a step behind him when he stopped. "Know what we need to do?"

I was afraid to ask, but did anyway, "What?"

"You knew Michael Hardin."

"Barely," I said.

"And you found his body."

"Yes."

"It's fate, you knowing who he was and finding his body. That says it all."

"What does it say?"

"You've got to figure out who killed him. The best news is I'll help." He smiled and nodded. "You're welcome."

Tell me again why I decided to visit Charles's apartment.

Charles looked at his bare wrist. "Whoops. I have to

deliver two packages for the surf shop. While I'm doing that, you start working on a strategy to figure out who killed bookie man."

Charles picked up extra cash making local deliveries for Dude. Up until when Charles had purchased a car to make the move to Nashville, all his deliveries were within a few blocks of the surf shop. He could now travel farther, yet Dude said he preferred to use "them big ole brown clunky trucks" for those deliveries. That's UPS for those who don't know Dudespeak.

Before Charles left me standing in the street, I asked what he would be contributing to the task of finding the killer. He'd said that, since I was the college graduate, I would need to strategize, outline our alternatives, and design a plan of action. I repeated my question about his contribution, to which he said, "I'll come up with all the stupid ideas so you can shoot them down. That'll help you figure it out."

I bit my tongue and didn't remind him that he claimed to be the private detective, nor had I agreed to his half-baked idea that it was fate that I should figure it out. I shared what I knew with Cindy. Her job, and the job of the Sheriff's Office in Charleston, was to catch bad guys. I had no reason to get involved.

I was sticking to that story.

Chapter Fourteen

The phone rang as I settled into my kitchen chair, preparing a labor-lite lunch of peanut butter on rye and Doritos.

"Chris, this is Theo. Could I ask a favor?"

I told him he could ask, although I couldn't promise that I'd be able to do whatever it was.

"Fair enough. Could you come to the house? There's something I'd like to talk to you about while the guys are out. I'd come to you, but I'm waiting for a plumber."

I was intrigued enough to tell him yes. I finished my sandwich on the ride over and was greeted by Theo before I'd reached the top step to his porch. He was dressed in blue jogging shorts, a T-shirt with Maryland Terrapins in red block letters, and his usual knee-high support socks. I hoped he wasn't taking sartorial lessons from Charles. He looked around like he was afraid someone was watching then waved me in. He led me to the great room filled with sturdy, light-colored, wood furniture, and original oil paintings on the walls. I sat on the couch and waited for him to tell me why I'd been invited.

Theo apologized twice for asking me to come on short notice. He fiddled with the elastic waistband on his shorts, went to the large windows overlooking the marsh and the Folly River, stared out, then returned to the couch. He was nervous, and I was starting to catch his affliction. Theo was getting to the reason for the meeting, as slow as he walked. He had the reputation in the walking group as being slower than coal turning to a diamond. With the average speed of the walkers zipping along at zero miles per hour, that was telling.

Before I started pacing with him, I asked, "What's bothering you?"

He looked at me like he'd forgotten that I was there. "I don't know how to start. I'm not sure, don't know what to do."

"Have a seat, and start at the beginning."

He slowly lowered himself onto the couch and again adjusted his shorts. "I've been robbed. I think it's one of the guys."

That wasn't on my list of things I figured Theo had called about. "Tell me about it."

He took a deep breath then pointed at the table against the wall. "See those silver figurines?"

My eyesight wasn't what it'd been years ago, but I couldn't miss three, six inch to a foot-high sculptures. One was a cat, another the head of an eagle, the tallest, a llama. I'd seen them during previous visits but paid little attention since to me they were merely dust catchers. I nodded.

"The designer we hired to furnish the house said they would add a touch of life to the room. They'd be exceptional conversation pieces. I thought they were hunks of silver that cost more than my first car. My wife, God rest her soul, said I had to buy whatever the designer recommended, so I bit my tongue, wrote the checks."

His story was interesting, although I didn't see what it had to do with him being robbed. "Okay."

Theo sighed again. "Three days ago, there were four."

"Oh."

"A silver frog was perched beside the llama."

"You think one of the guys took it?"

"Chris, I'm embarrassed to say that silly little frog cost $700. I was an inventor, an engineer by trade, so I had to do a lot of math. Granted, I'm not a math savant, but I sure as shootin' can tell the difference between three and four critters over there."

"Could something else have happened to it? Misplaced, or could someone else have taken it?"

"I have a cleaning lady who's been with us, just me now, since I moved here. I'd trust her with my life. A couple of workers have been in the house in the last couple of days. They could have swiped it, but I don't think so."

"Why not?"

"There's more."

Theo's phone rang before he could elaborate. He answered it and moved to the kitchen.

I went over to the table and lifted the cat figurine. I was struck by how heavy it was and by its intricately-detailed features.

"Danged plumber," Theo said as he came back in the room. "He can't get here until tomorrow. Sorry for having you come over. I could've met you somewhere."

"That's okay. You said there was more."

"I keep a safe in my closet. It's one that's fireproof, but not heavy. You could easily carry it off if you wanted to."

"It's gone?"

"No, but I keep $3,000 or so in it. If I ever need cash, I want it handy. Stupid, but I've always done it. This morning, I was in there to get money for the plumber, the danged one who isn't coming until tomorrow. He gives a cash discount. I'd forgotten to get it from the bank, so I went to the safe. Now, I don't know exactly how much I had, but it was more than what was there this morning. I'd guess it's $900 short. None of the workers who've been here were on the second floor, so they couldn't have taken it."

"Was it locked?"

"No. I'm usually alone here. I wanted to keep the money safe from fire, not theft."

"Have you filed a police report?"

"And tell them what? A little statue's missing, and there's some cash gone. Or, hey, my brother, or one of his pals, is a thief."

"It probably wouldn't help, but you never know."

"I might call the cops." He shrugged. "I'm not leaning that way."

"You really think it was Sal, or one of his friends?"

"Honest to God, Chris, I don't want it to be." He sighed. "Regardless what I want, it's probably one or more of them."

"Do they think you wouldn't notice things missing?"

Theo fiddled with his shorts again and stared out the window. "When they showed up, I was excited to see them, at least to see Sal. I didn't know the others. I became less excited when Sal said he was afraid that I was having memory troubles, thought it would be good for them to hang out here to help me. I told him that my memory was fine, or as fine as an old man's memory can be. Since I got these, everything was okay." He pointed to his hearing aids. "He beat around several bushes before the real reason for them coming started to come out. I could be off, although, I'd bet I'm not. They're broke, pennies away from being flat broke."

"Did he tell you that?"

"Not in so many words." He shook his head. "Do you know what they've paid for since showing up?"

"Not much?"

"How about not anything? They've made up stories about how checks from their investment portfolios have been delayed, or residuals from television appearances from the 1980s are being held up by agents and lawyers, or, oh, never mind."

"You don't believe it?"

"You know I've been fortunate. I sold my company for a tidy sum. I'm not as stupid to the ways of business as some may think. From living as long as I have, I can detect some things a mile away."

"Such as?"

"Such as pure, unadulterated bullshit."

"Any idea who did it?"

"Not really. I hope it isn't my brother. That's hope only. It could be any of them. If, umm, never mind."

"What?"

"If I had to guess, I'd say Wallace."

"Why?"

"His memory has me buffaloed. One minute, he's making sense, knows what's going on." Theo pointed to the top of his head. "Other times, he starts talking about something from the past, or forgets what he said seconds earlier, or looks off in space like he's seeing life in another dimension. It wouldn't take much imagination to see him stealing without knowing he did it, or, this is terrible to say, I've thought, a couple of times, that he's faking his problems."

"What makes you say that?"

"He forgets things or changes the subject when it's to his advantage. It's like when he doesn't want to answer something, he goes into his mental disappearing act. I can't put my finger on it. It's a feeling, that's all."

"You could be right," I said. "That doesn't make him a thief."

"I know. They're all broke, so any of them could've taken the money or snatched the frog to hock."

Or more than one of them working together, I thought. "What do you want me to do?"

Theo smiled for the first time since I'd arrived. "Listening to this old man spew accusations helps. I don't know that there's anything you can do. I was certain that if there was anyone on Folly who might be able to help, it'd be you."

I was glad Theo felt that way. I told him that I agreed with him when he said he didn't know anything I could do.

"Think about it," Theo said. "Next time you run into them, maybe you could pay more attention, or ask questions that could get one of them to say something suspicious. Crap, I have no idea."

I told him that I would.

He thanked me for listening and said our discussion made him want to take a nap.

In a matter of five hours, not only was I challenged to find a killer, but I added finding a thief to my to-do list.

Chapter Fifteen

In addition to today's near-impossible challenges, I added getting a good meal to my expanding list. The peanut butter sandwich worked for a few hours but, unless I wanted to fix another one for supper, I'd have to leave the house to find food. I made the block-long walk to St. James Gate, on the corner of Center Street and Ashley Avenue. The Irish restaurant was one of the easiest locations to give directions to since it faced the town's only traffic light and was painted black, not a typical beach color.

I'd been told that the deep browns and blacks that dominated the interior would be at home among the many pubs in Dublin. I was greeted by a smiling hostess and seven men sitting at the bar, most likely drinking one of the many craft beers the restaurant was known for. I wasn't a beer drinker, so the subtleties of the various brews were lost on me. I did know the restaurant served outstanding fish and chips.

The tables were full, so I sat at the bar where the bartender was in front of me as soon as I was situated. He said he was Richard and asked what I wanted to drink. He didn't let it show, but I suspected Richard was disappointed when I said I wanted water instead of Guinness. He smiled when he figured his tip would increase when I ordered food.

Richard was quick with the water, while I was much slower trying to figure out what I could do to help Theo or the police. I had suspected that Sal and his friends weren't as successful as they wanted everyone to believe, so I wasn't surprised by Theo's comments about them being broke. I could see one, or more of them, stealing cash, while wondering if he, or they, would have enough contacts in the area to fence the figurine. I realized that I was staring at a rerun of a golf tournament on the flat screen television on the wall behind the bar rather than thinking about my challenges. The fish and chips were delivered with a flourish. Richard set the plate in front of me and said, "In cod we trust."

I responded with a chuckle and bit my tongue, not to ask if he was ready to go on the road with the Legends comedy tour.

I was alternating between taking bites of cod and glancing at the television when a familiar face slid onto the seat next to me. I'd seen the man a couple of times. Unlike Charles, whose goal in life was to meet every human on earth, I normally wouldn't have spoken to the newcomer. Recent events made me more curious.

"Aren't you Neil Wilson?"

"Yes," he replied. He then turned to Richard and said, "Guinness."

Richard went to get Neil the drink that I was supposed to order.

Neil seemed larger up close than he had when I'd seen him in Bert's. He said, "I've seen you in Bert's. You're?"

"Chris Landrum."

Neil's eyes narrowed. "Yeah, I've heard about you."

"Good, I hope."

"Mostly. Someone there told me you live near the store and help the police when they're stumped."

That wasn't how I wanted the suspect in Michael Hardin's murder to think about me.

"Luck. People exaggerate."

He smiled. "Ain't that the truth?" He shifted on the chair trying to get his tall, wide frame comfortable.

"Work around here?"

I knew he didn't yet know what else to say. He hadn't had his first Guinness, so it was too early to ask if he killed Michael Hardin.

"Private security in Charleston and bouncer in a bar," he said as Richard delivered the beer.

"Oh."

"Know any jobs over here? I need to pick up something to keep me busy."

He sipped his beer and yawned. My eyes had adjusted to the dark interior, and I noticed that his were bloodshot. I wondered if it was from lack of sleep or alcohol.

"Afraid not," I said. "Give me a number. I'll call if I hear of anything."

He nodded but didn't offer a number. He returned to his drink, and I continued to eat. All we shared for the next fifteen minutes was the golf replay. He ordered a second beer while I wondered how to get him talking about Michael Hardin.

I didn't have to. The bartender did it for me. "Hey, Neil. That was terrible about your friend."

Neil said, "Friend?"

"Michael Hardin."

Neil turned from the TV to Richard. "Terrible." He said and stared in his mug like he was watching a fly doing the backstroke in the brew.

"Weren't you close?" Richard said.

Go, Richard, go!

"Not really," Neil said, as he continued watching whatever was happening in his mug. "More a business relationship."

Richard took the bar towel from his shoulder and started drying a mug. "All I know is I saw the two of you in here a few times. Hear what happened?"

"Nothing other than he was killed." He shook his head. "He was a nice guy. Don't know what the world's coming to."

Neil turned back to his mug, and I was afraid the conversation would go the same direction as had Michael.

I said, "What business were you and Michael in together?"

He looked at me. I was afraid he wasn't going to answer until he said, "I was one of his customers."

Richard had returned from getting more beer for two men at the other end of the bar, and said, "Michael was a bookie."

I refrained from shouting, *Thank you nosy Richard.* "I heard that. Someone told me he had several customers on the island. I never met him. From what I hear, he did a good business and was honest."

Richard was summoned by a thirsty customer, and Neil glanced back at the golf match. I figured our conversation was over, so was surprised when he faced me. His arm, the size of a giant sequoia, brushed against me as he turned. I reminded myself to never arm wrestle him.

"Michael was a good guy. I know some fellas who're constant losers. Michael gave them extra time to pay. You don't find that happening anywhere else. I'd done quite well with him. I hate that he's gone."

That was far from the version that Cal had shared. I couldn't figure out how to bring up the argument that Cal had told me about and his speculation that Neil owed Michael a *piss-pot full* of money; couldn't bring it up without Neil inflicting harm on me. I thought about asking where he was when Michael was killed, which would have been a wasted question since I hadn't heard when it happened. Besides, what would've been an innocent way to ask?

"You knew him pretty well," I said. "Have any idea who may've killed him?"

"Not really. He and I were good, but there are always disgruntled customers." He shook his head for the second time. "I suppose one of them could've fallen in the trap of killing the messenger. I see that a lot at my bar job, drunken show-offs, trying to pick fights with poor bartenders minding their own business doing their job. They're pissed about something and take it out on whoever happens to be around. Michael didn't lose horse races, games, tennis matches, or whatever. All he did was take bets. He didn't hold a gun to anyone's head to bet with him." He gave one more shake of his head. "Damn world's going all to hell."

I couldn't argue with that. I was searching for something to say when he grabbed a bar napkin and wrote a number on it. "Here. I'd appreciate it if you'd give me a call if you hear of any work."

I said that I would.

He gulped down the rest of his beer and mumbled that he needed to get home to get some sleep. He punctuated it with another yawn as he slid off the chair.

All I concluded from my conversation with Neil was that he was a world-class liar. I didn't know if he was responsible for Michael Hardin's death. I equally knew Cal had told me the truth about Neil's tirade directed at Michael. Neil probably hadn't stolen the figurine or the money from Theo, but he was now at the top of my suspect list for killing the bookie.

Chapter Sixteen

Boring another hole in my belt hinted that I needed to cut back on my traditional French toast breakfast at the Lost Dog Cafe. Over the last month, I'd been successful, so decided to celebrate my lower caloric intake by having French toast. Did that make sense? Of course not. Did that stop me? Nope. I rationalized it by walking instead of driving several blocks to the Dog where I was greeted by Amber, my favorite server. She was approaching fifty, five-foot five, with long auburn hair pulled in a ponytail. We had dated for a couple of years when I first arrived on Folly and have remained friends ever since; a relationship I cherished. It was already a good day. It was made better when she led me to my favorite table.

With a radiant smile, she said, "Coffee and fresh fruit parfait?"

"Out of mud-covered gravel?" I asked the lady, whose sense of humor equaled her beauty.

She knew I was more likely to order gravel than fresh fruit parfait.

"How about French toast?"

"You took the words right out of my mouth."

"But not the calories," she said as she punched my arm then left to put in the order.

She returned with coffee. "Wrangle any more guys fishing for mackerel in the middle of Center Street?"

In addition to being great at her job, Amber was exceptional at collecting rumors.

"No."

"How about bodies in the bush?"

I sighed. "No."

"You're slipping. Figure out who killed the bookie?"

"Who said I was trying?"

"Let's see." She rubbed her chin. "Chester Carr said you were sticking your nose in again. Charles told me that you almost have it figured out. Dude—"

I looked toward the window leading to the kitchen. "Think my food's ready?"

She laughed and headed to the kitchen.

Marc Salmon was standing beside my table before Amber returned with my celebratory breakfast. "Morning, Chris." He stared at the seat across from me.

I took the hint. "Join me."

"I can spare a few. Houston isn't here yet."

Marc and his fellow councilmember, Houston Bass, met most mornings in the Dog. Marc claimed they discuss the "intricacies of the difficult issues" facing the council. Granted, they could be overheard discussing the business of governing the island, although most of the time, they were chewing on breakfast and the rumor *de jour*. It was said they had a decent handle on the "pulse of the community," and a firm grip on "all the gossip worth repeating."

Amber returned, set a mug of coffee in front of Marc, and

told me my food would be up as soon as the cook stuffs the calories in.

I faked a smile and watched her move to a nearby table to see if there was anything else she could do for the couple seated there.

Marc took a sip, and said, "What's the latest on the dead guy?"

"I suspect you know more than I do."

He chuckled. "Won't know until you tell me what you know."

The gossip-collecting councilmember came by his reputation honestly. I shared what little I knew, skipping over my conversation with Neil Wilson.

"Nothing new there," he said, more to himself than to me.

"Got a question," I said.

"Shoot."

"Do you know Janice Raque?"

"Why?"

"I asked first."

A childish comment, I admit. Unless I got Marc talking, I'd never get anything out of him.

"Yes, she is one of our fine citizens, attends some of the council meetings, and shares her opinions whether asked or not. She lives at Mariner's Cay."

Mariner's Cay is a condo complex and marina on Folly Road the other side of the Folly River, but a short walk to the retail stores and restaurants on the island, as well as the beach. I wasn't about to ask Marc if he thought she was capable of killing the bookie and found it hard to believe he didn't know anything else about her.

"Is that it?"

He looked up from his mug and narrowed his eyes, irritated that I was disappointed because he didn't know more about Janice.

"She's married. I suppose he lives with her. I've only seen him once, and she clams up when anyone asks about him." Marc smiled. "She smiles a lot. She's also a bit feisty if you ask her something she doesn't want to talk about."

Marc said it like he had first-hand experience.

Amber returned with three plates, set the one with French toast in front of me, and took the other two to a couple behind us.

Marc pointed to the door and started to stand. "There's Houston, better get to discussing city business."

He grabbed his mug and was gone before I could ask, "What city business?"

Amber returned, looked around the room, and took the seat that Marc had vacated. "Heard you talking about Janice Raque."

"I was asking Marc what he knew about her. You know her?"

"She's been in a few times. Don't know much about her, except that she's got a temper and a gambling problem."

"How do you know?"

Amber leaned closer to the table. "A couple of weeks ago, she was sitting right over there." Amber pointed to a table in the center of the room. "Shantel, a server on her second day, was waiting on her. Somehow, Shantel grabbed the wrong plate and plopped it down in front of Janice. Well, you would've thought that Shantel took a plate of wiggly-worms to the bitty. I was afraid Janice was going to stab poor Shantel with her butter knife."

"What happened?"

"Zack was the manager on duty. He was nearby and stepped between Shantel and Janice. He managed to settle down the knife-wielding woman. Janice didn't apologize to Shantel. She did leave a decent tip; probably because we comped breakfast."

"You mentioned a gambling problem."

Amber saw a customer on the other side of the room raise her hand. She said she'd be back. My breakfast was getting cold, but it didn't stop me from sopping it in syrup and enjoying each bite.

Amber returned and said, "That's what I hear."

I assumed she was talking about Janice's gambling problem, "What did you hear about it?"

"Now, mind you, this came from someone who's accurate more often than not. I can't swear to how true it is. From what I hear, Janice placed a large bet on a horserace with a bookie. The horse she bet won, and she would've won, get this, $3,500."

"Would have won?"

"Good catch. Janice called in her bet with the bookie. The next day, the bookie told her she didn't get it in before the race went off. The person who told me said Janice wasn't spittin' nails, she was spittin' railroad spikes. She didn't have to pay the bet, but lost a ton of money because it wasn't placed. She swore she had it in plenty early. Who knows?"

"That's bad, though it doesn't mean she has a gambling problem."

"Oh," Amber said, "Didn't I tell you that she already owed the bookie $3,000 before that bet? She planned that the bet she won, and didn't win, would get her out of the hole."

I nodded. "The bookie was Michael Hardin?"

Amber smiled.

Chapter Seventeen

The Comedy Legends World Tour was mere hours from its Folly Beach debut. Theo had called three times since sunrise. During the first call, he said that Sal told him, before going to bed, to call me first thing in the morning to see what time their *opening act*, a.k.a. Country Cal Ballew, would finish his first set.

I promised myself not to tell Cal about his *opening act* status. If I had, the Legends tour would have been cancelled, as Cal would say, "in a hummingbird's heartbeat." I told Theo I'd have to ask Cal and suggested that he could call him instead of me relaying the information. He said he didn't want to bother the bar's owner. I took it as a compliment that he felt comfortable pestering me, or so I told myself.

I gave Cal a couple of hours to wake up before I called. He said that the *funny guys* should be ready to go on at 9:00, that he'd be starting his second set at 10:00 sharp. He repeated *10:00 sharp*.

Theo called a second time before I could call with the starting time. "Sal wants to know if there will be reporters from the Charleston television stations at the performance. If so, did they want to interview the Legends before or after the performance?

I started to ask if he was serious. Instead, I said, "They'll be there if Cal's is on fire."

"Oh. I'll tell them you weren't sure."

Wise. With the public relations questions out of the way, I told Theo what Cal said about their starting time.

His third call came two hours before Cal was to begin his set.

"Chris, Sal wanted to let you know that I will be chauffeuring the Legends in my Mercedes. Sal said all the top promoters they've worked with provided a limo to their *sold-out performances*." He lowered his voice. "He wanted me to wear a chauffeur's outfit, including one of those silly hats. I said, "No way."" He chuckled. "Actually, I said, 'Hell no!'"

Visions of trick-or-treat popped in my head. "Why a limo?"

I heard him sigh. "Sal said if television cameras are there, it's a good visual for the Legends' arrival."

I told him I'd keep that in mind and that I'd see him tonight. I also wondered if anyone would notice if I jumped off the Folly Pier rather than attend the Comedy Legends' Folly debut.

Charles said he'd meet me at the bar an hour before Cal started his set. We could get a good table for the historic event. That meant my friend would be there by 6:30, so I walked four blocks to Cal's and was there around the time I figured Charles would show. I was surprised to see Charles and Pete, or Marvin Peters, at the front of the room, sliding together three tables near the raised stage. They had already moved eight chairs to the tables. I waved at Cal, who was standing behind the bar, drying a wine glass. He cocked his head in the direction of Charles and Pete.

Johnny Cash was singing "Ring of Fire," from the Wurlitzer as I headed over to see what Charles was doing.

"Good timing," Charles said. "We're done."

I smiled and shook Pete's hand. He was dressed in raggedy jeans and a black T-shirt with *THE COMEDY STORE* in red and white letters on the front. It looked as old as Pete.

He saw me looking at his shirt. "In addition to being one of the Legends, I'm filling in as advance man. Our regular guy couldn't make flight arrangements. Got to make sure the venue's ready. I'll walk back to Theo's and get in my stage garb before our grand entrance."

It was more than I wanted to know. "Oh."

He looked at his watch. "Better get going. Got to get dressed then decide which jokes to open with." He nodded goodbye to Charles and me then went to the bar to shake Cal's hand and thank him for his hospitality, things I figured a good advance man would do.

The bar was beginning to fill. I knew some of the regulars, plus several newcomers. I asked Charles about them, and he said that Sal had taped posters around town announcing the Legends' Tour and left a stack of flyers at the Tides.

Charles looked around for Cal and whispered, "You may not want to mention the posters to Cal. Seems his name was left off." He rolled his eyes. "An oversight, I'm sure."

"Right."

The sounds of Tanya Tucker's "Delta Dawn" and the smell of frying burgers filled the air. All but two tables were occupied, so Cal had a grin on his face as he made his way over to Charles and me.

"Best Sunday crowd I've had since, well, since I don't know

when. Word must've gotten around that I'm doing a couple of sets. Don't usually sing on Sundays, you know."

Charles looked at me and gave an abbreviated shake of his head, roughly translated as, "Don't you dare mention the posters."

I didn't need the reminder. "Great group, Cal. Word got around."

Cal looked at the empty seats at the double table. "What time is my undercard getting here?"

In addition to not telling Cal that the comedians are considering him their opening act, I won't mention to the comedians that Cal has called them his undercard. It's beginning to look like a night to keep my mouth shut.

Charles helped me with that plan when he said, "Don't know. I'm sure they'll want to hear you sing."

"No doubt," Cal said. "Chris, you did tell them when they'll go on, and off?"

I told him I'd shared that information with Theo.

He nodded and said that he'd better help Joy, his server, distribute beer to his "adoring fans."

Charles watched the country crooner head to the bar. "It'd be best if we could keep the 'undercard' and the 'opening act' as far away from each other as possible. I'm not big on bar brawls."

I agreed and noticed a couple at a table between us and the bar. The room was dark, and I couldn't make out their features, but thought the woman looked familiar and fit the description I'd been given of Janice Raque. I asked Charles if he knew who they were.

He squinted in the direction of the couple. "Not certain, but I think the woman's Janice Raque. I've seen her a few times but remembered because of her unusual last name. Why?"

I gave him a rundown on what I'd heard about Janice and her relationship with Michael Hardin.

"When were you going to tell me?"

Charles was peeved that I knew something and hadn't shared it a millisecond after I'd learned it.

I told him that we hadn't had a chance to talk recently.

He reminded me that he had a phone.

I conceded that I could've called and gave a half-hearted apology.

He huffed but seemed mollified. Jumping off the Pier was becoming more appealing.

Randy Travis had finished "On the Other Hand" when a blaring automobile horn grabbed the attention of all but the noisiest customers. It continued to fill the air with its irritating bellowing.

Charles headed out to see what was going on.

I followed, but not as enthusiastically.

Theo's Mercedes was in front of the bar; its horn continued to blow. The back door opened, and out stepped three-fourths of the Legends. Sal was out first, dressed in the same robin-egg blue three-piece suit he'd worn when he first met Cal. Wallace, in all black, was next to scoot out of the seat, followed by Marvin Peters, excuse me, Pete Marvin. Yes, he had on his red sport coat and black ascot. They reminded me of going to the circus when I was a kid and watching approximately seventy-five colorfully dressed clowns exit a Volkswagen. Ray Bentley stepped out of the front passenger's seat. He wore jeans, faded green T-shirt, and looked like he would rather be anywhere but here.

The three clowns, excuse me, comedians from the back seat looked around, probably for television cameras. Theo was still in the Mercedes limo and wiggled his finger for me to stick my head in the window.

"They made me sit on the horn, something about alerting the media that they're here."

In the dim light of the car's interior, I saw Theo blush. I felt his pain.

We watched the comedians straightening their clothes, pulling their shoulders back, and entering Cal's like they were entering Madison Square Garden to perform for thousands.

It wasn't an exaggeration to think this would be one of the longest nights of my life.

Chapter Eighteen

"Guys and gals," came Cal's powerful voice through an oversized speaker on each side of the stage. He wore his trademark rhinestone-adorned white coat, black jeans, cowboy boots, and Stetson, with his gray hair inching out around the sides. "Thanks for coming out. Ya'll are in for a treat. Not only will I be performing country classics and my top-ten hit, we have a group of comedians from out of town who've agreed to share their funny business with us." He looked over, nodded to the tables where Sal and his group were seated with Theo, Charles, and me. He clapped his hands in the direction of the entertainers like he was applauding their attendance. The only other sounds coming from the room were beer bottles clanking, plus a man at the bar asking about his burger.

"Without further ado, I'll kick off the festivities with 'Hey, Good Lookin',' a ditty made famous by my good friend Hank Williams Sr."

I knew ole Hank and Cal were good friends because Cal

had confided that he met the fabled country singer twice; the second time, Hank had called him "buddy."

Wallace whispered to Sal, "That tall drink of water needs to work on his introduction of the Legends."

Cal finished his first song and swung into "Your Cheatin' Heart," another Hank Sr. classic. He'd performed the same songs for more than forty years, yet sold them to the audience like it was the first time. The noise level in the full room rose in time with the volume of Cal's singing.

I turned from the stage just in time to see the man who had been with a woman who fit the description of Janice Raque push his chair back, throw cash on the table, and storm out.

Cal's server, Joy, a new addition to the staff, had been behind the man as he exited before she came to our table to see if we needed more drinks.

I tilted my head toward Janice's table. "What's going on over there?"

Joy looked the direction I'd nodded. "Nothing unusual, I hear. That's Horace and Janice. I'm told they come in every so often, get in a fight most every time. One of them usually charges out. Good tippers though. Why?"

"Curious. What do they fight about?"

"You name it. One of the other servers told me if Horace says the sky is up, she'll say it's down. If he says water's wet, she'll argue it's as dry as the desert. Gotta keep moving. Cal's croonin' turns beer sippers to guzzlers. Ya'll need anything else?"

Sal said, "Another round for all of us. Stick it on Theo's tab."

Joy said it'd be right up, Cal switched to songs from another of his "good friends," George Jones, and Wallace kept glancing at his watch, no doubt wondering how much longer he'd have to listen to the undercard.

From the stage, Cal said, "I'm going to finish my first set with 'Don't We All Have the Right,' a song made famous by my good friend, the late Roger Miller."

Three minutes later, he finished the song with, "Don't we all have the right to be wrong now and then?"

A nice round of applause filled the room, none louder than from the comedians. I suspected because he was finished rather than appreciation for his singing.

Cal's curved spine leaned toward the silver mic. "Now, guys and gals, Cal's is privileged to have some funny guys entertaining until I start my next set in an hour. I'm plum piss-poor at remembering names, so I'll let Theo Stoll's brother Sal serve as MC for their part of the show." He snapped his fingers. "Almost forgot, Cal's doesn't have a budget large enough to pay the group their normal rate, so feel free to slip some paper money out of your pocket, after you pay your bar tab, that is. Before you leave, slip the cash in a bucket that I'll be parking on the corner of the stage."

I glanced over at Sal and could almost read his mind thinking, *He ain't paying us anything, much less something from his budget,* and, *That was a "plum piss-poor" way to turn the stage over to the Legends.* He gritted his teeth and faked a smile as he made his way to the mic.

"Thank you, Cal, for the nic—umm, introduction. I'm Sal Stoll. I'm honored to be one of the stand-up comics who'll entertain you tonight. I'll also be master of ceremonies and will introduce my fellow famous comedians so they can bring hilarity to your evening." He paused, looked around the room. "I was over at my brother Theo's this morning. There was a tap on the door." Sal gave a stage nod. "Yep, his plumber has a strange sense of humor."

The other comedians laughed like it was the funniest thing they'd ever heard.

A handful of others in the room chuckled.

Once again, I considered jumping off the Pier.

Sal smiled. "Now that we're off to a good start, let me bring to the stage one of the best comics who ever stood behind a microphone. He's travelled all over the country, bringing laughs to thousands, no, millions, at comedy clubs, Las Vegas stages, and television variety shows. Let's have a big hand for Pete Marvin."

Pete moved to the microphone, lifted it off the stand, and unwrapped the cord from the stand. In the stage lights, I noticed how much more frayed his and Sal's outfits were. "Thanks Sal." Pete stepped toward the front of the stage and tapped on an imaginary door. "Knock, knock." He moved to the other side of the door. "Who's there?" He scooted back to the spot where he'd said, "knock, knock." Held his arms out wide. "It's me, ladies and germs. Your entertainment!"

That got a laugh from the comedians.

No one else in the room cracked a smile. Several groaned.

Sal leaned over toward me. "That gets them every time. They were expecting a knock, knock joke. What makes comedy funny is the unexpected."

I suspected the most stupid, childish knock-knock joke would've been funnier. But, hey, what'd I know about comedy? After all, Pete was the Legend.

Pete didn't let the lack of laughter deter him. "This morning, Theo over there," he hesitated and pointed at Theo, "told me to follow my dreams. Now Theo's a wise man, so I followed his advice. I went back to bed."

That did garner laughs from some customers, probably from those who had consumed the most beer. There was hope.

I began to lose faith after Pete shared several more jokes.

From what I could tell, customers at three of the tables thought he was funny. That would have been good if there weren't four times that many tables in Cal's. One of the three tables was occupied by the rest of the Legends.

Pete looked around, gave a wide stage smile, then thanked the audience for being so enthusiastic. I wondered if he'd been in the same room as I had for the last ten minutes.

"Now I'm going to welcome Sal back to the stage to share his unique brand of humor."

I wondered if unique could mean the same thing as not funny.

Sal returned and took the mic from Pete.

"Let's give Pete another big hand," Sal said and clapped his hands together with the sound echoing through the speakers.

How had I missed the first big hand the audience had given Pete? He returned to the table and received pats on the back from Wallace, Ray, and Theo.

Sal waited for the applause from two drunks by the back door to die down, leaned toward the microphone, and looked at Cal who was standing by the bar. "Hey, Cal, I didn't know you were Chinese."

Cal looked at Sal and held out his hands like, "What're you talking about?"

Sal pointed to Cal's guitar on top of its case in the back corner of the stage. "That last song you sang, remember: 'Don't we all have the right to be Wong now and then?'"

Pete slapped his hands on his knees and leaned over to me. "Sal loves to bring local flavor to his set. See how he weaved in the country music?"

I saw how he'd insulted the owner of the bar who was giving Sal a chance to perform. I said, "Hmm."

"Speaking of Cal's," Sal continued from the stage, "a

termite walked in here last night. It said, 'Is the bar tender here?'"

I heard three people laughing behind me but didn't turn to see who they were. I was confident Cal wasn't one of them.

Sal did three jokes about marriage, and a couple about priests, before saying, "Time for me to get off the stage to turn it over to Wallace. Before I go, here's one for the road. A snake slithers into Cal's, and my country buddy refused to serve him. The snake was miffed, if snakes can be miffed. It asked Cal why. Old Cal tipped his fancy hat to the snake. 'You can't hold your alcohol.'"

That did bring laughter from a couple of tables that had been acting like they were at a funeral visitation rather than a comedy show.

Sal thanked the audience for being so attentive then introduced Wallace.

Wallace bounded on the stage with a burst of energy that I hadn't seen from him during our fateful meeting in the street, or the other times I'd seen him. He grabbed the mic, thanked Sal for the kind introduction, gazed out at the audience, and said, "Yes, I know what you're thinking. You expected a comedian. Instead you got Johnny Cash." He moved his hand up and down his all-black garb. "Before I upstage Cal and burst into 'I Walk the Line,' let me give you some advice. You may want to write some of this down, so I'll give you time to get out a pen and paper."

He looked at his watch then at the audience. If he was waiting for pens and paper to appear, it would be a long night.

"Okay, here goes. First, no matter what they tell you at the store, don't waste money on expensive binoculars." He paused, looked around before leaning closer to the tables, and whispered in the microphone, "All you have to do is stand closer to what you want to see."

There were chuckles from two ladies at the bar and from a couple of tables near the rear.

"Thank you," Wallace said. "Here's something that's even more important. Never get in line in the bank behind someone wearing a ski mask."

I heard a few more chuckles, a smattering of laughter, and, of course, more than a smattering from the comedians at our table. Apparently, they thought their reactions would be contagious. They were wrong.

Wallace smiled at the audience. "Thank you, thank you. Ready yet for 'I Walk the Line'?"

"No," yelled a man leaning against the bar.

I'd venture to guess that he was speaking for most everyone in the room, although, I wondered if Wallace's singing was worse than his opening jokes.

Wallace smiled. "Your loss. Okay, did you hear about the proctologist who …" Wallace hesitated, looked at the floor, then stared at the silver microphone. "I remember once, while I was headlining in Vegas at the Sands. Been a while back. Well, umm, who's that singer who's called green eyes?"

Ray, Wallace's son, was sitting beside me. He mumbled something, looked at his dad, and yelled, "Frank Sinatra, old blue eyes."

Wallace smiled, "That's it, Frank Sinatra. What was I saying about him?" He looked at the audience.

I was expecting, no, hoping for a joke.

Most of the others in the room were wondering where Wallace was going with the story.

Wallace shook his head and giggled. "Did you hear about the agnostic dyslexic insomniac? He stayed up all night wondering if there was a dog."

That received the most laughs of anything Wallace had said. I wondered if it was because the audience felt it was that funny or were relieved that he managed to share a whole joke.

Wallace took a deep breath and laughed. "That's more like it. Hey, when we got here, Cal told me that beer won't make you smarter. Wrong. I said it made Bud wiser."

Cal pulled a chair up beside me on my right. He leaned over and said, "Know where I can get a shepherd's hook to yank him off the stage?"

Charles said, "Don't know many shepherds on Folly."

"Not many?" I said.

"Okay, none."

From the stage, Wallace said, "Did I tell you about that time I found little Ray out back smoking … what was it again, Ray?"

Ray slammed his hand on the table and whispered something to Sal, who started to respond, before Ray said, "No! I'm out of here." He pushed his chair back, shoved his way past a couple at the table behind us, and stomped out of the building.

Most of the patrons didn't notice; they were staring at Wallace, probably wondering what he would say, or not say, next.

Pete said something to Sal, who stood and moved to the side of the stage.

Wallace saw him, looked at his watch, and shook his head. "Sorry folks, out of time. Won't be able to sing my big hit." He turned to Sal and said, "Want me to introduce Ray, or are you?"

Sal rushed to the microphone, took it out of Wallace's hand, and put his arm around the much shorter comedian.

"Ladies and gents, we're running a bit long. I know you want to hear more tunes from the legendary Cal Ballew, so Ray has agreed to skip his set. Let's put our hands together for Pete, Wallace, and, of course, me." He took an extended bow, while the audience gave a more than generous round of applause.

Cal's next set wasn't scheduled to begin for twenty minutes. Like the professional he was, he strapped his Martin acoustic guitar over his shoulder then took the microphone from Sal.

"Great job, boys. Great job. Now Sal is too humble to ask, but remember, the tip bucket is right there." He pointed to the tin bucket on the corner of the stage. "Be sure to plop some big bucks in there for these here Legends of Comedy."

I wouldn't have associated the word humble with Sal. Cal had been nice to remind the audience about tips.

Cal strummed a chord on his Martin. "Now, let's go back a few years. Here's one made famous by my good buddy Roy Acuff called 'Wabash Cannonball.'"

Charles tapped me on the arm. "Chris, have we been here a week yet?"

It was the funniest thing I'd heard all night.

Chapter Nineteen

Cal had been kind enough to give the stand-up comics the stage, so I wanted to support him and stay until the bitter end, emphasis on bitter. There was little more I wanted to say to the comics, and Charles had remained quiet—quiet for Charles. I hoped that Theo's guests would leave.

Instead, they stayed at the table and ordered two more rounds of beer during Cal's second set. Most of the customers had drifted out. Those who remained spent more time staring at their drinks than paying attention to what was happening on the stage.

Janice was still at a table, so I thought it would be a good time to meet her. Cal began John Anderson's hit, "Would You Catch a Falling Star," as I walked to Janice's table.

"Oh," I said, like I'd just noticed her. "Aren't you Janice Raque?"

Her eyes narrowed. Instead of saying anything, she nodded.

"Thought so. I was on my way to the bar and saw you. I'm

Chris Landrum. You were talking to Michael Hardin one afternoon in Bert's. Someone told me who you were. Just wanted to say hi."

I didn't remember seeing her before and hoped, at some point, that she'd had a conversation with Michael in Bert's.

She maintained her skeptical look. "You know Michael?"

"Not well," I said.

"He handle your bets?"

"No, but I know several of his customers. You?"

"Huh, yeah. Some of the biggest mistakes I've ever made. Can't say I'm sorry. He got what he deserved."

I moved to the seat across from her. She didn't ask me to leave.

"Mistakes?"

Cal was singing "Chiseled in Stone," so I leaned closer to Janice to hear her.

"He cheated me out of a lot of money. You're fortunate you didn't give him any."

"Sorry to hear it. Any idea who killed him?"

She looked to see where I had come before staring at me. "You a cop?"

I chuckled and shook my head. "Hardly. I'm here with some friends. We were over there talking about Michael's murder. You knew him, so I thought I'd ask."

"You can tell your friends that I didn't. The cops have already talked to me." She grabbed her purse off the floor. "I gotta go. Nice meeting you."

She headed to the exit without looking back. None of her words, body language, or attitude said that she thought it was nice meeting me.

I returned to our table where Charles whispered, "You need to work on your pick-up lines. She left like you'd stuck her butt with a straight pin."

Cal finished his song. I started to respond when I heard Wallace tell Sal, "I know I killed him."

I turned to Wallace and started to ask the comedian what he meant.

Charles also heard him. He pivoted away from me and said, "Kill who, Wallace?"

Sal slipped his arm around Wallace then turned to Charles. "Wallace said that we killed the audience. Isn't that right, Wallace?" Before Wallace responded, Sal added, "That means we were a hit."

Wallace had a glazed look in his eyes. Each of the comics had consumed several beers, so I didn't know if the look was alcohol-induced, or if he was drifting from reality.

Theo was behind Wallace, and he shook his head.

From the stage, Cal said he was taking a "pause for the cause," as opposed to having to "take a piss," as he often announced. He was on his best behavior in front of the Legends.

Sal took advantage of the quieter room to say, "Well, Theo, Charles, Chris, what'd you think of our show? Like Wallace said, I think we killed them."

I was relieved at not having to say a slow death by razor blades, when Pete said, "We were a little rusty. I screwed up a couple of jokes. It's been a few nights since we preformed."

"Few nights," Wallace said. "How about months?"

Sal jumped in, "He's always joking. Good one, Wallace."

Charles, the peacemaker, said, "I've been a regular at Cal's since our friend took over seven years ago. That's the best comedy show I've seen in here."

"I've got to agree with Charles," Cal said as he walked over to the table.

I wondered if the comedians realized that it was the only comedy show in Cal's history. I also wondered how I could bring the conversation back to what I heard Wallace say and not what Sal wanted us to believe Wallace had said.

Wallace tapped his beer bottle on the table and pointed it at Pete. "Pete, remember the other night when we were waiting in the green room to appear with Johnny Carson on the Tonight Show? You said I should tell my joke about the Rabbi and the priest. Remember what I said?"

Pete said, "Now Wallace, that was a few years—"

Wallace laughed. "I said not that joke, because … Umm, guess it was funnier then."

Sal said, "Think we'd better call it a night. We're not as young as we used to be."

Theo said, "Good idea, I'll get the car, the limo."

Cal headed to the stage to finish his set, the comics wobbled out of the bar, and I wondered what Wallace meant about killing someone.

Charles and I were the only customers left when Cal finished singing.

Joy was picking up bottles from the tables.

"I'm too old for these late nights," Cal said as he flopped down in a chair at our table.

Joy yelled from across the room and asked if he wanted anything.

"Peace, quiet, two new feet, a new ticker."

She grinned. "How about a beer?"

Joy was back to the table with his drink before he said that it was his next choice.

Cal took a gulp and said, "Now that they're gone, what'd you think about their show?"

I said, "They had some good jokes but, like Pete told us, they were rusty. I could tell they were better back in the day."

Charles smiled. "Looked more like the over-the-hill gang than the Legends. And what's with Wallace? Forgetting lines, screwing up times, *The Tonight Show* the other night. Get real."

"Think the geezer's gone bonkers," Cal said.

That showed the singer's high-level grasp of psychiatry. Or did it? Granted, I'd seen Wallace dazed, confused, and struggling to maintain a grasp of reality. I'd also seen him remember some of his routine and appear normal during a couple of conversations. And there was his statement about killing someone.

"Charles, what's your take on his comment about killing him?"

"Don't know. I'm certain it didn't have anything to do with their performances."

Cal leaned forward. "What're you talking about?"

I explained what Wallace had said while Cal was singing.

Cal took another draw on his beer, slipped a chair in front of him, and put his feet up on the seat. "Think he was talking about Michael Hardin?"

Charles glanced at me then back at Cal before pointing his cane at the stage. "The boy's performance up there was schizoid: memory accurate, memory sucked, loss-of-reality powerful. From what you said, his other performance, the one in the middle of the street, would qualify for a straitjacket. Think I'm leaning toward Cal's bonkers diagnosis although, by the time they left, they were a few beers passed soused. They were all jabbering nonsense." He looked at the table where Janice Raque had been seated. "Why'd you leave our outstanding company to hit on that Raque chick?"

Cal pointed at me. "In the middle of my set."

I smiled at the aging singer. "Guilty. I wanted to see how she'd react to me mentioning Michael Hardin."

"Well?" Charles said with his usual amount of patience.

"Don't think she'll be sending flowers to his funeral."

Cal took his feet off the chair and leaned toward me. "Think she killed him?"

I shrugged.

"What'd she say?" asked Charles, not satisfied with my shrug.

I filled in the details, at least, the few I knew from our brief conversation.

Charles said, "That the best you can do?"

I said it was. Charles stretched and clasped his hands behind his head. "This's been quite a night. Got to see some Legends, or maybe that's Legends in their minds, right up on Cal's stage. Got to know about two people who might've killed the bookie. And got to watch Chris stay up two hours past his bedtime. Will wonders never cease?"

I didn't know about all that, but knew I was leaving Cal's with more questions than when I'd entered. Did the "Legends" believe that they were Legends of comedy? I didn't, but wondered if they did. Did Janice have something to do with Michael's death? Then there's Wallace. Did he kill someone, or see someone get killed? If he did, why did he say what he did?

Chapter Twenty

The phone rang not long after I'd fallen asleep. I wasn't aware of research to back me up although, from personal experience, the odds were mighty slim, like being-struck-by-a-meteor slim, that a call at three o'clock in the morning would bring good news. It only took me saying, "Hello," to confirm my suspicion.

"Could you come to the house? Oh, yeah, this is Theo."

"What's wrong?"

"It's dreadful. My God, horrible. Dead, he's dead. Please come."

"Who's dead?"

"Please."

I was sitting on the edge of the bed and realized that Theo was so shaken, it'd be useless to ask anything else.

"On my way."

I shook the cobwebs out of my head, got dressed, and drove through the deserted streets to Theo's. It became apparent as soon as I turned on his street that I wasn't the first person summoned. Flashing red and blue lights from two Folly Beach patrol cars, one fire engine, an ambulance from Charleston, and two unmarked police vehicles reflected off street signs, each other, and windows from nearby houses.

I pulled off the street a half-block behind the emergency vehicles and headed toward a familiar face, Officer Trula Bishop, who was standing in the middle of the street ready to direct traffic for any curious citizens who might be driving by. Traffic at this hour could be counted on one finger, so she had little to do.

"Good morning, Mr. Chris."

I'd met Officer Bishop shortly after she'd started on the force three years ago. We'd talked on numerous occasions, and she'd helped me out a couple of times when I'd managed to find myself in awkward situations.

I nodded toward Theo's house. "Trula, what's going on?"

Instead of answering, she looked at her watch, then said, "What brings you out at this ungodly hour?"

"Theo Stoll, the owner of the house, called to ask me to come over."

She smiled. "Then you know what happened."

"No. Theo sounded in shock. That's all I know."

She nodded like that'd made sense. "Seems that someone fell down the steps, broke his neck. Killed him."

I exhaled. "Who?"

"Don't know. I haven't been in. Two officers and the chief were already on the scene. She asked me to stay out here to keep riffraff, like you, away."

She was teasing about me being riffraff, or so I hoped. I asked if it was okay for me to see what had happened. I reminded her that the owner requested my presence.

"If I had to shoot you to keep you away," she smiled, "I'd get in trouble for shooting wildlife out of season." She flicked her wrist toward the house. "There should be one of our guys at the door. Check with him before you go in."

I thanked her and wished her well on riffraff patrol.

I reached the door and lucked out, the second time since arriving.

Officer Allen Spencer met me. "Chris, is there some reason that I see you at as many death scenes as I see the coroner?"

He said it with a smile, although it was only a slight exaggeration.

I shrugged and told him that Theo called. Then I asked what'd happened.

Allen moved aside.

I moved to the entry and saw several cops, medics, plus someone from the coroner's office standing around a body at the bottom of stairs. The object of their attention was already in a body bag. The coroner, with the help of one of the cops, was hefting it on a stretcher. I asked Allen who was killed.

He moved me out of the doorway, so the body could be wheeled out, and said, "One of the visitors staying at the house with Mr. Stoll, in fact, the son of one of the visitors."

"Raymond Bentley?"

"Think that's it."

Theo and two of his houseguests were seated in the great room. I wanted to learn what I could before joining them.

"How'd it happen?"

"According to Mr. Stoll, Theo, not his brother, the group performed at Cal's last night. They consumed more adult beverages than their bodies could handle. Mr. Stoll said he was driving for the group and had a couple of beers, but the others were inebriated when they dragged in here around midnight. He said they barely staggered their way upstairs."

"Did anyone see what happened?"

"You're beginning to sound like the chief."

"She's my role model," I said, smiled, and reworded my question. "Witnesses?"

Allen looked toward the group in the great room. "I was second on the scene. Officer Fish beat me by a few minutes. When I got here, the body was where it was when you came in, Theo and the others were where they are now, and Fisk was calling the Sheriff's Office. If any of the guys in there, except for Theo, had been driving and I pulled them over, they'd be spending the night in the drunk tank. Their eyes are redder than Santa's suit. They weren't making sense. When the ambulance got here on a wasted trip, they'd settled down. From what I could gather, they'd been in their rooms when it happened."

"Who else is here?"

"The chief and Detective Callahan got here fast. They had each of the guys move to separate rooms, so they could question them individually. Callahan is still with one of them."

"No one saw him fall."

"Only Raymond Bentley." Allen shook his head. "He won't be telling us much."

Chief LaMond started down the steps and saw me talking to Allen. Instead of greeting me with an insult, she said, "Hi, Chris."

"Chief," I said then waited for her to say something snarky.

"Glad you're here."

If I had false teeth, they would've fallen out when my jaw dropped. "You are?"

"Theo asked if he could call you," She looked around the stairs to the group gathered in the great room. "He was so shaken that I was afraid he was going to drop dead in the middle of my crime scene. I was beginning to worry about him so, in a moment of weakness, I said he could call."

I asked her the same question I'd asked Allen. She said that from the statements each of the guys made, no one saw him fall. They claim that when they got home from Cal's, they were pooped and went to their rooms.

"Did they tell you Ray left Cal's before the others?"

"One of them did." She flipped open her notebook. "Marvin Peters, who said he would rather go by Pete Marvin." She shook her head. "Hell, I'd rather go by Jennifer Lawrence, but I'm stuck with Cindy LaMond."

"Pete's the only one who mentioned Ray leaving Cal's? That seems strange."

"Detective Callahan is upstairs talking to Theo's brother, so I don't know what he's said. The confused one, Wallace, is so out of it, I doubt he knows if he was at Cal's tonight, umm, last night, or climbing the Eiffel Tower. That boy's got a spittoon full of screws loose."

"Anything else?"

"Crap, Chris, want me to email you the police report when we get it finished? Even better, if the coroner's wagon hadn't skedaddled, I'd let you go with them to help with the autopsy."

I bit my lower lip to keep me from smiling. "So, nothing else?"

Cindy pointed toward the great room. "Get in there. Work your calming charm on poor Theo."

I saluted, said, "Yes, chief," and joined the comics and *poor Theo*.

Sal's questioning must have ended because he was back in the room, wearing blue and white horizontal striped pajama bottoms with a navy-blue top. He stared at the floor and held his head between his hands. Pete was staring out the window at total darkness. His bright red PJs would've made a stop light feel anemic. Wallace had on the same clothes he wore in Cal's. The only things missing were shoes and socks.

Theo looked up. Not only did he look up, but he pushed himself off the couch and hugged me. His white robe tickled my chin. His arms were more powerful than I would've imagined. I had to pull them away to break his grasp.

"Thank you for coming. I didn't know what to do. Didn't know who to call."

I was pleased that he felt comfortable calling, although I would've preferred a more decent hour. I told him I was glad to come.

He turned to the other three sitting on the couch. "Guys, Chris is here."

They weren't as happy to see me as Theo had been.

Only Sal's nod acknowledged my presence. He didn't speak.

I was confident that I knew, but still asked Theo what happened. He told me the same story I'd heard from the police. He added that he was asleep when he heard commotion in the hall outside his bedroom. One in the group screamed for someone to call an ambulance. Theo didn't know who yelled. He ran to the top of the stairs, looked down, saw Ray, and called 911.

"How's Wallace?" I whispered, although Ray's father looked like he was in a trance and couldn't hear anything.

Theo glanced over at him and whispered, "How do you think? He found his son dead at the bottom of the steps. I can't imagine what's going through his head."

Wallace must've sensed that we were talking about him. He shook his head, looked at Theo and me, and said, "My wife wanted to see the world, so I bought her an Atlas."

I smiled, and Theo faked a laugh.

Pete returned to the couch and put his arm around his friend. "It's okay, Wallace. Everything will be fine."

And I thought Wallace was the one losing touch with reality.

Cindy and Detective Callahan conferred by the front door while the comics, Theo, and I sat in the great room.

The detective left.

Cindy came in, said the police were done in the house, and told the assembled group to call if anyone thought of anything he hadn't shared. If the guys heard her, they didn't acknowledge it.

Theo and I walked Cindy to the door.

We watched her go, then Theo looked back at the group, still unmoving in the other room. "Chris, could you spare a few more minutes?"

I would've been hard-pressed to come up with a reason to be somewhere other than in bed at 4:00 in the morning. I nodded.

Theo ushered me to an office off the kitchen. "Chris, do you think Ray's death was anything other than an accident?"

"Why ask?"

Theo closed the door. "Just letting my mind run amok."

"Go on."

"Sal's the only one of the group I knew before they showed up at my door. Ray has been fighting with each of them since the day they arrived. He may be funny on stage but, from what I saw, he was a royal asshole. He made fun of the others behind their backs. He kept bragging about how many high-paying, prestigious gigs he had recently, and never hesitated to tell the others they were has-beens."

"Did he get along with his dad?"

"Not that I could tell. When Wallace was making sense, not that often, I might add, he tried to defend his overbearing, obnoxious son. He talked about how horrible a childhood Ray had with Wallace traveling all the time. Wallace may've taken up for Ray although, if you ask me, Ray treated his dad like crap. The others tried to get Ray to calm down." Theo smiled for the first time tonight. "I remember a couple of days ago, Pete had to step between Ray and Wallace to keep Ray from punching his dad. Pete pointed his seventy-five-year-old bony finger in fifty-year-old Ray's face, and said something like, 'You're fortunate that I don't flatten your nose.'"

"Was he serious?"

"I don't know. After he said it, Ray laughed, and Pete joined in. Besides, each of the other guys felt that way about Ray and told him so since they were here."

"Because Ray was obnoxious doesn't mean someone killed him."

"True," Theo said. "I don't know about Ray because he left Cal's before the rest of us. I know the other guys had so much to drink that they were probably seeing double when we got here." He smiled for a second time. "Doubt they'd know which of the two Rays they were seeing to push him down the steps."

"Theo, do you know what got Ray so upset that he stomped out of Cal's? Wallace made that joke saying that he remembered when Ray was young and was smoking something. Why did that bother him so much?"

"That may've been the last straw. I'll tell you it was only part of a larger hay bale. Ray was pissed when they piled in the car for me to take them to Cal's. Before you ask, I don't know why."

"Was Ray here when you got home?"

"I think so, but I didn't see him. His door was closed, so I figured he was in his room."

"What was he wearing when you found him?"

"Same thing he had on at Cal's. Why?"

"Curious. A minute ago, you mentioned something about

when Wallace was making sense. He seemed to be having a tough time with reality when he was performing. Has he been getting worse?"

Theo looked at the closed door. "You know I don't like to talk unkindly about anyone."

Other than calling Ray a royal asshole, I thought. I motioned for him to continue.

"I never know what year he's living in. One minute he's as coherent as can be; the next, he's talking about something that happened three decades ago."

"What do the others think?"

"They go back a long way. Other than Ray, they get along well, occasionally finishing each other's jokes. They listen when one of them tells a story that I know the others must've heard countless times. I think they would do anything for each other. That's all to say that, if they know Wallace is drifting out of reality, no one mentioned it. Think it's something they've come to expect."

I didn't know how to casually broach the topic, so I didn't try. "Remember the other day when Wallace said he'd seen a body. He was confused about when?"

"Sure, turned out to be that bookie."

"Remember last night when Wallace said something about *killing him*?"

"When Sal jumped in and tried to make us believe that Wallace was referring to killing the audience?"

Theo was old by many standards. In the walking group, he had been teased about being as fast as a snail on Ambien, but anyone who thought he wasn't as sharp as a chef's knife didn't know him. It wasn't by accident that he'd been a successful business owner and inventor.

"Exactly," I said. "Any idea what he was talking about?"

"No. I wanted to get him aside later and ask. Then this happened." Theo waved toward the stairs.

"To answer your question about what I thought, I wasn't here, so I have no idea what happened. Unless someone changes his story, none of your guests saw what happened."

"That's what I figured. Anyway, thanks for coming out in the middle of the night. I suppose I need to get back in there to escort the guys to their rooms. I doubt anyone will go back to sleep."

Theo walked with me to the door. The others hadn't moved since Theo and I'd been talking.

"Chris," Theo said as I was stepping off the porch.

I stopped and looked at him.

"You'll figure it out, won't you?"

"I'll try."

"Good."

The thing was, I didn't know what I'd agreed to figure out.

Chapter Twenty-One

I grabbed a quick supper at Planet Follywood and headed home for what I hoped to be an evening without thinking of what had happened at Theo's this morning or playing over in my mind the trauma of finding the bookie's body. Television was no help. I watched two sitcoms touted as the best of the year. Compared to the TV shows, I began thinking that Sal and the rest of the Legends might be funnier than I'd first thought.

I turned the TV off and grabbed a copy of a photography magazine and flipped through pages until I realized that I wasn't paying attention to what I was seeing. Regardless how hard I tried, I kept coming back to the dead bookie, Wallace's confusion over having seen the body, plus his confusion about nearly everything, and Ray's abrupt exit from the giant comedy club called Earth. And, why in heaven's name did I tell Theo that I would try to figure it out, whatever *it* was?

The death will be ruled accidental, unless the medical examiner comes up with something to indicate otherwise. Ray was inebriated, staying in a strange house, and it was early in the morning; all factors that could contribute to him falling.

So why did I keep coming back to it? Was it because it happened close to when I discovered Michael Hardin, the death where there was no question about cause? How about because Wallace said something about seeing Michael Hardin's body? He was also within a few feet of Ray when he fell? Were the deaths related? Or did I think it was suspicious because Ray was not liked by the others? He made fun of them. He arrived at Cal's angry, then when something was said stormed out. Add to that, he was rude, egotistical, disrespectful. Or was my imagination working overtime?

I wanted to call Theo to see how he was doing but figured he'd be exhausted, with luck, asleep. I called Charles after I left Theo and got his answering machine. I'd left a message but hadn't heard from him. That wasn't unusual since he had the irritating habit of leaving his phone in his apartment then forgetting to check messages.

I tried his number again with better luck. I asked if he ever checked his messages.

He gave feeble excuses about the phone being in another pair of slacks, about the battery being dead, he never got important calls anyway. After a litany of these he got around to asking why I'd called.

I shared what happened at Theo's. In return, I was the recipient of a thirty-second rant that could be summed up with him wanting to know why I didn't spend every waking hour since I left Theo's trying to find him so I could tell him about it. He was irritated with himself, taking it out on me. That's what friends are for, or so I continued telling myself.

He calmed and said, "Do you think Ray's death was accidental?"

"There's nothing to indicate that it wasn't, although, it

strikes me as strange coming so close on the heels of his father claiming to see the body of the bookie, and how others in the house didn't like Ray. That's only a gut feeling."

"You told Theo you would figure out what happened."

"No, I told him I'd try."

"How are we going to do that?"

"We?"

"You need my help."

"I do?"

"You said Wallace drifted in and out of reality. The whole group is delusional about their success. From what I heard at Cal's, they seem confused about how funny they are."

I waited, but no more was forthcoming.

"So?"

"Who do you know who's an expert on drifting in and out of reality? Who have you accused of thinking he's funnier than he is? When you think of delusional, who comes to mind?"

"You?"

"Duh. These are my kind of people. You need me."

I started to respond when he interrupted. "For the candle on top of the icing, on top of the chocolate cake, don't forget, I was with you when you found Michael Hardin. I'm smack dab in the middle of being connected to the case."

Somewhere between the icing and the cake, I took a deep breath and realized that I didn't know about Theo, but I knew that I was exhausted. I told Charles I'd think about it and we could talk tomorrow. I hadn't planned to think about it; I wanted to get off the phone.

The next morning, I brewed a pot of coffee instead of going next door to Bert's for a dose of caffeine. Charles and I had agreed to meet at noon at the Dog, which meant 11:30, so I had a few hours to kill. I sat at the kitchen table and flipped through the photography magazine I'd skimmed yesterday. I had little interest in reading the reviews of the latest, greatest cameras with numerous features more than the twelve-year-old digital Nikon that'd served me well, nor did I care about the newest drone technology that gave photographers the ability to view the earth from three hundred feet. Perhaps my age was showing. I had enough trouble capturing interesting images from my five-foot-ten vantage point. What the magazine did achieve was keeping my mind off the murder, the theft, and the motives of Theo's guests.

The more I looked at the magazine, the more I thought about my numerous walks around the island with Charles and how happy I was having someone with whom to share my interests. Photography was the excuse we often used to make the lengthy treks. We did take photos, yet the best part of the trips were our conversations. Other than an interest in photography and being retired, we had little in common.

It'd taken me a few years to realize that, while Charles was seldom without something to say, talking about his past was not among the things he dwelt on. I knew the basics: where he was born, about being raised by his grandmother, what he'd done before coming to Folly, how he'd spent his time while on the island. But, after the hundreds of hours we'd spent together, he'd never revealed why he wore long-sleeve shirts, regardless of the weather; why he carried a hand-carved, wooden cane, even though he was as mobile as anyone I knew, or, why he'd accumulated more college and university sweat-shirts and T-shirts than the marsh had oysters. It wasn't for the lack of asking, although I'd given up after the first couple of years, once I realized that the answers were as elusive as catching a rainbow.

I was with him when he met Heather. I observed their growing romantic relationship until she left a few months ago. I learned how much he loved his Aunt Melinda during her brief time with him until she succumbed to cancer.

He was getting over these heartbreaking losses, yet still had a way to go. Each time I thought he was making progress, he said something about Melinda, Heather, or acted depressed. I didn't think it was clinical depression, but bouts of sadness and anger over them being gone. His self-proclaimed position of executive sales manager at Landrum Gallery had given him purpose and a feeling that he was accomplishing something— something that he'd felt lacking before I'd come along. It was unavoidable, yet I knew how much I'd hurt him when I closed the gallery.

I poured another cup of coffee, threw the magazine in the trash, and realized, as strange as it may seem, the happiest, most energized and self-confident I had seen my friend over the last three years was when we were up to our eyeballs in police business, things that we shouldn't be involved with. Good or bad luck, depending upon who was telling the story, had propelled us into situations that almost cost us our lives. Falling on the side of good luck, we helped the police catch people who had killed some of our acquaintances, were out to kill someone close to us, and nearly had succeeded in ending our lives.

That realization gave me a different perspective on what I was going to say at lunch. My initial thought was to remind him that whatever had happened wasn't our concern, that it was in the competent hands of the police. Neither of us knew the bookie. We had seen him a few times but, on an island as small as Folly, that wasn't unusual. The death of Ray Bentley appeared to be a case of an inebriated man missing the top step and tumbling to the hereafter. Tragic, yes, and sad that it was Wallace's son, who happened to be a friend of Sal, who happened to be Theo's brother, who was one of our friends. It was still an accident. Yes, I'd told Theo that I would try, but we'd be better off leaving it to the authorities.

The best way to help my friend was to agree with him, do everything I could do to find out what had happened and who was responsible for Michael's death. We may not succeed, but I'd be doing something to bring back the positive, helpful, cheery friend whom I'd come to love.

Chapter Twenty-Two

I arrived at the Dog at 11:30 to find Charles at a booth along the back wall.

He looked at his imaginary watch and nodded his head to indicate that I was on time.

I slid in opposite him and noticed his eyes were red, his eyelids at half-staff. "Rough night?" I asked.

"Trouble sleeping. So, how're we going to catch the killer?"

Amber was quick to the table, set a mug of coffee in front of me, and asked if I knew what I wanted for lunch.

I thanked her for the coffee, although I'd had too much of the stuff, and said, "Mahi Salad."

Amber put her hand over her heart. "Whoa. That's almost healthy."

I smiled. "I'll get over it."

"No doubt," she said then asked if Charles needed anything else.

He told her no, and she headed to the kitchen with my almost-healthy order.

This is where I would normally argue that the police were

paid to catch the killer. It was none of our business. Instead, I said, "I think we need to start by learning everything we can about Michael Hardin. Who else placed bets with him? Did anyone have stories about how he'd cheated them? Did anyone owe him a large amount of money?"

Charles's eyes opened wider. "Really? I thought you'd tell me to butt out."

"You said *we* needed to figure out what was going on. It's a good idea."

He sighed. "Thanks a lot. Now you've done gone and screwed up everything I planned on spending all day arguing with you about."

"Like what?"

"Like you were going to say we that we didn't know Michael Hardin, so we had no reason to stick in our noses. I was going to say that it was true, but our friend, Theo's brother, is a friend of Wallace Bentley, Wallace said he saw the body, or said he saw a body. That made it our business. Sal's friend got killed at the house where he was staying, the house of our friend, Theo. See?"

"You're right."

Charles pointed his fork at me. "You messin' with me?"

"I'm agreeing."

He leaned back in the booth and stared at me like I was a three-headed sloth.

Amber returned with my salad and a hot dog for Charles that he'd ordered before I arrived. She said, "What's wrong, Charles? You look like you've seen the Ghost of Christmas Past."

Charles continued to stare at me. "An alien's done swooped down and planted itself in Chris's brain."

Amber smiled. "That explains the Mahi Salad." She patted my balding head and left to see if the couple seated in the middle of the room needed anything. She didn't appear as worried as Charles.

Charles blinked twice, took a bite of hot dog, looked around the room, then back at me. "Think I'm over the shock. How do we find out who else had reason to kill the bookie?"

I pointed to the table on the other side of the room, where Chief Cindy LaMond was lunching with two of her officers. I saw them when I came in and started thinking about Charles's question before he asked it. "First, we need to find out who the police have eliminated as suspects."

"And you think Cindy's just going to waltz over here to tell us?"

I laughed. "No, she'll say it's not our concern. If we keep meddling in her job, she'll shoot us before the killer does."

"That'll help us how?"

"I didn't say she wouldn't tell us. I said she'd first give us a bucket of grief."

"How are we going to get her over here without her lunch mates?"

"I'll figure something out."

Before I had a chance to do much figuring, Chester Carr magically appeared beside our booth.

He nodded at Charles and said to me, "Thought I'd find you here."

I didn't ask why. First, because it didn't matter. Second, because Charles was asking him to join us.

Chester slid in beside Charles. "We're halfway through a .5 group walk. Made it all the way to the River Park, where I left the rest of the folks gasping for air."

Chester started the .5 walking group two years ago. The name came from the half-mile distance Chester wanted the group to walk, from the end of East Ashley Avenue to Lighthouse Inlet, where we could view the iconic Morris Island

Lighthouse, then trek back to East Ashley. One of the requirements to be in the group was that the member had to be sixty or older. That, along with the physical condition, or lack of condition, of most of the members made a .5 mile walk as easily attainable as hiking to the top of Pikes Peak. Regardless, the name stuck.

Charles faked surprise. "You deserted your group?"

Chester said, "Since you think you're too good to walk with us, I couldn't tell you what I found out if I stayed with the others."

That perked Charles up.

I said, "What?"

"You asked me to let you know I if learned anything new about the bookie?"

"Yes."

"After the .5 group left the Pier to head up Center Street without two of its members who're sitting here feeding their faces—"

"Subtle," I interrupted. "You were walking up the street, and?"

"David Darnell was talking about how busy his insurance business is recently. Most of us couldn't care less about insurance, so we weren't paying attention, until he said something about Horace Raque. That's Janice's husband, remember, the lady I told you about who was arguing with Michael Hardin?"

"I remember."

"David was telling funny stories about things his clients say. David's a big talker. It's a wonder anyone has time to buy insurance with him doing all the talking." Chester shrugged. "'Course David's semi-retired, so I guess it doesn't matter if he sells anything."

Charles took the words out of my mouth when he said, "What'd he say about Horace?"

"Horace, right. I missed the first of it. I didn't want him to know that I wasn't listening, so I didn't have him start over. Horace was talking to David about car insurance then got off track and said he didn't need more life insurance." Chester closed his eyes, opened them, and tapped his finger on the table. "Oh, yeah, David laughed. He said that Horace told him that as mad as Janice gets, he's afraid she'd kill him. He didn't want to give her added incentive with a bigger policy."

"Was Horace serious?" I asked.

Chester looked across the room at Chief LaMond's table and turned back to me. "David thought Horace was joking. I don't know. Remember how mad Janice was at the bookie? She has a temper. I can see her being that mad at Horace. I sure can."

"Did Darnell say anything else?"

"Yeah, he went off on a story about one of his customers driving into a ditch. The guy swore that a fly landed on his nose and made him veer off the road."

"Anything more about Horace?" Charles said.

"No, but I reckoned since you and Chris are detectives, you'd figure what David said was a clue."

Every other time we'd been accused of what Charles's imagination had created, I denied it. Not today.

"Yes, it was," Charles said.

Chester started to slip out of the booth before saying, "I'll try to catch up with the crew. Shouldn't be hard at their speed."

I thanked him for coming to find us. As Chester walked away, Charles cleared his throat and nearly fell out of the booth leaning toward the table where Cindy and her officers had been. The two cops waved goodbye to the chief and headed to the door. Cindy looked our way. I motioned her over, and Charles pointed at the seat Chester had vacated.

Cindy looked at the seat, at Charles, then at me. "Am I going to regret this?"

Charles said, "Of course not."

I didn't lie to her; I smiled as she joined us. I'd wager it wasn't her first choice.

Charles asked, "How's your day?"

Cindy pointed to the table where she had been seated. "One of my guys told me he was quitting and moving to his wife's hometown somewhere in the middle of God's country in Arkansas. The other one said his doctor recommended he take a leave of absence because of job stress. Can you believe that?"

I could, but I limited my response to, "I'm sorry."

"Now two troublemakers summon me over. So, Charles, how do you think my day's been?"

Charles smiled. "Looks like it sucked until you joined us."

"I assume the two of you didn't ask me over to see what kind of day I was having. What's up?"

"Chris wanted to know who you and the Sheriff's Office are figurin' as suspects in Michael Hardin's murder." Charles pointed his fork at me. "He thought it was one of the bookie's disgruntled customers."

Cindy glared at me. "He did?"

"That's not exactly right, Cindy," I said, although it wasn't far off. "I was curious how the investigation was going."

Cindy shook her head. "If I could stick you behind bars for lying to a police chief, that salad would be the last good meal you'd be getting in the next few weeks, months, maybe years."

"Chief," Charles said, "before you haul Chris's pasty white rear end off to the hoosegow, do you have any good suspects?"

"There's room for both of you," Cindy said, looked to see if anyone was nearby, and sighed. "I was on the phone with

Detective Callahan before my department was reduced by two. He'd taken the bookie's notebook as evidence and has a detective following up on the names in it. The word most of Michael's clients shared was that he was a stand-up guy, honored his losses. If there was such a place, they'd nominate him for the Bookie Hall of Fame."

"Not everyone believed that," I said.

Cindy looked around, got Amber's attention, and ordered a Diet Coke. I took it as a sign that she wasn't going to rush out.

"Chris, there's nothing to indicate that his death was related to his bookmaking. It could be anything. Someone could have hated that damned hat with a feather in it. Who knows?"

I nodded. "Anything to say he was reverting to his drug-pushing career?"

"None that's come out."

"What about Janice Raque?"

"What about her?"

"How solid is her alibi?"

"She claimed to be visiting friends, but there're holes in the timeframe. Two women she'd visited live on opposite sides of Charleston and there was a significant gap between when they saw her. Have you heard anything more about her?"

"Chester Carr was in here a little while. Said that while he was with his walking group this morning—"

Cindy interrupted, "Crawling group."

She'd told me a couple of months ago that when Chester's group gets to some of Folly's intersections, one of her cops often stopped traffic to let them cross like a raft of ducks.

"Okay, crawling group. Anyway, David Darnell was telling him something that Horace, Janice's husband, told David."

"Do I need a subpoena to get it out of you?"

I told her what Horace had said about Janice getting so mad that he was afraid she'd kill him, and she didn't need an additional incentive by having more life insurance.

Cindy looked down at the table. "Chris, you're single, so I'll forgive your ignorance. We married chicks are always telling our husbands that we're going to kill them. Crap, some of the time we mean it. But you know how many of us do it?"

"Can't say that I do."

"How many?" asked trivia collector Charles.

"Don't know," Cindy said. "It ain't many, otherwise there wouldn't be any married women left. They'd all be in jail, which thinking about it, doesn't sound bad. Three square meals a day; we don't have to cook. No nagging husbands." She looked off into space.

"Janice Raque still a suspect?" I said to bring Cindy back from dreaming about an idyllic life in prison.

"Detective Callahan is trying to pin down her alibi. She may be."

"What about Neil Wilson? The last time we talked, you didn't know if anyone had questioned him."

"He was on Callahan's list. Neil was at work in Charleston around the time the bookie was killed. Like Janice, there's a gap in his alibi since the ME can't pin down the time of death as accurately as I'd like." She sipped her Diet Coke and looked at her watch. "Guys, I'd love to stay and let you tell me who killed Michael, but I've got a budget committee meeting at City Hall. I can't tell you how excited I am about it."

"One more question," I said. "Is there anything suspicious about Raymond Bentley's death?"

"Chris, is there a possibility, even a teeny-weeny, remote possibility that somewhere in your circuit-shorted brain that could entertain the thought that a person could die of some-thing other than being murdered?"

"Yes."

Charles waved his hand in front of Cindy. "What about Ray?"

Cindy shook her head. "I'm beginning to look forward to my meeting in City Hall. No, no, and no, there's nothing to indicate that anything other than a damned drunk man fell down the steps and prematurely ended his career in comedy. Is that clear enough?"

She didn't wait for an answer.

Charles watched her go and said, "So, which of Theo's guests shoved Ray down the steps?"

We discussed the possibilities for twenty minutes before deciding two things. First, when it came to people who may've killed Michael, we had no idea, although, we could identify two possible suspects, but acknowledged that considering Michael's profession, that number could swell dramatically. Second, we decided that our lunch was outstanding, even if the Mahi Salad was healthy.

Chapter Twenty-Three

I called Theo late that afternoon to see how he and his houseguests were doing.

His voice cracked as he spoke, yet insisted he was okay. He shared that, earlier in the afternoon, Pete had taken Wallace to the funeral home in Charleston to make arrangements once Ray's body was released from the coroner's office.

I asked if he'd heard anything from the police. He said that Detective Callahan had returned to ask more questions, saying that they were "routine" and to "follow up" from his middle of the night visit. I doubted there was anything routine about them. Theo was still traumatized, so I didn't share my thoughts. Callahan hadn't said anything new about what the coroner found, although he told Theo that he was still investigating the death.

"Has Wallace said anything about funeral plans?"

Theo hesitated before saying, "He's the only family they have left, and Ray didn't have close friends. His son wanted to be cremated with no funeral. Wallace tried to make a joke out of it by saying that they would be able to carry Ray's ashes to gigs. To be honest, I'm not sure it'd been discussed and would venture to guess the decision was because Wallace didn't have money for a funeral."

"You still think they're broke?"

"Wallace asked if I could lend him the money for the funeral home. He fabricated some far-flung story about CDs not maturing until November. I gave him my credit card."

"You don't believe him?"

"I know broke when I see it. Besides, Wallace first said his CDs were maturing in June, changed it to early next year, now November. I can't tell if he thinks I don't remember what he told me, or if he doesn't remember."

"How's he taking the death?"

"Don't know. He'd been in his room until he left with Pete."

"Is he still getting confused?"

"I suppose."

"What's that mean?"

"I hate to say anything, because I don't know him like his pals do. Like I mentioned before, it seems his confusion comes at the most opportune times."

"You still think he's faking it?"

"Honest to God, I don't know. Something doesn't feel right about it. Again, I don't know him enough to tell."

Have you asked Sal?"

"I tried. He kept changing the subject."

"Are they sticking to the story that no one saw what happened?"

"Funny thing is, none of them are saying anything. They're acting like nothing happened."

"They could be in shock."

"I know I am. I don't know what to say or do around them. I'm sick about what happened, yet, well, I'm sick."

Theo was leaving words on the table, so in the spirit of Charles, I said, "What aren't you saying?"

"I hate saying this. I don't know how much longer I'll be able to stand company. Sal's my brother, but we're not close. I've gotten comfortable being in the house by myself."

"I understand and feel the same way. Have they said anything about leaving?"

"Nothing. My gut says they don't intend to go anywhere. They haven't mentioned scheduled appearances outside the area. With the tragic death of Ray, this wasn't time to broach the subject."

I told him to call if he needed anything. He asked if I knew of any good comedian exterminators. If it hadn't been so close to the tragic death in his house, it would've been funny. I wished him a peaceful evening.

———

The Chamber of Commerce perfectly described the next day. The temperature was in the low seventies, a breeze was blowing out of the west, with not a cloud to be seen. I decided to walk two blocks to the ocean and stroll along the beach. After yesterday's healthy Mahi salad, and now a walk in the sand, I could picture pounds falling off my slightly overweight frame, my cholesterol sinking to acceptable levels, and contemplating running in a mini-marathon. I wondered how different I was than reality-challenged Wallace. I started to laugh at the comparison, when I saw Pete Marvin sitting in the sand with his bare feet touching the water as each wave inched ashore. No one was nearby, and he was staring at the horizon like he was watching for his ship to come in.

Pete was so focused that I hesitated to approach then

figured, if I wanted to learn as much as possible about Ray's death, this would be my chance. I said, "Hi."

He looked up and for a second didn't appear to recognize me.

A smile appeared on his face. "Oh, hi, Chris, you startled me. Have a seat. Wiggle your toes in my kiddie pool."

I lowered my body to the sand, keeping my feet back from the water lapping over his feet.

"A terrible thing about Ray," I said as I scooted my deck shoes in the sand. "Are you okay?"

He shook his head. "It could've been any of us. We had too much to drink. Theo's steps are steep." He shook his head again. "You never know. It could as easily have been me."

"Were you and Ray close?"

"Not really. I've been friends with Wallace since Columbus sailed the ocean blue. I've known Ray since before he was born. Don't get me wrong, I liked him as Wallace's son." He hesitated and chuckled. "He was easier to like when he was a kid. The older he got, the harder it was to be around him. He'd diss his dad, as well as the rest of us. The other day he told Sal that Sal's IQ came back negative. He called us old farts, said we were as funny as a toadstool. The only time he showed a sense of humor, or for that matter, humility, was when he was on stage. He could be funny standing behind a microphone. When the spotlight was turned off, so was his sense of humor."

I'd heard that many comedians weren't that funny when not preforming. Pete had more experience with them than I had, so I said, "Is that unusual for comedians?"

"There are more like that than you might think. Still, most of them, most of us, aren't always hostile. Some of us even like other people, something Ray lacked."

"Have you always been a stand-up comic?"

"Wanted to be a boxer when I was young. After entering a few amateur bouts and getting the snot knocked out of me, I decided on something less dangerous."

I pointed to his tree-trunk-sized arms. "Looks like you would've been good at boxing."

He laughed. "After I kept getting whipped, I started weightlifting." He patted his left forearm. "These things used to be all muscle back in the day. I bulked up then got tired of exercising, watched them turn to flab. That's when I turned to comedy. I hung out in some bars. When the bartenders got bored, they asked me to tell a few jokes. Wasn't long after that when I met Sal."

"Guess it was safer than boxing."

"Safer, no less brutal. I was decent at it. I figured I wouldn't be good enough to do it for a living, not a successful living. For a few years, I switched to the management side of comedy. I got to know a lot of the guys on the tour. A couple of them asked if I wanted to be their manager, booking gigs, helping them with their money, stuff like that. That's when I learned that most were nice guys. Oh, sure, some had problems, drink, drugs, anger, paranoia, but most were okay."

"Do you manage any now?"

His laugh came easily, and he shared another one with me. "Can't seem to manage myself. Nah. Gave up managing a decade ago and re-hitched up with Sal, and with his buddy Wallace. We've been together ever since."

"When did Ray start traveling with you?"

"A year ago. He kept telling everybody that he's between big TV deals. If you ask me, it's bullshit. He's worked more than the rest of us, although, I think TV deals were in his imagination. It doesn't matter now." He looked out to sea, then back at me. "Ray was a prick. His dad's a good guy. For that reason, I hated to see anything bad happen to Ray. It could've been any of us."

"Where're the rest of the guys?"

"They're torn up about the accident. Sal was heading upstairs to see if he could get some sleep. None of us got much after it happened. Poor Wallace said he needed to get away and took the Lincoln to Charleston. He made up some story about buying new stage duds. I think he wanted to get out of the house. I hope he makes it okay."

"Is there a reason he might not?"

"He lost his son. His memory is on the fritz. And, he's driving around in a strange town in a car the size of the Queen Mary. What do you think?"

"He does seem confused at times," I said, stating the obvious.

"I suppose. I'd better get back." Pete hopped up, brushed sand off his feet, and slipped his shoes on. "Good talking to you."

I watched him go and repeated what he had said about Wallace's confusion: "I suppose." Something about the way he'd said it didn't feel right.

Chapter Twenty-Four

On the way home, I stopped at Bert's to grab a sandwich. Ty, one of the clerks, was kneeling and in a deep conversation with a mid-sized dog that appeared to be a pure-bred mongrel. The clerk was conversing with the dog; the dog was waiting for Ty to give it a treat.

The pooch, person conversation ended, the dog gobbled down the treat, Ty looked up at me, and said, "Want a treat?"

I declined, so Ty stood and wiped off his knees, before asking, "Hear about that funny guy falling down the stairs at Theo Stoll's house?"

I told him that I had.

"Don't know why I bother telling you anything. I'm beginning to think you know about terrible things before they happen. And I thought Charles's ex-gal Heather was the psychic."

I thought about how much truth there was in his comment. "Theo's a friend. He called me after it happened. Tragic."

"Speaking of tragic," Ty said, "you figured out who killed the bookie?"

I rolled my eyes. "It's in good hands with the police."

"You're one of the best I've run in to for not answering a question while the person asking thinks you did."

"Thanks, I think."

Ty held his head back and laughed.

"What's so funny?" someone said from behind me.

I turned to see Neil Wilson. He wouldn't have been easy to miss as his six-foot-three, former college football player frame towered over me. He wore black slacks and a light-weight, black jacket with a generic red, white, and blue shield-shaped patch on the arm. *SECURITY* was printed in the middle of the patch. He was holding a six-pack of Budweiser and looking over my head at Ty.

"I was asking Chris if he'd figured out who killed Michael Hardin. He was avoiding answering me."

I stepped out of the way of their conversation.

Neil looked at the clerk but nodded toward me. "Why would he figure it out?"

Ty smiled. "Chris gets in the middle of every murder. He claims to be a simple, retired bureaucrat, but there're rumors he's like one of those superheroes you see in the movies. He's got a tight-fitting, stretchy body suit under that red golf shirt."

Neil turned to me like he was waiting for me to pull my shirt off and bend steel barehanded.

"Ty's teasing. He knows I've lucked into helping the police a couple of times."

Neil seemed unconvinced and I was in a hurry to change the subject. "Had any luck finding a job?"

Neil set the six-pack on the table beside us and started to answer.

Ty interrupted and said he needed to get back to work.

Neil crossed his arms. "Not yet. Hear of anything?"

I told him that I hadn't but still had his number in case anything came up.

"So, you're trying to help the cops catch the guy who killed Hardin?"

"No," I said. This was the last conversation I wanted to have with the giant of a man who I considered a suspect.

"Anyway, I hope the cops hurry up and catch whoever did it. Would you believe one of them came to my work, pulled me in the office, and started asking questions?"

I did believe it since Cindy had already told me. "What kind of questions?"

"Where I was when he was killed. Word was that I owed Michael a few dollars. I guess the cops thought I was a suspect."

"You had an alibi, didn't you?"

His eyes narrowed as he smiled. "You playing superhero?"

I'd hoped Neil had forgotten Ty's comment. I smiled. "Do I look like a superhero? The police chief, Cindy LaMond, is a friend. The other day we were talking. She said they'd interviewed several people who may've had a motive. She told me that they all had alibis, so I figured you might've been one of them."

"They asked about a four-hour block. I figured that's when he was killed. I told them I was working about that time. I think they verified it with my boss. That was the end of it."

"Good."

Neil picked up the six-pack. "Better get this home before it gets warm. Don't forget, you said you'd let me know if you hear of work. Don't have to be security. I've also done some cooking in my day."

As he left, I couldn't help remembering that Cindy had

said that his alibi was for only some of the hours, then how he'd lied to me about feeling bad about Michael's death.

I got home and chewed on my sandwich and on what Neil had said. I didn't know what the police were thinking. To me, the security guard was a prime suspect. I called Cindy and was rewarded with her voicemail. It was late, so I told her I didn't need anything important. I asked her to call in the morning.

Fifteen minutes later, the phone rang. Cindy must've missed talking to me so much that she couldn't wait until the morning. I was wrong, something that was happening far more often than I liked.

In a barely-audible voice, I heard, "Chris, this is Theo."

"Hi, Theo. Is everything okay?"

"Umm, yes."

"Why're you whispering?" I asked, hoping he didn't want me to come to his house.

"I'm in the kitchen. Can't talk. Sal and Wallace are in the other room."

I heard glasses clanking. Theo yelled, "I'm on my way, guys." He went back to whispering. Can you meet me at the Dog in the morning?"

"What time?"

"Seven, if you can make it. Not a creature will be stirring around here that early. No one will miss me."

"I'll be there. What's going—"

The phone went dead.

Chapter Twenty-Five

Theo was easy to recognize when he entered the Dog. He wore his USS Yorktown ball cap, an oversized, white T-shirt, Carolina-blue jogging shorts, and knee-length black support socks. He's always looked older than mid-eighties. Today, he looked like he could be starring in a zombie movie. His eyes were blood-red from what I could see of them. They were half closed. I worried that he wouldn't make it to the booth.

Amber arrived at the same time and asked if Theo wanted coffee. He perked up, lowered himself onto the bench seat with great effort and a groan, and told her, "Yes, lots."

"Rough night?" I asked.

He bowed his head like he was praying and mumbled something that I couldn't understand. I asked him to repeat it.

"I'm scared. Don't know what to do. Chris, I'm at wits' end."

I leaned closer to my distraught friend. "What's going on?"

Amber set coffee in front of Theo.

He didn't look up, so I thanked her.

She shrugged, and I told her I'd wave if we needed anything.

Theo put his hands around the mug but didn't lift it. "Wallace and Pete spent a lot of time yesterday talking about their trip to the funeral home. I was in and out of the room. I swear to God, Wallace told Pete a thousand times what the funeral director said. Pete listened, listened, and listened. If Wallace had repeated himself that many times, I would've walked away. Anyway, that's not why I'm upset."

"You think Wallace kept forgetting he'd told Pete, or was nervous and kept repeating it?"

"Hard to tell. It's what he told me later that made me call you."

Theo blew across the coffee and took a sip. I wanted to ask if Wallace and Pete had learned anything else about Ray's death yet didn't want to interrupt whatever Theo wanted to share.

He set the coffee down. I motioned for him to continue.

"Pete must've gotten tired of listening to Wallace, said he had to do something in his room. I was coming out of the kitchen when Wallace asked me to walk out back with him. I followed him to the deck. He stretched out in a chair, I sat next to him, and he told me." Theo sighed and looked in his mug like his next words would appear on the surface of the liquid. "You know what he told me?"

Of course, I didn't, so I remained silent.

"Said he killed the bookie. Wallace said it to me right there on my deck." He shook his head. "What should I do?"

"Was he serious?"

"Sounded like it."

"Remember, he told me that he'd seen the body, yet was confused about when it was. You told me that he seemed to drift in and out of reality."

"You weren't there, Chris. The man looked me in the eye, said he smacked the bookie in the head and left him in the weeds."

"I find it hard to believe he knew Michael Hardin. Did he say why?"

"I was so taken back that I couldn't speak, much less ask questions. What should I do?"

"You need to tell the police."

He took a deep breath then looked down. "I know … I know. I don't want to get anyone in trouble. They're my houseguests."

"Theo, I understand, but the police need to know."

"What if poor Wallace was hallucinating, or confused? He could've made it all up?"

"That's possible. The police will figure it out."

"I hate to impose, but would you go with me?"

That wouldn't have been in the top one-hundred items on my to-do list, but Theo was a friend.

"Of course. Let me call Chief LaMond to see if she can meet us at her office."

She answered on the second ring. "Crap, Chris. I just got your message from last night. Is there a reason why you couldn't wait until I got coffee in my bloodstream before pestering me again? I was going to call, scout's honor."

"That's not why I'm calling. Theo Stoll and I are at the Dog. He has something to tell you. Could we stop by your office in a few minutes?"

"I'll do one better. Where do you think I was going to get my caffeine fix? Don't answer, I'm pulling in front of the Dog. I'll be there before you can say, 'Cindy LaMond, you're the best police chief in the world.'"

She wasn't far off. She was standing at our booth,

motioning for Theo to move over before I finished telling him she was on her way.

Cindy smiled. "Who said cops are never there when you need them?"

She was too cheerful for Theo. He didn't return her smile, and I would rather have had our conversation in the privacy of the chief's office. That wasn't in the cards.

Amber was quick to the booth with Cindy's coffee and asked if Theo and I needed anything.

I deferred to Theo, who said he was fine. I said the same.

Cindy took a sip, exhaled, and said, "So, what'd you call about last night?"

"It can wait. Theo has something to tell you." I motioned to him.

Three false starts later, he told her about his conversation with Wallace.

She asked the same question I posed. "Was he serious?"

Theo gave the same response.

Cindy turned to me. "What do you think?"

"I wasn't there. From my conversations with Wallace, it could've been something out of his fantasy world."

Theo interrupted. "You're right, you weren't there. I'm no expert on warped minds, but I think he was serious."

Cindy said, "Where is he now?"

"My houseguests operate on three time zones west of here. They were asleep when I left the house. They're sawing logs in their, in my beds."

Cindy looked at her watch. "Tell you what, Theo. Mosey on home, I'll come-a-callin' in a couple of hours."

Theo nodded. "Are you going to tell him where you heard it?"

"Did he tell anyone else?"

"I don't know."

"He'll know, unless he told other folks. I won't mention you unless I have to."

Theo nodded. "Will you arrest him?"

"Theo, I'll start by talking to him and play it by ear. That's all I can promise." She glanced at her watch. "Head on home. I'll be there in a couple of hours."

Theo had looked beaten down when he came in; he looked like he'd been run over by the comedians' Lincoln when he shuffled out.

Cindy shook her head as she watched Theo leave. "What's your take, Chris?"

"Wallace is a mystery. There's no doubt he confuses reality on a regular basis, yet I keep getting the feeling that it may be more fake than real. Theo said the same thing."

"What makes you and Theo believe that?"

"Gut feelings. It appears that Wallace's at his worst when it suits his need, if that makes sense."

"Not much. I'll take your word. What doesn't make sense is that, after you dragged him out of the middle of Center Street, he felt the need to tell you he'd seen a body. I never would've made a connection between Theo's visitor and the death of a bookie."

I caught Amber's eye. I motioned her over, ordered French toast, then asked if Cindy wanted anything to eat. She said that she didn't want to be rude and sit there and watch me eat, so she told Amber to double the order.

"If Wallace was having trouble with reality, he could've stumbled on the body, was confused about when he'd seen it. If the comedian was faking mental problems, and killed the bookie, he might have seen someone notice him near the body. Acting confused and claiming to see it, would explain why he was there."

Cindy looked at the ceiling and said, "Why would he confess to Theo?"

"Great question. That'll be up to Folly's *best police chief in the world* and the detectives from the Sheriff's Office to figure out."

"Thanks."

I smiled. "Glad I could help."

"So, what'd you call about last night?"

I told her about my conversation with Neil Wilson and asked if she had learned anything more about his alibi or if Detective Callahan had made progress. I told her about Neil asking if I was playing a superhero.

She laughed until coffee spouted out the side of her mouth.

I told her I didn't think it was that funny.

She said she agreed. It wasn't funny, it was hilarious.

Our food arrived and I said, "Callahan learn anything?"

"Don't guess it matters. It seems we've got a confessor bunking at Theo's."

Chapter Twenty-Six

Cindy called as I was sitting down for a supper feast of Velveeta on rye. "Didn't disturb anything important, did I?"

"No, the Food Channel just left after filming me fixing supper."

She laughed. "And you think Wallace has problems with reality."

"Speaking of Wallace, did you catch up with him?"

"I did. At eleven-hundred today, I knocked on the door of one Theodore Stoll and was greeted by the homeowner, who looked more like he wanted to slam the door in my face than welcome me to his far-from-humble abode."

I interrupted, "Chief, are you auditioning for a movie role as a stuffy cop? You sound like you're reading a poorly written script."

"The mayor's been on my ass, umm, excuse me, on my case—again—to start acting and sounding like a professional law enforcement official. I'm practicing."

The mayor, Brian Newman, had been the city's police

chief for many years before being elected mayor three years ago.

"He's failing."

"Affirmative. Now, if I may continue. Against his wishes and better judgment, Theo let me in. He headed upstairs to get Wallace. Half past an eternity later, Theo inched his way down the stairs with Wallace following. The old comic was dressed in black and looked like Theo's shadow as they made it to the great room where I'd been twiddling my thumbs."

I took a bite of sandwich instead of twiddling my thumbs while waiting for the Cindy to get to the reason for the call.

"Theo made an inane excuse why he had to go back upstairs, and left Wallace with me. I told the funny guy that I'd heard that he had confided in *some people* that he'd killed Michael Hardin. When I told Theo later, he was pleased that Wallace didn't ask who."

"What did Wallace say?"

"He looked at me like someone would look at the devil walking down the street while wiggling his bony finger for the person to follow him. Wallace's body shook like he was exorcising bad memories. He said, 'I did? When did I say that?'"

"Cindy, that's what I meant about him drifting out of reality at opportune times."

"Hang on, Food Channel star, it gets weirder."

"I'm not surprised."

"Let me get my notes." Papers rustled in the background. "I'm back. Wallace looked at me and said, 'I found a shell on the beach. Luckily, it didn't explode.'"

"He told a joke?"

"I'll say yes if you add *stupid* in front of *joke*."

"What'd he say next?"

"Let me get the exact quote. Here it is, he said, 'Ha, ha, ha.'"

I sighed. "After that?"

"He said, 'Speaking of the beach, did you say I killed someone out there?' He pointed toward the ocean. I repeated what I told him when I first came in, to which he said, 'Oh yeah, I remember.' I thought we were getting somewhere. I was wrong, way wrong. I asked him what he remembered. The poor boy looked around the room. He put his finger to his lips like he was trying to hush me. He slipped four steps under reality and said that he, and this is a quote, 'Conked a man with a candlestick in the library.'"

"Was that another joke?"

Cindy hesitated and then continued, "Chris, my professional opinion is that Mr. Wallace Bentley is, in official police lingo, wacko. After he described the murder, he grinned and held out his hands like he wanted me to slap on handcuffs."

"What'd you do?"

"Pinched myself to make sure I wasn't dreaming. I wasn't. I asked if he knew where he was, what day it was, if he knew who he was staying with, even his name. I wanted to see how far from reality he'd drifted."

"What'd he say?"

"Funny thing, he knew the answers, even told me that he was at the funeral home yesterday making arrangements for his son's cremation. He knew the name of the funeral director, how much the cremation cost, where he and Pete had gone to eat after leaving the mortuary." Cindy hesitated and said, "He put his head down and started crying and saying how much he was going to miss Ray and how horrible a father he'd been to his only child. It was an awkward ten minutes before he wiped his eyes and asked if I had more questions."

"Did you?"

"I asked him to tell me again about the body on the beach.

He cocked his head and frowned before saying, 'Sorry, I don't know what you're talking about.' That's all he said."

"What are you doing with him?"

"I told him I didn't have anything else to ask and for him to go upstairs and send Theo down. Wallace left, Theo returned. I wanted to see if he could remember exactly what Wallace told him about killing someone. Maybe he knew something specific that would help determine if Wallace killed Michael. He didn't. Wallace hadn't told him when he killed him, or where. All he said was he smacked him in the head. Theo didn't know about the candlestick in the library."

"Now what?"

"My hands are tied. Wallace didn't say anything that led me to believe the crime he'd committed had been anywhere other than in his warped head. Michael's murder was committed by a one-inch thick oak branch, not a candlestick, nowhere near a library. What was I to do? He didn't appear to be an immediate threat to himself, or others so, when he came back downstairs, I smiled, thanked him for his time and for sharing his flight into fantasy."

On that note, she said she needed to help her husband clean out a closet and invited me to help.

I declined the generous offer.

She wasn't surprised.

Cindy was right about Wallace not giving her anything to implicate him in Michael's death, and I couldn't think of anything that would tie him to the bookie. Wallace and his friends were new to Folly so, most likely, he wouldn't have known that Michael existed. So why did I have such an uneasy feeling about Wallace's sojourns in and out of reality?

Neil Wilson struck me as a better suspect. He owed the bookie a bundle and had lied about liking Michael. He had size and strength to send Michael to the great bookmaking joint in the sky with a blow to the head; his alibi had a hole in it. I would also add Janice Raque to the suspect pool. Her alibi had as many holes in it, as did Neil's; she had a quick temper and had been seen arguing with Michael.

I finished my sandwich, used my culinary talents to unwrap a Hershey bar for dessert, and wondered what I could do to unwrap the truth about Michael Hardin's death.

Chapter Twenty-Seven

The next two days were taken up with the type of hassles that come from owning an older home in a humidity-rich beach community. I got an expensive respite from thinking about Michael Hardin, his two customers, and the comedians, when the air conditioner decided to take time off.

After I'd called the AC repair shop, stared at my watch for four hours waiting for someone to fix it, a tech arrived, rolled up his sleeves, and stuck his head in the unit's innards. He fiddled with the mechanism and said, "Hmm" and "That's what I was afraid of," which I translated as expensive, before he said that a blown electronic something-or-other in the unit needed to be replaced.

He didn't have what it needed, so he had to go to the parts house to get one. While I waited for his return, the power in the kitchen kicked off, apparently, a sympathy strike for the silent air conditioner. A call to an electrician was next, followed by laughter from the lady who answered the phone when I asked if someone could come to the house today.

The first half of the next day was spent waiting for an electrician, but at least a working air conditioner made the wait tolerable. I knew as much about the AC unit and the house electrical system serving the kitchen as I knew about the Huli Wigmen tribe in Papua, New Guinea. My contribution to both technicians was to point to the electrical box and the air conditioner.

Cindy called while I was listening to the electrician ramble on at an extraordinary high hourly rate about why I needed five hundred dollars' worth of repairs.

I asked if I could call her back.

She said I could and, if I was lucky, she'd answer.

My checkbook was one more check and several hundred dollars lighter when I returned her call.

She answered with, "What are you pestering me about now?"

I reminded her that I was returning her call.

"Whatever. The coroner's office called this morning with the autopsy results on Ray Bentley."

I waited for her to continue, but she didn't say anything.

"Well?"

"Hold your palomino, I'm trying to find it. Okay, got it. Let's see, he says in all sorts of words I don't understand, but I think they mean Ray is still dead. Wait, there's more. In laymen's terms, Ray died of a broken neck."

"No surprise."

"Since you think every death is murder, I should add that the coroner said there were no signs of a struggle. Ray's BAC, that's blood alcohol content for you common citizens, was .16, twice the threshold for drunken driving. He wasn't in a vehicle when he tumbled down the steps, so he won't be posthumously cited for a traffic violation."

"It was accidental?"

"It looks like he was so drunk that he didn't see the stairs and staggered straight when the floor fell out from under him. The medical examiner agreed. It's ruled accidental, a result of alcohol, stupidity, and gravity. I added the last two."

I asked if Cindy found it strange that one of Theo's houseguests claims to have seen a body, presumably Michael Hardin, or has killed the bookie, depending upon his mood and, days later, another of his houseguests falls to his death.

"Of course I find it strange," Cindy said. "If you've been a cop as long as I have, you'll have seen way more things strange than normal. Still, I can't see a connection between the two. Can you?"

I hated to, but I agreed.

Cindy said, "Welcome to my world of strange."

———

My spirits were lifted when I met Barb for supper at Rita's Seaside Grille. It was a couple of hours before sunset, and still warm, so I arrived at the restaurant before Barb and was fortunate enough to commandeer the last available patio table.

Rita's was on a prime piece of property across the street from the Pier, catty-corner from the Tides Hotel. Customers were standing two deep at the outdoor bar. The rest of the tables were filled with a mix of locals, vacationers, and four men at one table who probably had played hooky from a meeting at the hotel. They wore coats and ties and appeared as uncomfortable as balloons at a porcupine party. The din of festive diners was a welcomed relief after spending hours in silence in my house the last two days.

My spirits were boosted further when I saw Barb walk across the street. She wore a short-sleeve red blouse, tan linen slacks, and a gleaming, white smile as she weaved her way around two tables and greeted me with a kiss.

The server had been waiting for her to arrive, was quick to the table, and asked if she needed a drink.

"Do I ever?" she asked before ordering a bottle of Sam Adams Rebel IPA, way more words in the beer's name than the beer choices of my other friends.

"Rough day?" I asked.

"Not really, but super busy with customers arriving in bunches. I can sit there for an hour without anyone coming in, then a couple of people are buying books, three are waiting to sell books, and someone wants to talk about the muse, or some amorphic symbolism in a book she 'loved, simply loved.'"

I'd spent several years in the space when it was the unsuccessful Landrum Gallery, so she lost me on *people buying*. I nodded like I understood as her drink arrived.

She took a sip and asked about my day. I shared my fascinating AC and electric stories while she pretended to be interested. After her heart rate slowed after being so excited about my air conditioner's new electronic part, she told me someone had come in the store who claimed to know me. I asked who. She said she'd tell me later. Her priority was getting food. I waved for the server, and Barb ordered fish and shrimp tacos, while I went with the fried shrimp basket.

The server left, and I said, "Back to your story?"

"An older guy, I'd guess in his mid-seventies, all-black clothes. His hair was so black it looked like he put shoe polish on it. He looked like he was going to a Halloween party. It was one of the times the store was empty. The gentleman walked over to me and said, 'Hi, I'm Wallace Bentley, you may have heard of me. I'm a comedian. Who might such a lovely lady as you be?'"

"What'd you say?"

"I smiled, told him my name, and said I had heard of him. I didn't tell him it was because you screwed-up his fishing trip in the middle of Center Street."

"Wise," I said. "How'd he seem?"

"Flirty, smarmy. Why?"

I told her about Wallace's son's accident, how he'd told Chief LaMond about killing someone, and how delusional he had appeared to be when confessing.

"He seemed fine, well, not fine, but didn't say anything that was out of the ordinary—ordinary for a smarmy flirt."

"Why'd he come in?"

"After we talked, he strolled around the store like he was killing time rather than looking for anything, then he bought a book on Jewish humor. He paid from a wad of cash and asked if I had other joke books. I told him I didn't think so." Barb chuckled. "He said that was okay. Said that, unlike one of his friends, he was funny enough without stealing jokes. I thought that was humorous since he'd just bought a book of jokes."

"He say anything else?"

"He said if I wanted to have a smokin' good time with a man's man, I was looking at him. I told him I'd keep that in mind. I wanted to tell him that he was a funny guy, but I smiled instead."

It didn't sound like Wallace was too broken up by his son's death. Either that, or he was doing something he appears to do well, avoiding reality.

Our food arrived, and Barb asked if I'd heard anything new about the death of the bookie I gave her my thoughts about Neil Wilson and Janice Raque.

Being a good attorney, she homed in on the differences between what I knew and what I suspected. I knew what she was getting at, but we weren't in court. She asked if I'd shared my thoughts with the police.

I told her that I did.

She reached across the table and put her hand on mine. "You've done all you can. Now it's up to them."

I nodded, recognizing it was time to drop the subject.

We spent the next hour enjoying a perfect evening watching diners around us soaking in the island's atmosphere while enjoying a delightful meal.

I was again reminded why I had chosen to retire on Folly Beach. The best part of the evening, other than spending it with a lovely lady, was that I didn't give another thought to the murder, or murders.

Chapter Twenty-Eight

Theo called the next afternoon to tell me Ray's body had been cremated. He'd taken Wallace to the funeral home to pick up the cremains.

I asked how Wallace was, and Theo said he was quite well for someone who'd just lost a son. He went on to mention that, during the trip, the comic never strayed from reality. I thought that was a good sign, although curious.

Theo then admitted that there was another reason for his call. Sal cornered him as soon as he got back from the funeral home and wanted him to call me to see if I'd meet him at Cal's tonight. Theo said Sal thought that, since I was such a good friend of the bar owner, it'd be good if I was with Sal when he asked about another appearance. I could tell Cal how good the idea was.

I'd rather have another visit by an electrician than pimp for Sal and his band of comedians, so I asked Theo what he wanted me to do.

He stated that Sal was his brother and that family members must stick together. Not a rousing yes.

I told him that if he was there, I'd be.

I entered the nearly-full bar as the distinct voice of Hank Williams Sr. singing "I'm So Lonesome I Could Cry" filled the air, along with the comforting smell of frying hamburgers. Two couples at a nearby table were clinking their beer bottles together toasting something. At another table, four middle-aged women were laughing. Cal was behind the bar, pointing a finger at Chester Carr, who stood in front of the bar nodding at Cal.

There were two empty tables beside the stage and nobody else entering, so I didn't have to rush to grab one. I headed to the bar to say hi to Chester and warn Cal about Sal's visit.

"Chris," Cal said as he tipped his Stetson my direction. "Glad you're here. Tell this old man I'm right."

I smiled and turned to Chester. "Old man, Cal's right."

Cal pulled his shoulders back. "I told you so."

Chester shook his head. "Chris, you don't know what he's talking about."

I patted Chester's shoulder. "Don't need to. It's his bar, so he's right."

Cal slid a beer to Chester. "Chester, you could learn a lot by paying attention to this here youngster." He pointed at me.

Cal's mood was often influenced by the size of the crowd. He was excited about the mid-week numbers. My mood was influenced by someone calling me a youngster. Maybe tonight wouldn't be as bad as I'd anticipated.

From the jukebox, Johnny Cash was bemoaning how bad his Sunday morning was, two men stepped up to the bar and asked for more Buds, and Chester put a damper on my mood when he asked if I'd caught the bookie's killer. I would rather he'd told me what he and Cal had been arguing about. I said no.

He took a sip, looked around the room, and leaned closer to me. "If you ask me, it's Janice Raque."

"What makes you think that, other than the argument you told me about?"

Chester looked around again, then turned to me, "Last night—"

Cal set a glass of wine in front of me, nodded in Chester's direction, and interrupted, "You convinced my pard here that I'm always right?"

"Yes," Chester said before I could. "You're always right, Cal. You remember when I was in here last night sitting by the table near the door?"

"I'm old, not senile. Of course, I remember. You were with Horace and Janice Raque. Am I right, or am I right?"

"Did you notice that Horace left before Janice?"

"That slipped by me. What's your point?"

Chester motioned for Cal to lean closer. "I was telling Chris that I think Janice killed Michael Hardin."

Cal took off his hat and rubbed his hand through his hair. "Because her husband left before she did?"

Chester shook his head. "You know why he left?"

"I'm a broken-down, country-singing barkeep, not a psychic."

"Why'd he leave? I asked, hoping to move the deteriorating conversation along.

"Janice started to tell me how much she lost when the bookie claimed he didn't place her bet in time. Horace snarled at her and said that he's sick of hearing her tell that story and how happy she is that the blankety-blank bookie's dead."

Somehow, I'd missed how that made her a murderer. I said, "Is that why you think she killed him?"

Chester hesitated and whispered, "When Horace was

storming out, Janice mumbled, "That's why I freakin' killed him."

"Whoa," Cal said. "That came from nowhere. You sure that's what she said?"

"I barely heard her. It surprised me. I asked her what she said. She looked embarrassed, like she didn't know that she said it out loud."

Cal reached over the bar and punched Chester on the arm. "Don't keep us in suspense. What'd she say?"

"She stammered, 'I, umm, said, I'm glad Michael is dead.'"

"You sure that's what she said?" Cal asked.

Chester tapped his beer bottle on the bar. "That's what she told me. That ain't what I heard. Not what I think I heard."

Two men at the other end of the bar called for more drinks.

"Damn, just when it's getting good," Cal said and moved to the thirsty customers.

"Chester, you want to tell the chief what you heard?"

"Chris, that's all I've thought about since last night. I've tried to think how I could've misunderstood her. If I didn't, if she was serious, umm, it was loud in here. My hearing's not what it used to be. The more I ponder it, the more I'm not sure. I don't feel comfortable blabbing to the police."

"Sure?"

"Yes."

Roy Acuff's version of "Blue Eyes Crying in the Rain" filled the room as Sal sauntered in wearing his three-piece, robin-egg blue suit. He was followed by Pete and Theo.

Sal saw me and shrugged.

I motioned them to the empty table by the stage and turned back to Chester. I offered to go with him to see the chief if that'd help. He promised to keep my offer in mind, threw a ten-dollar bill on the bar, said he was tired, and wanted to get home.

Sal and Pete had taken seats at the table; Theo was talking to a nearby couple. I moved to the newcomers, even though I would rather have spent more time trying to convince Chester to share his story with the police.

Theo finished talking with the women, and he and I took the two vacant chairs.

Sal thanked me for meeting them and waved for the harried server to take our order.

She was quick to the table and said it would be a few minutes before she could get back with the drinks.

I asked, "Where's Wallace?"

Theo looked at Sal and answered, "He stayed home. Said he was torn up by Ray's death, didn't feel like seeing anyone."

"News to me," Sal said. "Wallace couldn't stand being around Ray when he was alive. Now he wants to stay in his room to stare at a box of ashes."

Pete spoke for the first time. "Ray's a lot nicer in a box than when he was alive."

"Come on, Pete," Sal said, "that's a horrible thing to say."

Pete smiled. "It's true."

Cal brought our drinks and welcomed my table mates.

Sal moved around the table to shake Cal's hand. "Great to see you again, good buddy. How's business?"

Cal shook Sal's hand and gave me a sideways look. He'd told me that, after several decades of being on the road entertaining and encountering countless managers, promoters, and bar owners trying to take advantage of him, he could spot BS a mile away. He was even better spotting it at three feet.

"Good," was all Cal said before Sal interrupted and asked the singer to join us. He reached over to pull another chair to the table before Cal could escape.

Cal looked around and didn't see anyone needing his attention. He gave me a dirty look as he sat.

Sal smiled. "Pete, Wallace, and I were checking and uncovered a couple of open slots in our schedule. We thought since you were so happy with our performance, we'd be willing to do an encore. We know we can't compete with your incredible singing talents, but we could give you a break you know, fill in between your sets. What do ya think?"

I don't know what Cal thought, but I thought it was the biggest crock I'd heard in Cal's.

"Tell you what, guys," Cal said and set his Stetson on the table, "Chris knows this, but you may not. Each Tuesday, I have open mic night for crooners. We draw a good crowd and a handful of wannabes. I was thinking we could try a few open mic nights for comedians. I've had customers mention it, even say they might could lay some jokes on an audience. We could do it Sunday nights. If you could work it in your busy schedule, we could feature the Legends Tour the first few weeks to get us off to a rousing start. I bet the newcomers could learn a bunch from you professionals. How about it?"

Not only could Cal spot BS, but he could also sling it. It was interesting that he chose his slowest night of the week and, with other joke tellers, there was a chance of hearing something funny from the stage.

Sal looked at Pete then turned to Cal. "Of course, we'll have to talk to our agent and our booking company. There's a decent chance we'll be able to break free to help you get your event off to a good start. Our business manager will want to know the pay."

Without hesitation, Cal said, "Same as last time."

Sal stared at the ceiling then at Cal. "That'll work."

Pete said, "Now, about something else, smoking. It's a proven fact that people don't hear things as funny unless there's smoke in their eyes. Seems I've seen folks smoking in a couple of places over here. So, it can be okay during our performances, right?"

Cal said, "I'm a country singer. I don't tell jokes or funny stories. I'll tell you what I do. I make payments on this bar. I own those speakers up there." He pointed to the stage. "I own that big ole silver microphone that's hooked into my amp that's hooked to the speakers. And, I make the rules. When ya'll asked about smoking the last time, it was no joke when I said no, N-O. If you don't like it, there's the door." Cal glared at Pete. "That clear enough?"

Sal put his hand in front of Pete. "Don't get all worked up, Cal. Pete was just asking,"

Cal nodded. "I think that Dylan guy said it good when he warbled 'The Times They Are a-Changin'.' Change your hang-up about people puffin'."

Cal had said he couldn't tell a joke, yet he's talking about changing, talk coming from a man who's so stuck in the 1960s that he thinks music written after that should be banned.

"Good point, Cal," Sal said. "It's easy to see why you have such a successful bar. We'll let you get back to your job. Someone will call you tomorrow to let you know what our support staff says about the Legends headlining Sunday."

Headlining. Support staff. Sal was funny.

Cal was quick to leave. No one was waiting for drinks, so it was to escape from the Legends rather than to get back to bartending.

I finished my drink and left Theo and his houseguests enjoying drinks, country classics, conversation, and a night out of the house where Ray had fallen to his death and his dad was conversing with his son's ashes.

Chapter Twenty-Nine

Charles was waiting for me the next morning at the Dog. I'd called him on my way home from Cal's to see if he had breakfast plans. He said that he did but, because I was such a good friend, and had offered to pick up the tab, he'd shift his schedule around to free up breakfast—all that to say he had nothing to do.

Amber and I arrived at the table at the same time, and she placed a steaming hot mug of coffee in front of me.

A group of five ladies on the other side of the room waved for Amber's attention.

She acknowledged their signal but, before she left, she said, "When it slows down, I've got something to tell you."

We ordered, and Amber moved to the other table.

Charles watched her go. "What does she want to tell you?"

I shook my head and took a sip.

He continued to stare at Amber. "Suppose we'll have to wait until she gets back." He ran his hand through his hair. "I've been thinking."

I nodded in response since that was his second comment that didn't warrant a response.

"Aren't you going to ask what I've been thinking?"

I smiled. "No, you're going to tell me whether I ask or not."

"You're no fun. Anyway, I did a heap of pondering last night. I think Neil Wilson killed the bookie."

"Go on."

Charles tapped the table with his forefinger. "First, he owed money." He tapped again. "Second, he could no more pay it than I could become Governor of South Carolina." Another tap. "Third, he's a brute. It would've been easy for him to clobber the life out of the bookie." One more tap. "In addition to being big, he's a cop, so he's got hand-to-hand combat training. Bookie-man wouldn't have had a chance." He hesitated and looked at the ceiling. "And, whatever the next number is, Cindy said Neil didn't have an alibi. That enough reasons?"

I didn't think a security guard would be considered a cop. I also questioned whether Neil had combat training, hand-to-hand or otherwise. I didn't think Charles's reasons were anywhere close to proving Neil's guilt. I couldn't fault him for trying and didn't want to challenge him since he's been so fragile. My guess was that he's thinking about the bookie's death more to get his mind off losing Heather than to solve the murder.

"Good points. The police know all of that, so I doubt they've cleared Neil."

Charles peeked at his wrist, then looked around the room. "When's Amber coming back?"

"Patience, she'll be here. You could be right about Neil. Let me throw something else in the mix."

I shared what Chester told me about Janice, what he

thought she said about killing Michael, and what she told him she'd said after he questioned her about it. Charles asked if Chester was sure he heard her say that she killed him. It was the same question I'd asked, so I gave Charles the same answer I'd received.

"When were you going to tell me? Why'd you let me go on about Neil when you already knew who the killer was? Why did—"

I held my coffee mug up in his face. "Could I have stopped you?"

Charles bit his lower lip and said, "No, but—"

Amber was standing by the table, set our breakfast down, and interrupted Charles. "I've only got a minute. I figured you'd want to know that Janice was in yesterday, got here right before closing. Remember her temper tantrum when Shantel got Janice's order wrong?"

I nodded.

"She did it again. This time, she was mad when she walked in the door, and didn't try to hide it. Shantel was stuck with her. I was behind the counter by the coffee urn. Since I knew what happened the last time, I kept an eye on them. Shantel bent over backwards to be nice. Janice ordered. Shantel went to put the order in and bring Janice water. I thought Janice was going to knock the water on the floor. She pounded the table and said, 'Could you be any slower?' Poor Shantel didn't know what to do. She'd done everything right, had the water there as quick as any of us could have." Amber rolled her eyes. "I would've been tempted to smack Janice. Shantel apologized, backpedaled from the table, then went to the kitchen to get away from the irate customer. Next thing I know, Janice slammed her chair against the chair behind her and was out the door. She didn't pay for anything." Amber shook her head. "Shantel was in tears."

"That's terrible."

Amber looked around, didn't see anyone seeking her attention, and said, "That doesn't prove anything, other than Janice is a hothead and won't be on Shantel's Christmas card list. I figured you'd want to know since you're trying to catch the bookie's killer."

I thanked her, and she headed back to work.

Charles said, "Okay, you've got me. Neil just slipped to number two on my list."

"Like Amber said, all it proves is that Janice has an explosive temper."

"True, but when you add that to what Chester told you, it paints a nasty picture about good ole Janice. You need to tell Cindy." He took a bite of breakfast then pointed to my phone.

"I don't want to talk to her from here. I'll call later."

"You bet you will. I'll be there to make sure you don't leave anything out."

I changed the subject and told him about the comedy Legends meeting with Cal and the decision to hold open-mic comedy night on Sundays, that is, if the Legends' staff approves.

"Staff, you mean their imaginary manager?"

"That's the one."

"Cal figures if he can get some amateurs to embarrass themselves on his stage, his customer won't have to be exposed all night to the Legends."

I said, "Do you blame him?"

"Cal didn't get old by being stupid."

We continued eating and agreeing on Cal's wisdom.

Charles said he knew a couple of folks who might have the guts or were stupid enough to stand on stage and try to be funny. He would try to recruit them. I wanted to ask if he was okay, but decided he'd tell me he was whether he was or not. I kept the conversation light and was pleased to see him smile more than he had the last few times we'd been together.

He stuffed the last bite in his mouth then pointed at my phone.

I took the hint, asked Amber for the check, paid, and Charles followed me to the small park adjacent to the Dog. Instead of calling Cindy, I punched in Chester's number. He must've had the phone in his hand because he answered before I heard it ring. "Hi, Chester."

Charles flailed around like he was being attacked by a gaggle of gnats and mouthed, "That's not the chief."

I held my hand over the mic and said, "Chill."

"No, I wasn't talking to you, Chester. I wanted to see if you were certain about what you told me that Janice said about killing the bookie."

"Chris, I was up half the night thinking about it. I'm not sure. I think that's what she said. I'd hate to get her in trouble if I'm wrong."

"That's all I wanted to know."

"I wish I could be more helpful."

I told him I knew and wished him a pleasant day.

Charles put his hand over his eyes and shook his head. "Don't suppose you're going to call Cindy?"

"Not until I have something to tell her."

Charles sat back on the bench. "George W. Bush said, 'When I take action, I'm not going to fire a two-million-dollar missile at a ten-dollar empty tent and hit a camel in the butt. I'm going to be decisive.'"

I agreed, and the phone rang.

Charles said, "See, Chester changed his mind."

I didn't know about Chester, since Theo was on the other end of the call.

"Chris, could you come to the house?"

"When?"

"Now. The guys are still in bed. I have something to tell, no, to show you."

"Can Charles come?"

"Will that take longer? I want to show you before the guys wake up."

I told him that Charles was with me. We could be there in a couple of minutes.

Chapter Thirty

Charles and I were at Theo's door and greeted by the homeowner whispering for us to keep our voices low so we wouldn't wake his guests. We moved to the great room and sat close together on his oversized couch.

Theo whispered, "Notice anything different?"

It was the kind of question I hate. It was up there with someone asking if I'd heard the latest.

"Different?" I repeated back to Theo.

Charles looked at Theo. "You look older than I remembered."

"Not me," Theo said. "Anything different in the room?" He stared at the table along the side of the room, the table holding his silver figurines.

A silver frog was next to the eagle, cat, and llama that he had shown me during a previous visit.

I walked over and lifted the frog. "Is this the one that was missing?"

"One and the same."

Charles said, "So it didn't croak after all."

I carried the figurine to the couch and sat so I could keep my voice low. "How'd you get it back?"

"Don't know," Theo said. "I came in yesterday afternoon, saw something behind the table. It was on the floor in the corner."

I turned it over in my hands. "Could it have been there all along?"

Theo shook his head. "It's possible, although I would have thought the cleaning lady, or I, would've noticed."

Charles moved to the table and put his hand in the gap between the table and the wall. "The space is wide enough for it to fall."

Theo shrugged.

Charles said, "Frog's hop. I'm certain that silver ones don't hoppity hop on their own. If someone knocked it off, he, or she, would've heard it smack the floor."

"I agree," Theo said.

I pointed to the ceiling. "Do you think one of them took it and put it behind the table so it looked like it'd fallen?"

"That was my thought."

Charles said, "Why would someone steal it then bring it back?"

I stared at the frog. "He could've felt guilty about taking it, figured this was a way to return it without raising suspicion. Or he tried to hock it and couldn't find anyone who'd give him much for it. What about the missing money?"

"Still gone."

I returned the frog to the table, and Charles said, "Any idea which one of your guests absconded with the frog and the moolah?"

Theo shook his head.

Charles replied, "Come on, Theo, you have an idea."

"Could've been any of them."

"How about Wallace?" Charles asked. "He could've been in one of his weirdo moods. He took it then came to his senses and brought it back."

"Could be. If he did, his good sense wasn't strong enough for him to bring the money back."

"Sal?" I asked.

"I hate to think so." He shrugged. "We've had so little contact during the last couple of decades that I can't rule him out."

"What's all the racket down here? Did I hear my name mentioned?" Sal said as he came down the stairs.

Without skipping a beat, Theo said, "We were talking about your appearance tomorrow at Cal's. They were saying how excited they were to see the Legends perform again."

Charles turned to me and whispered, "We were?"

I smiled, said hi, and agreed with Theo about how happy we were.

"Fantastic," Sal said. "I think our performances will blow you away. Heard if there're amateurs who'll try their hand at comedy before Cal turns the show over to the pros?"

Charles said, "I know a couple of folks who might tell some jokes."

Sal headed to the coffee pot in the kitchen and poured a cup. I looked at Theo and wondered how he wanted to handle us being here. I didn't have to wonder long.

He said, "Chris, sorry you and Charles have to run. It would've been nice if you could have spent more time with my houseguests."

Charles returned Theo's lie. "Me too. We must get going. Besides, we'll get to spend time with them tomorrow at Cal's."

Theo mouthed, "Thank you."

I took one more look at the silver frog before we let ourselves out.

———

"What are the chances that that ugly, expensive frog hopped itself off the table?" Charles asked as we stood in front of Pewter Hardware a block from Theo's house.

"Zero. Theo didn't tell his guests it was gone. It makes more sense that whoever took it couldn't unload it then brought it back, hoping that Theo wouldn't notice it'd been missing. Let's see if Larry's here."

In addition to being Chief LaMond's husband and owner of the city's only hardware store, Larry had a checkered past and had spent eight years at taxpayer's expense after getting caught burglarizing homes. He'd used those years to reevaluate his career choice, moved to Folly, and became one of its most upstanding citizens.

"What're you going to do, ask if someone tried to pay for a Weed Eater with a silver frog?"

I rolled my eyes and told him to follow me as I opened the door to the compact store. The building was empty, except for Larry standing behind the counter, fiddling with a toaster-sized electric motor, and Brandon, Larry's only full-time employee, who was at the far side of the store restocking a rack of electrical tape.

Brandon looked up as the bell over the door announced our arrival. He saw who it was and went back to restocking.

Larry smiled, set the motor down, wiped his hands on a grease-stained towel, and said, "Welcome. What can I do for you today?"

Charles made an overblown stage wave in my direction. "This ought to be interesting."

Larry turned to me.

"Got a question." I said. "How easy would it be to find

someone to buy a less-than-legally acquired, expensive, silver figurine?"

Larry tilted his head and frowned. "I would know that how?"

I held up my hand and said in a voice low enough so Brandon couldn't hear. "Because I value your wisdom and vast experience."

Larry smiled. "That's a subtle way to say I used to be a thief who had relied on fences to unload my, umm, regifted items."

"Larry," Charles said, "I like the way you said it better."

Larry ignored him. "How valuable?"

"Seven hundred dollars."

"Most pawn shops would avoid it. They'd want to be sure of the person pawning it. How did he get it? Why was he hocking it? Those kinds of things. Even then, the owner would give you little for it. Now if the person hocking the item found a, how shall I say it, less than upstanding dealer, he might buy it no questions asked, but not for much. Nowadays, those guys are harder and harder to find, or so I've been told. Most likely they wouldn't have a shop, would do business through word of mouth."

"How easy would it be for someone from out of town to find one of those dealers?"

Larry stepped out from behind the counter and glanced over at Brandon. "Near impossible. No one would trust a stranger for fear that he was an undercover cop. Why?"

I shared what had happened at Theo's and why I'd suspected one of his guests.

Larry shook his head. "Chris, it's possible that the thief could luck out and stumble across someone who would give him a decent price. Possible, although I wouldn't bet on it."

Chapter Thirty-One

I arrived at Cal's an hour before the first-ever open-mic comedy night and second appearance by the world-famous, in their minds, Legends tour group. The island was blanketed by an April shower. While it was too early to know if it would bring May flowers, it was apparent that it didn't bring a large crowd. Two tables were occupied, one man sat at the bar and was in deep conversation with Cal. Two servers huddled in a corner, probably bemoaning why they were both there with so few customers.

Theo had asked me to save room for his group, so I slid the same two tables together that we occupied during the Legends previous appearance, set my Tilley on them to mark my turf, and went to see Cal.

The bar owner finished his conversation with the lone bar customer and tilted his Stetson at me. "Did you see a bus full of thirsty customers parked out front?"

"It's early. The rain's supposed to stop. Folks will turn out."

"Sure as holy hyenas, I hope so, or those gals will string me up." He hesitated and tilted his head in the direction of the frowning servers. "I told them that tips would be flowing as free as the tide tonight."

It was shy of a busload, but four people stepped in the door, looked around, and moved to the table closest to the stage.

"See," I said, "the crowd is arriving."

Cal watched the group take seats and Joy approach them to take their order. "That's part of the entertainment. The one who looks like a fat piñata is Vernon. He's a comedian, well he's a bean counter, but tonight he's playing comedian."

The man Cal referred to was in his thirties, with pasty white skin, and dressed in a colorful Hawaiian shirt and cut-off jeans. He looked more like a blimp caught in a paint store explosion than a piñata.

"How do you know?"

"He came in last night. Said he was here to, 'analyze the assets and liabilities of the venue' before tonight's appearance."

"That's how you knew he was an accountant?"

"Hell's bells, no. I said to him, "You want to dumb that down for this ole cowboy?' Then he told me he was an accountant and apologized for his highfalutin' talk."

Charles arrived next and shook the rain off his Tilley. He noticed my hat on the table, threw his beside mine, then joined Cal and me. He was wearing a navy-blue long-sleeve T-shirt with the head of a lion and the word *EMERSON* in gold on the front. "Where're the thousands of Legends' fans?"

I suspected he knew the answer but, since Cal looked so down about the numbers, I told him that I was sure they were on their way.

"They may need a boat to get here," Charles said.

Their ship must have come in because, during the next few

minutes, three more groups of soaked customers arrived and griped about the rain as they commandeered tables.

Cassis and Kristin had added smiles to their faces and a bounce to their steps as the rushed to serve the newcomers.

Cal began to get more enthusiastic about the crowd when two more people arrived. He got Charles a Bud Light, a glass of wine for me, and pointed at Charles's shirt. "Emerson?"

Charles smiled. "Wondered if anyone'd notice."

Cal asked, "What's the deal?"

I knew better than to comment on Charles's shirts.

"It's in Boston. The only college in the US of A that has what?"

"One fewer T-shirt?" I said.

"Wrong."

"I'll bite," Cal said. "What?"

"A bachelor's degree in comedic arts."

Cal said, "You're kiddin'."

"I didn't go there so I can't be kiddin'," Charles said like it made sense. "I got it for tonight."

I was impressed but didn't dare tell my friend.

"Wow," Cal said, "I'd love to hear more, but I'd better start acting like a bartender."

Charles and I left him grabbing drinks for Kristin then moved to the tables.

Charles looked at the table, where the colorful accountant was talking to the others with him. "I see Vernon made it."

"You know him?"

"I'm why he's here. I met him in Mr. John's Beach Store. He was gabbing with that skinny chick sitting with him. She was laughing at something he said. I didn't hear what it was, but figured it was funny, so I introduced myself and asked if he was a comedian."

Charles could get away with something like that. "What'd he say?"

"He looked at me like I was a tarantula he wanted to stomp on, then he grinned. He told me that he was an accountant, although some of the folks in his office told him he should be a stand-up comic. That was coming from accountants, so I didn't think he had to be funny to impress them. The lady with him, her name's Tanya, said he should go for it. I told him about open-mic comedy night. There he is."

"Don't know how funny he is, but his shirt will get laughs."

"Ah, ha," Charles said as he looked at the door. "There's my other recruit. Maybe I should supplement my private detective income as an agent to the stars."

He was looking at two women, both appeared to be in their late-twenties, with short, dark hair, wearing white blouses and skinny jeans.

"Both comedians?" I asked.

"Not sure about both. The one on the left is. That's Franny Foster. She works at Harris-Teeter. Every time I'm in there, she's talking about her three kids and her worthless husband. She's downright funny, so I invited her."

Franny waved at Charles as she followed the lady with her to a table.

There was one vacant table left, and Joy and Kristin were busy. Cal was in a better mood as he looked at his watch before moving to the stage.

He tapped the large, silver microphone. "Guys and gals, listen up. This is a big night for Cal's. You're in for quite a treat. We're going to unplug the jukebox and bring to this here stage some of the finest joke tellers that ever stepped foot on Folly Beach. That's right, we'll be opening with some locals who think, no, who know, that they're as funny as those funny guys you see on TV. Then, as quick as you can shake a hickory stick, you'll be laughing your as—umm, your rear end off when the true Legends of comedy get here." He held up both hands like he was holding back the excitement of the crowd.

It worked. No one applauded, laughed, or showed signs of excitement.

"So, let's get the fun beginning. Raise your hand if you want to share some jokes with us."

Two hands went up: Vernon and Franny.

"Fantastic," Cal said. "Let's begin with the young man who looks like he just got here from Hawaii. Vernon, umm, what's your last name again?"

The roly-poly man said, "Moore."

"Bring it on, Vernon Moore."

The three-other people at Vernon's table applauded as he moved to the microphone.

He squeezed it like it was a snake trying to wiggle free. "Hi, I'm Vernon Moore, and this is my first appearance here." He chuckled. "Umm, it's my first appearance anywhere. I've been told that I'm funny, and my sweet wife, Tanya, said I could prove it to you. So here goes." He hesitated, took a deep breath, then said, "During the day, I'm an accountant in downtown Charleston. Yep, I'm one of them. There are three kinds of accountants in the world, those who can count, and those who can't." He nodded his head toward the room.

Two of the three people at his table laughed. They must've been accountants.

"Okay," Vernon continued, "You know the definition of an economist?" Vernon waved his hand at the audience. No one knew. "It's someone who doesn't have enough personality to be an accountant."

Charles leaned over to me. "Is it midnight yet?"

"Do you know when a person decides to be an accountant?" Apparently, no one knew that answer, either. "When he realizes he doesn't have enough charisma to be an undertaker."

That elicited chuckles from several people who weren't sitting at his table.

Vernon was on a roll. He shared a few more accountant jokes, and I was beginning to wonder where the Legends were.

Vernon said, "I'd better finish up so, remember, if you ever want to drive an accountant insane, tie him to a chair, stand in front of him, and fold a roadmap the wrong way. Thank you, thank you." He bowed and received a standing ovation—from three people at his table.

Polite applause was sprinkled throughout the rest of the room.

Cal put his arm around Vernon and said, "Great job, great job. Let's hear it again for Vernon Moore."

Vernon returned to his adoring fans, and Cal motioned to the woman who'd said she wanted to perform.

She walked to the stage like she was stepping on eggshells.

Cal met her, leaned close, while she whispered something to the country crooner.

Cal grabbed the mic and said, "Folks, put your hands together on this historic night. Give a big round of applause for Miss Franny Foster."

Most of the patrons applauded, and Franny said, "Evening guys, like Vernon, this is my first time behind a microphone. As handsome Cal said, I'm Franny and I'm frazzled. I came out tonight with my friend, Laurie, to get out of the house. You see, I have three tikes at home, actually, it's four, because my husband's thirty years old, or ten in kiddie years." She sighed. "Let me tell you how smart he is. He put a knocker on our front door. Seems he thought it'd help him win the no-bell prize." It may have been my imagination, but it appeared that most of the women in the room laughed.

"I know, I know," Franny continued, "I've learned never to argue with an idiot. He'll drag you down to his level then beat you with experience."

This time, it wasn't my imagination.

Franny shook her head and frowned. "I don't know who's lazier, my hubby, or our dog Darwin. Whenever someone knocks on the door, Darwin looks at me like I should bark."

More laughter. Franny smiled, and said, "My husband claims I'm always negative. Yesterday, we were halfway to Columbia when he said, 'All you do is complain. Gee, I remembered the car seat, I remembered the diapers, I remembered the stroller. And all you do is gripe about me forgetting the baby.'"

Even Cal laughed.

Franny started another joke when she was interrupted by the constant blaring of a car horn.

I closed my eyes and shook my head. The Legends had arrived.

Charles asked if I wanted to go out and meet them.

I told him I'd rather slither under the table.

He said it wasn't a bad idea.

We turned out attention back to Franny who was trying to pretend that the horn wasn't disrupting her set.

"And kids," she said. "Don't get me started about kids. The other night, I came home and saw Timmy, my oldest, who's nine, sitting on a big stuffed horse and writing something. Now, being a keen observer, I asked him what in the world was he doing. He looked at me with his big brown eyes and said, 'Our teacher told us to write an essay on our favorite animal. That's why I'm sitting here and why sis is sitting on the goldfish bowl.'"

Cal's front door flung open and, for all practical purposes, Franny's performance was over.

———————————

Chapter Thirty-Two

In walked Sal, shoulders pulled back, looking as confident as LeBron James playing in a middle-school basketball game. His robin-egg blue, three-piece suit was replaced by a shiny, off-white suit and black dress shoes.

Pete was next through the door. Instead of his red sports coat, he wore a bright orange coat with a brown ascot.

I wouldn't have been surprised to see him followed in by Wallace in a red, white, and blue jumpsuit, with an elephant wearing a top hat. I was disappointed when Wallace walked in the door wearing a black shirt, slacks, and shoes. His wardrobe was black and new; the shirt showing packaging creases. He carried a plastic Walmart bag. It wasn't black.

Sal looked at Franny, gave her a thumbs-up, and moved, along with his companions, to the table. Their attire was loud enough to make up for his silence.

Franny seemed to lose her place, stammered, and said, "My time's up. Remember, folks, it's true that women don't work as hard as men." Two women in the audience groaned.

Franny held up her hand and smiled. "It's because we get it right the first time. Thanks."

Maybe it was because they had a beer or two, or because they thought Franny was funny, the crowd applauded, not just the lady at Franny's table. Sal yelled, "Bravo!"

He'd heard a grand total of one joke. The comic must've figured that if he praised her performance, she'd do the same when he finished.

The reason didn't matter to Franny, she beamed from ear to ear and nodded in Sal's direction. After all, how often does a legend of comedy praise a mother with three toddlers, four counting her hubby, after her first gig?

Cal had his arm around Franny. He echoed Sal's remark when he told the audience that he was taking a fifteen-minute break for everyone to order more drinks before he brought on the world-famous Legends of Comedy.

Theo had parked the Legends' limo and joined us while Krista and Joy were taking Charles and my reorder plus orders from the others.

"Nice outfits," Charles said to the Legends.

Sal said, "We wanted to look our best tonight. Wallace thought we could be good role models for the aspiring comics who came out to tell a few jokes. It's called leading by example."

"Good idea," I said, yet thought they looked like examples for aspiring clowns rather than comics.

Joy and Kristin returned with drinks when I noticed Janice Raque seated at the bar. She was by herself, so I went to say hi. She recognized me and said it was good to see me. I was surprised by her good mood. I asked if she was alone.

She said yes, so I asked if she wanted to join our group. She looked over to see who *our group* was, and said, "Why not?"

Charles saw us coming. He pulled an extra chair from a nearby table and patted its seat for Janice.

I introduced her to the group. If they cared, they hid it well. I wrote it off to nerves, or it could have been they truly didn't care. Theo, who didn't have to worry about his comedy performance, said he knew Janice and was glad that she joined us.

"Where's Horace?" Theo asked like he just realized that Janice was by herself.

"Don't know, don't care, don't ask," she said, then turned to Wallace. "I was sorry to hear about your son."

I was surprised that she knew about Ray. Charles beat me to asking, "How'd you hear?"

She hesitated and said, "Can't keep anything under rocks around here."

Cryptic, I thought, and so did Charles. "Who told you?"

Before she answered, Cal blew into the microphone, tapped it with his knuckles, and said, "Here's what we've all been waiting for. Let me bring up to the stage Mr. Sal, umm," he glanced at a piece of paper in his hand. "Salvador Stoll. He's going to serve as master of ceremonies for the Legends. It's all yours, Sal."

Sal looked like a skinny, short version of Colonel Sanders as he grabbed the mic like he owned it. "Thank you, Cal. Let's have a hand for the best bar owner in this half of the country."

Mild applause followed, some of it was because the people knew Cal and showed their appreciation, some was muted by people who were probably trying to figure out who the best bar owner was in the other half of the country.

"How about the great performances by the comics who opened for us tonight?"

Applause rang out from the tables where the previous

performers were seated. Sal nodded. "Great job, folks." He paused and smiled. "I was sitting over there a few minutes ago when my good friend, Chris, asked me if there were any famous men born on my birthday. I said, nope, only babies." Sal laughed at his joke and said, "Speaking of birthdays, I asked my wife what she wanted for her birthday. She said something with diamonds. Being the generous, accommodating husband that I am, I gave her a pack of playing cards." He laughed again. "And if you think that's funny, wait until you hear what my good friend, Pete Marvin, will be laying on you. I'll be back in a little while. Until then, let me present nationally-known comedian, entertainer extraordinaire, Pete Marvin."

I leaned over to Theo while Pete was making his way to the mic. "Those new outfits must've cost a pretty penny."

"Don't know. They didn't use my credit card."

I thought it strange since he'd said he'd been footing all their bills. "Where'd the money come from?"

"Pete said he got a payment he was owed by one of the clubs where they'd played last year."

"Do you believe him?"

"No reason not to. It was fine with me since I wasn't forking out the cash."

No reason other than someone stealing money from his house. I didn't share that thought.

Pete was introducing himself to the crowd as if Sal hadn't already.

"I don't know about you," Pete said, "I want to die peacefully in my sleep like my grandfather." He paused. "Not screaming and yelling like the passengers in his car."

Scattered laughter came from some of the tables, along with a spattering of groans. I wondered how sensitive a death joke was this close to Wallace's son's demise.

"The other day, I read where four out of five people suffer from diarrhea. Yep, four out of five. Does that mean one person likes it?"

The dead joke wasn't so bad after all.

"Speaking of my grandfather," Pete continued without waiting for the silence to die down, "I remember when he gave my grandmother a cemetery plot for her birthday." He shook his head. "Was she ever pissed. The next year, he didn't give her anything. That irritated her even more. She asked him why he didn't get her a gift. Gramps said, 'You didn't use what I gave you last year.'"

Three men at a table behind us thought it was funny, probably the reason they were in Cal's without their wives.

Pete told a few more jokes that received increased amounts of laughter. I could see how he'd been a success on the comedy club circuit. He finished, took a couple of bows, and introduced his "good friend," Wallace Bentley, the "star of comedy shows, television, and movies."

The room was full, Cal smiled like he'd discovered a way to increase Sunday business. Joy and Kristin were scurrying around the bar, distributing drinks while earning the kind of tips that they'd anticipated.

Wallace pushed up from the table, grabbed the Walmart sack, and moved toward the stage like he was walking in a pool of Jell-O. He set the bag on the corner of the stage and moved to the microphone. His shiny, black hair glistened in the lone stage light.

"Wasn't Pete great?" Wallace asked and applauded in the direction of Pete. His face smiled, but his eyes and clenched fist screamed pain.

Pete gave what I suspected was intended to be a humble nod but looked more like he was drifting asleep with his chin bouncing off his chest.

Wallace turned to the crowd and said, "Before I begin, I'd like to dedicate my performance to my son, Ray. He was a wonderful kid, a fabulous entertainer. He joins me tonight on the stage. He's gone now but will always be with me during my performances." Wallace moved away from the mic and stooped down in front of the Walmart bag. He pulled a rectangular, bronze box the size of a shoebox out and set it next to the mic stand."

A couple of people in the back of the room laughed, two tables of customers moaned, most everyone else didn't know how to react. Was it a joke? Was he serious? What do we do now? Everyone at our table understood. The comedians bowed their heads. I peeked at Charles and couldn't tell if he was rolling his eyes or shaking his head.

Janice mumbled, "Shit."

"Thank you," Wallace said.

For what, I didn't know.

He pointed at Pete. "Pete's a good friend. I love him like a mosquito, but tell you the truth, he comes from a stupid family." He then pointed to a table on the other side of the room. "How stupid, you ask. In the Civil War, his ancestors fought for the West."

Nervous laughter from not knowing what to do after Wallace's introduction of Ray, turned sincere.

"His sister's so dumb, blondes made jokes about her."

More laughter.

"Then there's my good friend, Sal. Wave Sal."

Sal frowned then waved.

Wallace nodded then gave a stage whisper into the mic. "Don't tell anyone, but Sal told me that his brother, Theo, the old codger sitting beside him, is so dumb that he once sold his car for gas money."

Most everyone in the room, except for Theo, Charles, and

I, thought it was one of the funniest things they'd ever heard—proof that cigarette smoke wasn't a requirement for people thinking things were funny. A couple of hours guzzling beer made the difference.

Wallace continued with a couple more jokes about marriage and two about humorous road signs he'd seen.

Most of his jokes were funny, but that's not what surprised me the most. He'd been on stage for fifteen minutes and transitioned from one joke to the next. Not once had he lost his place. He didn't drift into the past, and he seemed to have a grasp on reality. This was not the Wallace I'd become accustomed to observing. Instead of listening to his joke about a drunken hippo, my mind wandered back to what Theo had said about Wallace's lapses in reality coming at times that were convenient. Was it all an act?

I returned to reality when I heard him say, "Let me leave you with two bits of advice. First, when everything seems to be coming your way, you're in the wrong lane. And folks, a day without a smile is a day wasted. Thank you."

Sincere laughter and applause followed as Wallace bowed twice before reaching down and lifting the container holding his son. He kissed the box and walked back to the table.

It could have been the poor lighting, but I thought I saw a tear roll down his cheek. Was Wallace a killer, a man grappling with reality, or a grieving father?

Or, all three?

Chapter Thirty-Three

It was after midnight before the party at Cal's broke up. The comics were on a high after their performances. While Sal kept referring to the large venues where they had entertained on *numerous occasions*, the three seemed exhilarated by the reception they'd received at lowly Cal's.

Janice had drifted away after Wallace finished his set.

Several customers stopped by the table to congratulate the entertainers, which, boosted by several beers, gave them, as Sal had interpreted their comments to mean, "A night to remember."

The main thing I remembered as I fell out of bed the next morning was how late I'd stayed at the bar. I also remembered that, in a moment of weakness, I'd agreed to meet Charles for breakfast. Fortunately, showing a glimmer of wisdom, I'd suggested we meet at 9:00, an hour or so later than we usually frequented the Dog.

My friend was already in the booth when I arrived. He made a weak effort to goad me into feeling guilty about being late, which, of course, I wasn't.

Amber was quick with coffee, quick to let me know she knew where we'd spent last night. She asked if I had as much fun as Charles. I told her I didn't know since I didn't know how much fun Charles had. She told me comedy wasn't my forte. I told her I was serious. She said, "Whatever," before leaving to wait on another table.

Charles took a sip, rubbed his temples, and said, "Thomas Jefferson said, 'Beer, if drunk in moderation, softens the temper, cheers the spirit, and promotes health.' If last night's an indication, somewhere along the line, moderation must have been thrown out the window. I'm irritated, nowhere near cheered, and feel like I've been run over by a bull elephant."

He looked like it as well. He had on the Emerson College T-shirt he'd worn at Cal's, and his hair looked like it'd spent time in a food blender.

"What's wrong? Didn't you have a good time?"

He continued to rub his temples. "The guys were funnier than I thought they'd be. The wannabes weren't bad. I thought Franny was as good as Sal. But … oh, never mind."

"Charles?"

He lifted his mug then set it back down. "When the funny men were on stage, I kept thinking of Heather and how much she lived for standing behind that microphone, strumming and singing. I kept thinking about how much I liked … no, how much I loved her, how much I prayed that she could've had the life she wanted." He hesitated and looked toward the door. "Kept thinking about how I failed her, how I couldn't give her the one thing she wanted with all her heart and soul." He looked at me with his bloodshot eyes. "Now, she's gone."

I was at a loss for words when Charles looked at the door a second time and smiled.

I turned to see Cal in the entry.

Charles waved him over.

I thought Charles looked bad, although he actually looked like a GQ model compared to Cal. I must've missed the memo about wearing the same clothes from yesterday. Cal's rhinestone-covered coat appeared to have been run over by the same bull elephant that had stomped on Charles. His shirt was so wrinkled it made a mummy's face look Botoxed.

Cal put his arm around Amber's waist and whispered something to her before making his way to the table.

"What're you doing up this early?" I asked.

Cal removed his Stetson, put it on the seat beside him, and to no avail, ran his hand through his unruly hair. "Can't be up unless you've been down," he said, sounding like a line from a country song.

Charles asked, "You haven't been to bed?"

"Does it show?"

Instead of screaming yes, I said, "How come?"

"Was 2:00 when I ran out the last bunch of drunks. I had to do a heap of cyphering to try to get my cash drawer to balance."

Charles said, "Did it?"

"Nope."

Charles was on the hunt. "Off by how much?"

"Two big ones."

"Two hundred dollars," Charles said.

"That's what I said?"

Charles nodded, although it wasn't what Cal had said. "What happened to it?"

"If I knew that, I wouldn't be here looking like cow crap. I ain't got a clue."

I said, "Think it was stolen?"

"Did you miss *ain't got a clue*?"

I was tempted to smile, but Cal was serious.

Charles said, "What are you going to do?"

Amber set a mug of coffee in front of Cal.

"Thank ya darlin'," Cal said, as only he can without sounding sexist.

He took a sip then said, "Nothing I can do. No use crying over spilt C notes. Hell, it was a great night. Ain't ever seen that many customers on a Sunday, and I hate to admit, the Legends weren't half bad."

It was interesting how money disappeared whenever the Legends were around. "Are you going to have them back next Sunday?"

Cal chuckled. "Before he left, Sal inched up to me, said that he'd have to confab with his business manager. If a mutually prosperous arrangement could be lassoed, the Legends could break free for another gig. To this old cowpoke's ears, that meant I'd be hard pressed to stop them from doing their thing. They've got a business manager like I've got a mansion in Beverly Hills."

I said, "The tips were enough to keep them coming back?"

"Not bad, but I'll tell you one thing, they didn't come close to covering the tab for the Legends. The buds at Budweiser live for groups like the beer-guzzling Legends. My horse would've choked on the roll of cash Wallace pulled out of his pocket to pay for their night of partying."

That got Charles's attention, although not for the reason that struck me. He said, "You have a horse?"

Cal shook his head. "Charles, you read all those books, so I thought you'd grasp symbolism if I laid some on you. I ain't got a camel, a chimpanzee, or a horse. Wallace had a roll of cash."

Charles said, "Thought the funny guys were broke. Where'd he get a wad of cash?"

"Do I look like a money tracing, FBI bean counter?"

"A forensic accountant," Charles corrected.

Cal smiled. "See, you do get something out of those books. I don't have an idea the size of an atom where he got it. It was cash. That green stuff spends pretty good in Cal's."

Charles would be, in Cal vernacular, a great bronc rider. Once he grabs on, there's no letting go. "He didn't say——"

"Charles," Cal interrupted, "I don't know."

Charles paused and let Cal's definitive statement soak in before trying another approach. "What else did he say?"

"Charles, I ain't Leonard Bernstein, that Watergate reporter. I ain't got a recorder or one of those photogenic memories."

"Carl Bernstein," Charles corrected, referring to one of the reporters who uncovered the Watergate scandal, further proof that he'd read most of his books.

"Whoever. The point is, Wallace didn't share where the money came from. He was too curious to give me the history of his paper money."

"Curious about what?" I asked.

"Remember when Janice came over?"

I reminded him that I was the one who invited her to the table.

"After she left, Wallace asked me who she was. I figured, since everyone kept calling her Janice, that wasn't what he was searching for. I told him about her and her hubby and that she'd come in the bar a few times. I'm practicing being as nosy as you, Charles, so I asked him why he wanted to know."

Charles smiled and said, "You're a wise man, Cal. What'd he say?"

"Wallace said she looked familiar. I told him he could've seen her in the bar. He said that wasn't it. He thought he remembered seeing her somewhere in town."

Charles said, "He didn't say where?"

"Charles, my memory bank's overdrawn. He didn't say where. I didn't ask. That's that."

My memory bank wasn't in as poor a shape as Cal's. Something began to click. Wallace had told me that he'd seen the body of someone, presumably Michael Hardin, near the beach. Janice was irate with Michael because of a bet he claimed she didn't place, and she owed him money. According to both Cal and Amber, Janice has a quick temper. It didn't take an Olympic-length leap to think that Wallace, during a period where he and reality had split ways, could have seen Janice near Michael's body.

Chapter Thirty-Four

Charles said he needed to go back to his apartment to clean. He once told me that he cleans every eight months, whether it needs it or not. I took it as another sign of depression. Cal said he had to get home, needed to "sleep a spell" before opening the bar.

I wished him well and realized that I didn't have to be anywhere, or do anything, but wasn't ready to go home. It turned out to be a gorgeous day. The rain that disrupted Cal's open-mic comedy night had moved out to sea. It was in the mid-seventies with a few puffy, white clouds filtering the sun. A walk to the end of the Folly Pier would meet my need to avoid going home. On the way to the end of the pier, I stopped twice to take in the view of the beach and the Atlantic, to savor the moment and how fortunate I was to live where thousands of people save money all year to vacation.

I reached the end of the structure and saw a familiar face seated on one of the wooden benches, looking out at the waves. I almost didn't recognize Marvin Peters, a.k.a. Pete Marvin, since he wasn't in stage garb. He looked like thousands of other locals and vacationers in his tan shorts, a short-sleeve Reebok T-shirt, and tennis shoes.

He stared at me, did a double take before smiling recognition.

"Great show," I said as I leaned against the railing near his bench.

His smile widened. "You think so?"

I crossed my fingers. "Sure. Thought all of you were great."

"I appreciate that, but my timing was off. You'd be surprised how rusty I get after a layoff. Suppose it's like a pro athlete after off-season."

This could be a chance to get a non-PR version of what they've been doing.

"You've been off a while?"

"Wallace and Sal would kill me if they heard me say this." He looked around like they might be hiding behind the steps to the second level of the pier. "Hell, I don't care. Until that first night in Cal's, we hadn't had a gig in five months." He chuckled. "I'd say we're down to our last penny, but that'd make us sound rich."

"I'm surprised. You're so good, I would have figured you'd be booked all the time."

A little sucking up couldn't hurt, and it may keep him talking.

"I appreciate the smoke you're puffing up my butt. Stand-up comedy is a young person's game. Sure, there are a few old farts still making it. For most of us, big shows, big crowds, big paychecks are in the rearview mirror."

"Sorry."

"Don't get me wrong, entertaining is what keeps us going, and, umm, if you tell Cal I said this, I'll hunt you down and feed you to the sharks out there." He hesitated and pointed out to sea. "We'd play his bar without as much as tips, if he'd let us." He looked down and back at the ocean. "Sal and I would. Don't know about Wallace, poor guy." He looked down again.

"Why poor guy?"

His brow wrinkled. "We've been together a long time. When Sal first thought his brother was having Alzheimer's problems, he talked us into coming with him. He's a good guy, wanted to do what he could to help his brother. Hell, it's not like we had anything else to do, so we said why not. Wallace, sometimes, has trouble with what's real. He came, but he didn't like us butting in Theo's world, and hates us bumming off him. When we discovered that Theo's mind was okay, his problem was his hearing, Wallace flipped. He said we needed to move on and make some money."

Now that Pete had opened the door, I figured that I'd better slip through before it slams shut.

"Curious. I was thinking about Wallace's confusing things. Did he say anything about seeing the dead body on the beach?"

"I've been hanging with Wallace for years. A long time ago, he had trouble with prescription drugs. He had a bad leg break from a car wreck, got hooked on pain pills. He worked his way out of it. God knows, it wasn't easy. I don't know if it had anything to do with that or not, but his memory started slipping. He slips back in time, now more than ever."

I wondered if he'd forgotten my question about Wallace seeing a body. I didn't want to stop him from sharing. Charles would kick me out of the nosy club, but I was determined to wait.

"What do you mean?"

"Don't get me wrong, Wallace is a good friend; he'd do anything for the rest of us. Some days, I'm not certain that he knows what decade he's in. Other times, he's as lucid as an astronaut." He smiled. "About now, I reckon that you're wondering where I'm going with this story, if I'm going to get to your question about the dead guy."

I returned his smile. "It crossed my mind."

"I'm saying this because Wallace told me about the body. He could've been remembering something from thirty years ago as easily as what had happened the day he said it."

"What'd he say?"

"Said he was walking on the beach. Instead of walking near the water, he decided to move closer to the dune's fences that are up by the line of whatever those tall things are."

"Sea oats," I said.

"If you say so. Anyway, he was up there, saw a clump of dead guy, that's how he said it, clump. Said he was sure the guy was dead because of how his head was twisted."

"He say anything else?"

"He mumbled something about a person nearby."

"Did he say anything else about the person?"

"Don't recall."

Wallace had to be talking about Michael Hardin, not something he dredged from ancient history.

"Pete, I found the body. Wallace's description was spot on. Did he say anything that led you to believe that what he was talking about took place in the past, not the day before he told you?"

"No."

This is where it was going to get tricky. I knew what his answer was going to be.

"You know that Wallace had told a couple of people that he killed the man."

Pete looked out to sea and gave a tentative nod.

"Could he have?"

I was prepared for an outburst and a robust denial.

Pete continued to look out to sea. "It's possible."

That stopped me. I waited for him to continue, but he didn't.

I tiptoed on. "Why?"

"Remember what I said about us being broke?"

I nodded.

He turned back to me. "Did you notice our new stage outfits?"

"Yes."

"Theo's been paying for everything since we got here. He's been super generous. Wallace bought the outfits. Don't know where he got the money. He also bought our drinks after the show."

"You think he killed the bookie to rob him?"

"Wallace would never have hurt the guy, never would hurt anybody, unless the man put up a fight. Even then, he only would've tried to stop him. Wallace is a good man, a good friend."

"Did Wallace say anything about what he found? Tell me again what he said about a person being nearby."

"Just what I told you. A woman was nearby."

"You didn't say it was a woman."

He shrugged. "That's what he said."

That reminded me how Cal said that Wallace had asked him about Janice when he met her at open-mic night.

"Did Wallace say anything about a woman named Janice? She was at our table at Cal's."

"I remember someone introducing a gal. I don't remember her name. Wallace didn't mention anyone by name after that. He was excited that so many people enjoyed the show. Why do you ask?"

"Just curious. Wallace asked Cal about her, and I thought she might've been mentioned."

Pete smiled. "In his younger days, Wallace prided himself on being able to woo the young ladies from the audience into, umm, more intimate venues. He forgets that he's not the stud he used to be. It doesn't surprise me that he was asking about a chick. He must've forgotten by the time we got back to Theo's."

"Would you be willing to tell the police what you told me about Wallace and the body?"

He shook his head. "The police have already talked to Wallace. He told us he confessed to killing the man. I suppose they checked it out and didn't believe him since he's still on the free side of prison bars."

I don't know what Wallace had told Pete about his confession, but I knew he told the police that he killed the bookie with a candlestick in the library. Pete's version made more sense. I wasn't in a position to push him.

"Remember anything else he said?"

"Chris, I wasn't avoiding your question about talking to the police. Okay, I guess I was. You must understand, Wallace gets confused. When he was telling me about the body, he could have been talking about something from his memory that he thought he saw forty years ago. I don't want to get my friend in trouble over something that may not have happened in this century. Something that may not have ever happened. Memory is a strange thing, often wrong. You understand, don't you?"

"Sure," I lied.

Pete stood, straightened his shorts, and leaned on the railing and looked toward the Tides. "Enough about poor Wallace, how long have you been here?"

I gave him an abbreviated history of discovering Folly, retiring here, owning a gallery.

He listened without interrupting, something I wasn't accustomed to.

"Theo tells me you're some sort of detective that helps the police catch bad guys. That's got to be fascinating."

I told him that I had been lucky a couple of times, although I wasn't anything more than a retired bureaucrat living his last years on Folly Beach.

"Theo said you saved his life."

I told him that Theo was the hero and how he'd given me information that helped catch the killer.

Pete said Theo didn't take any of the credit. That's why he admired him so much.

I agreed with Pete then asked him, one more time, if he would be willing to go to the police. One more time, he said no.

I didn't tell him that I would.

Chapter Thirty-Five

Barb told me that if I picked up a pizza at Woody's she'd provide drinks so we could enjoy supper from her fourth-floor balcony overlooking the Atlantic and the Folly Beach Fishing Pier. She didn't have to say it twice. I arrived sharing a smile, a kiss, and a large pizza.

The weather was perfect, as was the company. Over the first slice of the Woody specialty pizza, I shared my strange conversation with Pete. Barb asked if I believed what he said Wallace had told him.

"Good question. You know about most of my conversations with Wallace. If you'd asked me after the first couple of times I talked with him, I'd say he was so far outside the realm of reality, that I wouldn't believe anything he said."

Barb poured a second glass of wine and said, "You've changed your mind?"

"Theo said he thought Wallace might be faking some of his problems; said he seems to use confusion when it's convenient. At open-mic night Wallace gave a flawless performance.

He didn't miss a punchline, he remembered all the jokes. He was in total control."

Barb took a sip and said, "Mel Tillis."

She'd been around my friends too long.

"Mel Tillis what?"

She smiled. "And you claim to be a country music fan."

"I am, so?"

"Mel Tillis was a chronic stutterer—"

"Except when he was singing," I interrupted.

"His speech disfluency disappeared when he performed."

"You think that's what happened when Wallace was behind the microphone?"

"Possibly."

"I would agree except, the first time I saw the Legends perform, Wallace was all over the map. Coherent one moment, out of it the next."

"Let's say Theo is right. Wallace uses his problem when it's in his best interest. The first time he performed was close to the time he claimed to have seen a body. Maybe he wanted to confuse everyone about his mental state. That would support his absurd statement to the police that the bookie was killed with, what did you say?"

"A candlestick in the library."

"Yes."

I shook my head. "It's all confusing."

"Perhaps Wallace wants it to be."

"Why did he say anything in the first place? Granted, his behavior was anything but normal when I pulled him out of the street, but why bring up a body?"

"You said before that he could've feared that someone saw him near the body. He wanted to give himself a reasonable explanation for seeing it while not being the killer."

"Yes."

"Makes sense."

She plopped a second slice of pizza on my plate, added another one to hers, and I said, "But why did he tell me that he saw a body, tell Pete that he saw a body, and told Theo he killed the person, then told the police the fantasy about a candlestick?"

"Chris, I'm a bookstore owner and former lawyer for the wealthy. I'm not a psychiatrist. It sounds like you'd need one to understand Wallace."

"No argument there. Let me add something else. Both Amber at the Dog and Cal told me one of their customers, Janice Raque, was angry at the bookie for not placing a bet she thought he should have. She owed him several thousand dollars. The bet would've paid him off with money to spare. They also told me Janice has a temper and blew up at a waitress in the Dog and at her husband in Cal's."

"Another suspect."

"Yes, and it gets stranger. At open-mic night, I saw Janice at a table by herself and invited her to join the group. Wallace asked about her after she left, and Pete told me that, when Wallace was talking to him about finding the body, he said that there was a woman nearby."

"You think it was Janice?"

I shrugged.

"That supposition wouldn't get you far in court." She held her hand up, palm facing me. "Don't say it, I know we're not in court. That is an interesting coincidence."

"I asked Pete if he would tell the police what he shared about Wallace."

"He said no."

"Correct."

"Why would he? Why would he want to get his friend in trouble? Wallace didn't tell him that he killed the bookie. Wallace had already been interviewed by the police. What could he have said to them?"

"The police think that Wallace is a kook, but they don't know about the money."

"What money?"

I told her about what Pete had said about Wallace paying for the stage outfits and the bar tab.

"Didn't Theo tell you that someone stole a statue and money from his house? It was probably one of his houseguests, right?"

"Yes."

"Wouldn't that explain where Wallace got money?"

"Yes, but what if the murder and the theft from the house were unrelated?"

"Wallace could've stolen the stuff from Theo's, and Janice killed the bookie."

I nodded.

Barb smiled. "Wallace could've seen Janice near the body and still be right about seeing the bookie without being the killer."

"Even if Pete didn't want to share what he told me with the police, I need to tell them, at least tell Cindy. She can share it with the Sheriff's Office."

"I agree," Barb said, "If you allow me to slip on my old attorney hat for a minute, I don't see a shred of admissible evidence in what you've said."

"I didn't think there was. It might give them a kickstart to the investigation that doesn't appear to be going anywhere."

She waved her hand toward the ocean. "Is this a fantastic evening, or what?"

It was Barb's way of saying that our depressing conversation about murder was over.

I told her that it was fantastic.

And so was the rest of the evening.

Chapter Thirty-Six

The next morning, I thought about walking to Bert's for coffee, thought about driving to the Dog for breakfast, and thought about what Barb had said about looking at the theft at Theo's and the murder of Michael Hardin being unrelated.

After more thought than I could handle, I fixed coffee at home, ate stale coffee cake for breakfast, and spent the rest of the time trying to figure out what I knew and didn't know about the offenses. The obvious thing I didn't know was who committed them, and that was only the beginning of the list. What was Wallace's true state of mind? Could Janice or Neil have killed Michael? And could Ray's tumble down the stairs have been something other than an accident? What I did know was that, regardless if he wanted me to or not, I had to tell Cindy about what Pete shared. The sooner the better.

She answered with, "What now?"

"I learned something yesterday from one of Theo's house-guests I think you need to know."

"Where are you?"

"Home."

"I'll be there in five minutes."

She was gone. No insults, no interrogation, no smart-aleck remark. What had happened to the Cindy LaMond I'd come to love?

She pulled her pickup truck in the drive, and I met her on the front porch. She walked past me into the living room and said, "Coffee?"

I led her into the kitchen and poured her some in my cleanest dirty mug.

She took a sip then plopped down on a kitchen chair.

"You okay?" I asked.

She held up the cup of coffee. "Working on it."

It didn't appear that she was succeeding. "What's wrong?"

"Tired."

It was more than that, so I played Charles. "Why?"

She looked at me, took another sip, and sighed. "I didn't get home last night, correction, this morning until two something. College students, a busload of them, were on the beach, acting like infants playing in a sandbox. Their Pablum had a high alcoholic content. They were raising such a ruckus that it woke up two families from Tennessee renting a beach house.

"Three of my guys and I had to pretend that we were adults and put a stop to the horsing around. We didn't haul any of the students away, although it took longer than it should have to round them up and herd them on their bus. The driver was sober, so he could get them off the island and out of our hair." She took another sip and shrugged.

It didn't sound like something that would put her in a foul mood. "And?"

"Larry decided that three this morning was the perfect time to express extreme displeasure about me being out. He was pissed, pissed on hormones. He dredged up every time in the last year he thought I should've been home rather than serving and protecting the citizens of this fine island. I wasn't in the best mood and blew a gasket. No blows were thrown but every profanity known in the Western World bounced off the walls."

Cindy and Larry were two of my favorite people and I hated to hear about their early morning fight. They were stubborn, opinionated, and madly in love with each other.

"What happened?"

"Not much. Neither of us wanted to act like things were normal, so neither of us slept in the bed. Larry spread out on the couch; I slept in the truck." She stopped and stared at me. "If I hear that you tell anybody about this, you'll be sleeping in a coffin."

"It doesn't leave this room."

"So, what in the hell did you drag me over here for?"

Instead of answering, I gave it one last try. "Are you going to be okay?"

"Of course, we are, I hope. I'm heading to the hardware store as soon as I leave here to give the little squirt a big hug, tell him I'll try to get home earlier, and see what happens. If that doesn't work, I'm moving in with you. Did you forget why you wanted to talk to me?"

I squeezed her shoulder.

Again, she asked why she was here.

I told her everything that Wallace had said to Pete about seeing a body and a woman. I also told her how Wallace reacted to Janice at the open-mic night, plus what Pete said about Wallace paying for drinks and their new stage clothes.

She asked if Pete thought Wallace had been making sense or was in one of his back-to-the-past moods.

I said I thought he was making sense.

She asked if he mentioned a candlestick beating in the library.

I shook my head.

"Why was Pete telling you?"

"He's worried about Wallace. I wouldn't be surprised if he isn't afraid that Wallace might break and kill someone else."

"The best I can do is talk to Wallace again. I didn't know about him paying for drinks and their costumes, so that's a reason to reintroduce myself. Thanks for letting me know."

I wished her luck.

"I'll need it. Also, thanks for letting me dump on you about Larry. We'll be fine."

———

Cindy left, and I had second thoughts about what I'd shared. Regardless, the police now know as much as I do. With luck and their resources, they should be able to get to the bottom of it. If Wallace hadn't killed Michael Hardin, there was still a good chance he'd stolen Theo's money and figurine.

As the old saying goes, *Man cannot live on stale coffee cake alone.* Okay, I made that up. Anyway, I was still hungry and decided to walk to Snapper Jack's for lunch. The colorful, multi-level restaurant faced the island's only traffic light and was popular with residents and vacationers. The eatery was crowded for early in the week.

Instead of taking up a table, I sat at the bar and faced a bank of flat-screen televisions and a college-aged bartender wearing a black Snapper Jack's T-shirt. She asked what I needed. I said a glass of wine and a menu. She smiled and said she thought she could handle it.

I was staring at one of ESPN's 300 channels on the set in

front of me when I was startled by a tap on the shoulder. I turned to see Neil Wilson smiling at me.

"Is this seat taken?" he asked as he pointed to the empty chair beside me.

I told him, "No."

He sat, looked at the television, and said, "You a sports fan?"

"Not particularly. I was daydreaming more than watching."

The bartender set my wine and a menu in front of me.

I asked Neil if I could buy him a drink.

He said yes before I got the question out and told the bartender he wanted Corona.

"How's your job search?"

"Remember the other day when I told you the cops came to my job and questioned me about that dead guy?"

"Yes."

"Know what my boss did yesterday?"

I said I didn't.

"Fired me."

The bartender slipped a Corona in front of Neil.

"Why?"

"Get this, he said it was bad for the image of his company to have cops interrogating his security guard about a murder. Can you believe that? It's a damned plastic fabrication plant. They make toys, for God's sake. You would've thought they built freakin' computer chips for the Pentagon."

I didn't tell him, but agreed that it seemed drastic.

"That's too bad."

"Yeah, and he threw up an old arrest from years ago that found its way on my background search when I was hired. He told me when he hired me that since the arrest was more than ten years old, he was willing to take a chance on me. The chance lasted until I was doing my civic duty and answering the cop's questions." He took a long draw on his beer and repeated, "Can you believe that?"

I didn't know what to believe, but wondered if there was something about the firing that he hadn't told me. He was here and seemed open to talking, so this would be a good chance to see what he would say about his relationship with Michael Hardin.

"Want some lunch?" I slid a menu in front of him.

"You buying?"

"Yes."

He waved for the bartender. He ordered fish tacos. I went with a chicken finger basket, and he added another Corona.

"I know the police learned you were working when Michael Hardin was killed. You'd bet with him, so I wondered if you could think of anyone who would've wanted him dead." I didn't mention there was a big hole in his alibi and that I was aware that he owed the bookie a significant amount of money.

"He was a nice guy. I can't imagine anyone would kill him."

Other than to wiggle out of paying off a huge debt, I thought. I also wondered how Wallace, who had been on the island for a few short days, could've known the bookie.

"I'd seen Michael around town a few times, but never talked to him. Did he take bets from anyone?"

Neil smiled for the first time. "Bookmaking is illegal, you know. Over the years, I've known a few bookies. You could say gambling is one of my hobbies." He pointed to one of the TVs playing highlights from last night's NBA games. "Won some, lost some. Most bookies are careful about who they deal with. Not just anybody could go to them. Most new clients are referrals from someone the bookie trusts. Understandable, don't you think?"

I agreed.

"Not Neil. What got him so much business was that he'd take bets from anyone. Well, not anyone. If he thought someone was an undercover cop, he'd act like he didn't know what the person was talking about."

No one would confuse seventy-five-year-old Wallace Bentley for an undercover cop.

Our food arrived, and Neil inhaled a large chunk of fish taco.

"Let me ask you something else," I said.

His mouth was full. He mumbled, "You're playing cop, trying to catch the person who killed Michael."

I didn't deny it. "I'm curious. Someone I know may've had something to do with the death. I was wondering if anyone else had information that would help the police."

"What's the question?"

"Did Michael carry a lot of money?"

"One reason Michael was so popular was that he paid winnings right away. Some guys make you wait a day before shelling out. Most betters I know need the money, need it now."

"So, he would've carried a substantial amount of cash?"

"Depends on what events were being bet on that day but, yes, I wouldn't be surprised if he'd be pocketing hundreds, even thousands some days."

Yet no money was on him when I found his body.

Time for a little white lie. "I hear he would carry some customers."

Neil swallowed another bite and smiled. "Yeah, he trusted a few of us. I owed him a little. He wasn't pressuring me to pay, knew I was good for it."

Other than asking if he killed Michael Hardin, I didn't see how I could get more from him.

"He sounds like a nice guy."

"Yes. It's my turn to ask something."

"What?"

"Are you sure you don't know anyone hiring? I was stretched thin before the idiot fired me. I've got one low-paying, part-time gig and no money."

"I don't, Neil. But I'll ask around. You'll be the first if I hear anything."

We finished lunch with minimal conversation. He wanted to talk about the pro basketball games guys on television were jabbering about. I had little, if any, interest and limited my comments to, "Hmm" and "Yeah." Dude would have been proud of my vocabulary.

"Sure you've got this?" Neil asked as he waved at his empty plate.

"Yes."

"Thanks, you're a pal." He headed to the exit.

Yeah, a pal who's trying to pin a murder on you.

Chapter Thirty-Seven

On the walk home, I reviewed my talk with Neil, leaving out anything about pro basketball. I hadn't learned much. He confirmed what I already knew about Michael Hardin. I'd learned that Neil had been fired and was desperate for a job, although the termination occurred after Michael was murdered so that, alone, couldn't have precipitated the killing. To listen to him, you'd think he and Michael were good buddies. Neil liked the bookie, and owing him a little money was no big deal. I figured none of that was true. Had I expected him to admit being so desperate that he'd killed Michael? If Barb was right that the thefts at Theo's were separate from the murder, Neil was my prime suspect.

I started thinking about what I knew about Janice Raque, the other suspect, when the phone rang.

Theo's name was on the screen. "Hi, Theo, what's up?"

"This is Sal, his brother. Is this Chris?"

"Yes," I said. "Is Theo okay?"

"Can you come to his house? Like now."

I heard noises in the background and repeated, "Is he okay?"

"Umm, sort of. Are you coming?"

Sal either didn't want to or was unable to tell me what was going on. "Yes."

I pulled in front of Theo's a couple of minutes later. I was relieved to see there were no ambulances, fire trucks, or police cars surrounding it. On the other hand, Chief LaMond's vehicle was in the drive.

Sal greeted me with, "Thank God, you're here."

I saw Pete on the couch with a drink in his hand and staring out the window at the Folly River. "What's going on?"

He pointed at the steps to the second floor. He didn't say anything, so I hoped he meant that I should go upstairs. A wide, center hall divided the second-floor rooms. This was the first time I'd been upstairs, and it was apparent that it had been decorated by the same professional who did the first floor. The wall covering had a muted floral pattern that was complimented by a patterned fabric on the two upholstered chairs on one side of the hall. Three original oils depicting serene Lowcountry scenes were on the opposite wall. They were the only serene things I found. One of the chairs was occupied by Theo, the other held Cindy LaMond.

I faced the chief, who was tapping her foot on the floor. She looked up and shrugged. Theo was twisting the sleeve of his T-shirt like he was wringing water out of it.

Cindy said, "What're you doing here?"

"Sal called and asked me to come."

She exhaled. "Okay, stay out of the way."

"Out of the way of what?"

Cindy pointed to a closed bedroom door, in a low voice said, "We have a bit of a problem."

Theo let go of his sleeve and said, "Thanks for coming. Sal

said you were the one friend he knew I had. He thought I needed someone with me. Sorry for the inconvenience."

I nodded at Theo then turned to Cindy. "Problem?"

She stared at the closed door. "I stopped by to ask Wallace some questions." She hesitated and patted Theo on the knee. "He told me that Wallace, Sal, and Pete were in the kitchen and asked me to follow him. We got to the kitchen, where things went sideways."

Theo made an audible groan and put his head down between his hands.

"What happened?"

"The funny guys were standing around the island drinking beer. Sal saw me with Theo, smiled and said, 'Umm, correct me if I get it wrong, Theo. 'Three seniors were out for a stroll. One of them said, 'It's windy.' Another one said, 'No way. It's Thursday.' The last one says, 'Me too. Let's have a beer.' I thought I was there to ask Wallace questions, not to be the audience at a comedy show. Sal slapped his knee, and Pete laughed at the joke. Wallace shot out of the room like a chicken with its tail feathers on fire."

Theo groaned again.

"Then?" I said.

"Wallace took off up the steps, went in his room, and slammed the door. Theo and I followed and asked him to come out. I told him I had a couple of routine questions. I emphasized routine. As you can see, he hasn't taken kindly to my request."

I turned toward Theo. "Does he have any weapons?"

"Been down that road," Cindy responded before Theo could. "He doesn't, well, not that Theo knows about. Sal followed us up and said that Wallace could stab us with his rapier wit. I didn't need more jokes and sent him downstairs."

"How long's he been holed up in there?"

Cindy looked at the door. "Half hour, tops."

I said, "Plan?"

"I don't want to go all SWAT on him. The door's got one of those little holes in the knob. I could get in with this." She held up a three-inch-long, thin wire that unlocks many interior residential doors. "Wouldn't have to kick it in. I called Officer Spencer and asked him to come in silently to join us. He should be here any minute. Before you came up, I told Wallace that I'd give him a few minutes to think. I'd be waiting out here."

"What'd he say?"

"Something about hell freezing over." She glared at the door. "I'm not waiting that long."

I said, "Think he's a danger to himself?"

"We can hear movement in the room and he mumbles something every once in a while, so he's going strong."

I heard the front door open and Sal talking to someone. Seconds later, I heard the heavy footsteps of Allen Spencer as he bounded up the stairs. He looked around, and Cindy gave him a thirty-second recap of the situation. I had always been impressed how calm Cindy became when faced with tricky situations. This would qualify.

Cindy leaned close to Theo and said, "Theo, this is your house. Do I have permission to search Wallace's bedroom once we finagle him out?"

"Oh," Theo said, like he'd returned from being zoned out. "Umm, sure, whatever you need, Chief."

Cindy stood and moved to the side of Wallace's door. "Wallace, this is Chief LaMond. I've got a couple of easy questions I'd like to ask you. How about you open the door and come on out? I'll ask my questions and be on my way."

The only sounds I heard were Sal and Pete talking downstairs.

Cindy tapped on the door. "Wallace, tell you what. Theo will go downstairs and get you something to drink while I'll come in and ask my questions. How's that sound?" She pointed at the stairs and Theo headed down.

Cindy closed her eyes and shook her head.

Allen moved to the other side of the door and rested his hand on his handgun.

Cindy started to insert the wire in the door knob, when the door swung open. Cindy jumped, and Allen started to pull his gun when Wallace stuck his head out the door. "Here for my next show?"

"Wallace," she said, "how about you and I move over to those chairs so I can get my questions out of the way?"

He was dressed in black. For the first time, I noticed that he was the same height as Cindy, although she outweighed him by thirty pounds. She appeared comfortable with that advantage in case he didn't cooperate.

Wallace smiled, said, "Why not?" then sat in one of the chairs.

"Officer Spencer," Cindy said as she took the other seat, "why don't you look around Wallace's bedroom while he and I talk?"

Wallace jumped up and pointed to his room. "You can't do that. You need a search warrant."

Cindy held her hand in front of him. "That's okay, Wallace. It's Theo's house. He said we could look. Have a seat, and let me ask you something."

Officer Spencer went in the room, Wallace returned to his seat, and I moved to the corner of the hall.

Cindy smiled and leaned toward Wallace. "I was wondering why you ran when you saw me stopping by to visit my friend Theo."

She said it like two friends having a conversation rather than an interrogation.

"I've been a little jittery. I've also had a couple of bad experiences with police over the years."

Cindy nodded and smiled. "That explains it. You don't have to be afraid of me." Her smile widened. "Someone said you'd been generous, bought your friends their new stage clothes. I must say, from what I've heard from people who were at your performance at Cal's, you all looked professional."

Wallace smiled. "Thank you."

Cindy chuckled. "I even heard you bought the drinks that night. That was nice of you."

Wallace leaned back in the chair, his shoulders relaxed, and he nodded.

Cindy leaned closer to him. "Somebody told me that it'd been some time since you'd received a lot of the money that you'd been owed by promoters or royalty checks. That's irritating, isn't it?"

He tilted his head and eyes narrowed. "Sure is."

"So, I was wondering about something. You can help me figure it out. Where'd you get the money for the clothes and drinks?"

It wasn't the best timing, but Theo returned and handed Wallace a canned Coke.

Wallace took a sip without taking his eyes off the chief.

"Chief LaMond, why am I getting the idea you didn't show up to visit your good friend Theo? Are you accusing me of something?"

"No, I'm trying—"

Wallace interrupted. "I already confessed that I killed that guy on the beach. You'd looked at me like I was an organ grinder's monkey. You didn't bother to arrest me." He leaned down, slammed the Coke can on the floor, and stood.

Cindy put out her hand. "Calm down, Wallace. I'd rather clear up these questions here. If you'd rather, we could go over to City Hall."

He looked toward the stairs and returned to the chair. His fists were clenched. If Cindy wasn't larger, I was afraid he was going to pounce on her.

"The money," he said and repeated, "the money. Oh, yeah, I got a cash advance when I used Theo's credit card at the grocery." He turned to Theo. "Sorry, I should've told you."

Officer Spencer cleared his throat. He was standing in the doorway to Wallace's room and holding an orange and red credit card. "Chief, could I borrow you a moment?"

She looked at her officer then said to Wallace, "Give me a minute. Chris, why don't you talk with Wallace until I get back?"

I translated is as, "Don't let Wallace bolt." I asked if he wanted anything to eat.

He said no and looked toward his room. "Chris, those cops need twice as much sense to be half-wits."

I was glad he hadn't shared that statement, joke, or whatever it was with Cindy, or he may've found himself getting an ant's eye view of the polished wood floor.

Cindy, followed by Allen Spencer, returned to the hall. She sat, scooted closer to Wallace, and waved the MasterCard in front of the comedian. "Wallace, please explain this."

Wallace looked at the card and shook his head. "Never seen it before."

"You sure?"

"That's what I said. Where'd you get it?"

"Officer Spencer found it under your mattress."

"Must've been there forever. Is it Theo's?"

"It appears to belong to Michael S. Hardin. That name familiar?"

Wallace stared at the card, looked at the floor, then back at Cindy. "How could I forget? That's the guy I told you I killed." He closed his eyes and whispered, "I did it, I knew I did." He shook his head. "Where did I get the candlestick?"

"Wallace," I said, "how do you know you killed him?"

"Oh, umm. I was told I did. I think it was in a dream, or one of the guys told me. I remember standing over him. He was dead."

I asked. "What guy told you?"

"Pete," he hesitated, "or could've been Sal." He snapped his fingers. "No, it was Ray."

Cindy held her hand in Wallace's face. "Before you say anything else, I'm going to have Officer Spencer read you your rights."

Allen Spencer Mirandized Wallace.

The comic slumped in the chair and came close to slipping out of it.

Cindy then told Spencer to take Wallace to the jail in Charleston.

Allen asked what he should charge him with, and Cindy said the murder of Michael Hardin. Allen took hold of Wallace's elbow as he escorted him to the steps.

Wallace stopped and turned to Theo. "I never saw that card. Honest to God."

Theo moved to the chair that Wallace had vacated and looked at Cindy. "I think there's something wrong with him— something wrong with his head."

Cindy reached out to touch Theo's leg. "Theo, that's for someone else to determine. My job is to haul the fish in; someone else has to weigh them."

I said, "Did Allen Spencer find anything else that would implicate Wallace?"

"Isn't the dead guys MasterCard enough?"

I shrugged.

"Chris, don't tell me you don't think he did it. He was broke, yet came into money to buy clothes and pay a hefty bar tab. He parked the dead guy's credit card under his bed and, oh, yeah, there's one other little pesky detail, he confessed."

"Cindy, he confessed to killing someone in the library with a candlestick. He seemed surprised when you sprung the credit card on him."

Cindy looked at her hand and at me. "Surprised because we found it, not that he didn't know it was there. Where did he get the money?"

I turned to Theo. "Why don't you tell her about the missing cash?"

Cindy turned to Theo so quickly that she could've sprained her neck. "Missing cash?"

Theo's face turned a dull shade of red. He told her about the missing money and the disappearing and reappearing silver frog.

Cindy started to take notes, but her pen didn't touch the notebook. Instead, she pointed the writing instrument at Theo. "You didn't think the heist was important enough to tell the cops?"

"Chief, I'm sorry. It had to be one of my houseguests, one of my brother's friends. I didn't want any of them to get in trouble."

I also thought it could have been his brother but didn't think it needed to be said.

Cindy mumbled, more to herself than to us, "The clothes and bar tab could have come from that money and not Michael Hardin." She sat straight in the chair and looked at Theo. "Any other crimes you didn't think I needed to know about?"

Theo said, "No, Chief. Again, I'm sorry."

"If you'll excuse me. I've got to get to the jail and try to make some sense out of this mess. Maybe Wallace will confess to killing JFK so we can clear up that conspiracy."

Theo's guests weren't the only comedians in the house.

Cindy left.

Sal and Pete were waiting for Theo and me at the bottom of the stairs. They were talking over top each other. Their basic question was, *What's going on?*

We moved to the great room, where Theo and I tag teamed them with an explanation.

Sal said, "He needs to be in the psych ward instead of jail. He's been losing it, more and more each day."

"Sal," I said, "weren't you suspicious when he bought you the new clothes? Did he tell you where he got the money?"

"No. I figured—don't know what I figured."

Pete added, "Theo, Wallace told me that you gave him the money. He could've been lying. The bookie probably had a bundle on him and, if Wallace killed him, he would've taken the cash and the credit card. Poor Wallace's been so confused, poor man. What can we do for him?"

Theo said, "He needs a lawyer. I'll call the one I use for estate planning. He'll be able to recommend a good defense attorney."

"He can't afford it," Pete said.

Theo replied, "I'll take care of it."

Pete shook his head. "That isn't fair to you. Won't a good lawyer cost a bundle?"

"Yes," Theo said. "If there's a chance that he's innocent, he'll need all the help he can get."

"What can we do?" Sal asked.

Theo said, "Damned if I know."

I couldn't have said it better.

Chapter Thirty-Eight

"Charles, I've got a story for you," I said on the phone before I pulled out of Theo's drive. "Where are you?"

My friend had trained me well. I knew the sooner I shared what happened with him the better. And, if by some strange circumstance he heard it from someone else, I'd never hear the end of it. He was in front of the Baptist Church and walking on his way to nowhere; said he was tired of being cooped up in his apartment, feeling sorry about his miserable life. That was more information than I wanted and suggested that I meet him in the Folly River Park, across the street from the church, and a couple of blocks from Theo's house.

The park was small, but popular, as it was within easy walking distance of the main business district. It was the home to art shows hosted by the Folly Beach Arts and Crafts Guild in warmer months, and Christmas decorations during the holiday season. Its pavilion was the site of musical performances throughout the year. It occasionally provided a shady spot for Charles and me to hang out.

I parked and saw my friend sitting at one of the picnic tables. He was leaned back on the table and looked like he may have slept under it. His Tilley was tilted sideways on his head, his hair was sneaking out from under the hat, his tennis shoes were untied, and his orange Tennessee Volunteers long-sleeve T-shirt had a rip on the sleeve.

"Been wrestling a bear?" I asked as I sat beside him on the bench.

"Funny," he said without a glimmer of cheer. "What's so important to interrupt my mindless, boring, depressing walk to nowhere?"

My first thought was if I should have waited another day to tell him about my trip to Theo's. I also figured that what I had to share could bring him out of his funk, at least momentarily. I started with the call from Sal and shared the highlights of my visit ending with Wallace being hauled off to jail and the conversation I had with Theo, Sal, and Pete.

Charles was clearly depressed since he didn't interrupt countless times.

I finished, and he said, "Let's walk out to the river."

A narrow walking pier went from the park over some of the marsh and ended a few feet over the Folly River. Charles didn't speak as we made our way to the river end of the pier. We leaned against the railing, watched traffic cross the bridge, and a fishing boat meander under it.

Charles continued to stare at the boat. "What's your take?"

I told him about seeing Neil Wilson and how, until this morning, I was leaning toward him as being the killer. I also shared my gut feeling that Janice could have done it.

"You eliminated them because the card was in Wallace's room?"

"Sure."

"You said Wallace seemed surprised that the credit card was there."

"True."

"And Wallace claims to have killed the bookie with a candlestick?"

"That's what he said."

"That says the boy's off his rocker, not that he's a killer. Let's say he needs to be in a padded cell rather than in a jail cell, then who put the card under the mattress to frame him?"

Charles was becoming more animated the more we talked. Bad topic; good sign. I saw the Charles of earlier days inching his way back.

"Sal, Pete, even Theo."

"Yes," Charles said, and rubbed his three-day old beard. "Don't forget Ray. He could've put it there before he took his tumble."

"Or Ray," I conceded. "If the bookie was killed for money and credit cards, it wouldn't have been Theo. He has all the money he'll ever need."

"That leaves the living houseguests, plus Ray. All had access to the room."

I was almost convinced it was one of the houseguests when I remembered what Neil had said about when he was hired in the job from which he'd been terminated. His boss had hired him, despite him having a record that dated back several years. It was a stretch, but I wondered what his crime had been. Cindy talked to him about the murder and could have run him through her databases. I made the mistake of mentioning this to Charles.

"Call her."

My choices were to get yelled at by Charles if I didn't call, or get yelled at by Cindy if I did. Charles was showing signs of improving, so I chose to incur the wrath of the chief.

Cindy greeted me with, "This better be good."

"Got a question." She could decide if it was good or not. "You said you'd questioned Neil Wilson about where he was when Michael Hardin was killed."

"Yes, and—"

I interrupted, "Did you run a criminal check on him?"

"Do you sit for hours at home in your big, plush easy chair thinking up things to make my life miserable, or do they just come to you?"

I chuckled and said, "Some of us have the gift."

"No."

"No to me having the gift, or no to checking his background?"

She sighed. "You have the gift. No, I didn't check. Dare I ask why?"

I shared what he told me about his recent termination and how he mentioned being arrested several years ago.

Cindy said she'd check when she got to a computer and let me know.

Charles was pestering me about when she would let me know before I had time to return the phone to my pocket. The old Charles was in sight.

We left the park and walked down Center Street toward the ocean. The sidewalks were more crowded than I'd seen since last summer. We stopped in front of Mr. John's Beach Store.

Charles looked at a large, inflated float shaped like a frog that was hanging on a pole at the side of the building and said, "Ray may've killed the bookie and hid the credit card in Wallace's room, but he didn't steal the cash from Theo and take the stupid silver frog."

"He was dead when the frog reappeared."

"Yep," Charles said. "Unless his ghost brought it back, or

the frog hopped back, you can mark him off the money and frog heist suspect list. That leaves Sal, Wallace, Pete, and Theo, who would have to be nuttier than Wallace to take his own stuff."

"Other than Wallace's confession that won't hold up, what do we know about the other three comics?"

Before answering, Charles stooped to pet a dog that was leading its master down the street. "You've been with them more than I have. I know they ain't knee-slappin' funny for being Legends. They probably played their last gig for George Washington and are broker than an amoeba. Speaking of Washington, he said, 'Truth will ultimately prevail where there are pains to bring it to light.'"

Getting to the truth has been a pain, and I was clueless about what to do next. Other than Charles stating the obvious, I didn't know how we, or the police, were closer to knowing what happened. Other than stumbling on the body and seeing Theo hurt from his experiences with his houseguests, I couldn't come up with a good reason to be involved. It would be easy to accept that the police had the killer in jail. It likely was the same person who stole money from Theo. Case closed.

Why did I have the feeling that I knew something or heard something that would lead to a different ending?

———

I was sitting in, as Cindy called it, my big, plush easy chair and instead of thinking of things to make her life miserable, thinking about each interaction I'd had with the comics. I thought of several things, but none of them brought me closer to what had been nagging at me. I got a reprieve when the phone rang. Cindy's name was on the screen.

"Good evening, Chief."

"If you say so. It's been such a fun-filled afternoon, I thought I'd fallen asleep and dreamed I was being followed around by a camera filming an episode of *America's Biggest Idiots*."

"What happened?"

"When I was a teeny-tiny sprout in East Tennessee, our next-door neighbor had an old billy goat. Ornery thing, about as smart as a piece of chalk, but not as useful. He'd sit in the corner of the yard and watch cars go by. Half the time, he'd run along the fence, thinking he was a dog chasing the car. Other times, he'd stand in the middle of his pen, think he was a Mexican jumping bean, and jump straight up in the air. Occasionally, he thought he was a gymnast. He'd stick his head on the ground and somehow push off with his back legs and throw his rear end up in the air and balance himself in his front legs and head. Get the picture?"

I said yes, but I wondered why I was hearing about her tiny-sprout days.

"Chris, Wallace Bentley makes that old goat look like Albert Einstein."

I repeated, "What happened?"

"Officer Spencer almost ran into a garbage truck when Wallace stripped naked and mooned an eighty-seven-year-old granny following the cop car in her 1977 Ford Granada. After he got to the interrogation room, he told Detective Callahan, in such a sincere voice, that he could be mistaken for the Pope, yes, he'd killed Michael Hardin, and had killed Adolph Hitler, and while he was at it, admitted killing David Letterman, who, unless you know something I don't know, is still walking among the living."

"Oh."

"You won't find this hard to believe. Instead of sticking him in one of the fine, well-appointed prison cells provided by the County of Charleston, Wallace is over at the hospital, handcuffed to a bed being evaluated by a head doc."

"That's too bad."

"There was a high-powered lawyer at the jail to talk with him but, after a few seconds, she decided that psychiatric care was needed more than legal care. The lawyer said Theo Stoll hired her. That was generous of your friend. So far, it's not going to help Wallace."

"Do you think he was faking?"

"Not after what I saw and heard today."

"Thanks for letting me know."

"Other than playing ringmaster in a three-ring circus, I did one useful thing for you. You're welcome."

"What?"

"Your boy, Neil Wilson, was arrested twelve years ago after he and three of his buddies got hopped up on something and broke into a drug store. It was in a town in Arkansas where everybody knew everybody. The guys got off light. Seems some of their parents were good friends with the pharmacist, and some were friends with the local judge. Neil had a shortage of influential friends and got the short end of the stick and spent two years behind bars."

"Why'd he get the short straw?"

"Seems he was the one who picked the drugstore lock. The other three guys just happened to follow him in. That was their story. They stuck to it, saw the light, and were back roaming the streets three months later."

I heard Larry in the background asking Cindy something. She said, "Yes, dear," and whispered to me, "Gotta go. I'm back in good graces with the shrimp. Need to keep it that way."

She didn't wait for me to say goodbye.

Chapter Thirty-Nine

The simplest explanation for everything was that Wallace met Michael Hardin, learned he was a bookie, and tried to rob him. Michael put up a fight, and Wallace hit him hard enough to kill him, or Wallace intended to kill the bookie and rob him. Often the simplest explanation turns out to not be so simple. If that's what happened, why did Wallace tell me he had seen a body? That admission was the first thing tying him to the crime. Next, why did he go off the deep end with the story that he killed Michael with a candlestick in the library? Two things could have accounted for that. He could've decided once suspicion had been raised about him, to make up the far-fetched story to craft an insanity defense, or he had actually hopped off the sane train.

I didn't have answers for those questions, although I knew that Wallace had come into an unexplained amount of money. It could have come from the bookie, or was the money taken from Theo? If Wallace stole it from Theo, it was possible that he didn't kill the bookie. That led me back to why he had said that he'd seen a body in the first place. The simplest answer is that he saw the body, but hadn't been the killer.

Then what about Neil Wilson? He owed the bookie and had asked me if I knew of part-time jobs. He was desperate for work, which meant that he didn't have the money to pay the debt. Now I learn that he possessed lock-picking skills, which meant that he could've broken into Theo's house and planted Michael Hardin's credit card in Wallace's room. If he killed Michael and planted the card, how did he know anything about Wallace? Silly question, I realized.

Rumors fly around Folly as fast as a speeding bullet, and it was no secret that Wallace claimed to have seen a body. Neil had been questioned by the police and could've figured they knew about the holes in his alibi, so he had to deflect guilt. What better way than to frame an outsider, someone who would have little community support, someone who was having troubles with reality, someone who had already said he'd seen a body, presumably that of Michael Hardin.

Returning to Barb's thought, there could have been two separate crimes and two criminals. The most likely candidates for stealing Theo's money and taking and returning the frog, would've been one or more of the houseguests.

The most likely person to have killed Michael Hardin would be Sal, Wallace, Pete, or even Ray, who could have killed him and slipped the credit card under Wallace's mattress days before his death. Add Neil Wilson as a long shot and, if I was objective, an even longer shot would be Theo. What about Janice Raque? She thought Michael Hardin cheated her out of enough money to pay off her debts. She has a temper and told more than one person that she resented the bookie. Each of them could be the killer but considering how difficult it would have been for Neil, or Janice, to have put the credit card in Wallace's room, they would be down the list. If I marked Neil and Janice off, and removed Theo, because he didn't need the money and I had known him long enough to trust him, that left Sal, Wallace, Pete, and Ray.

Sal, Wallace, Pete, Ray. I said the names several times and remembered something that was said the first time the comedians had been in Cal's. It didn't strike me as unusual at the time but, the more I think about it, the stranger it seems. Who said it? For the life of me, I couldn't remember. Cal had been there, so maybe he'd remember. A late afternoon walk to Cal's would get me out of the house and, with luck, an answer.

A dozen or so folks were enjoying drinks, conversation, and country classics from the jukebox. The bar's owner was wiping off the counter and singing along with Jimmy Rogers. Cal had his Stetson tilted back and wore a green Polo shirt instead of his rhinestone coat.

He waved me over. "What brings you out so early?"

I told him I had a question about the first time he'd met the comedians.

"It'd better be easy. I'd have to strain my brain to remember what happened this morning."

He looked around then pointed to a vacant table nearest the bar. "Lasso that table and I'll have Joy take care of the customers."

I headed to the table as Cal headed to the storage room to find the server.

A minute later, Cal set his Stetson on the table and said, "Okay, what's on your mind?"

"What do you remember about the first night the group came in and talked to you about appearing here?"

He ran his fingers through his long, gray hair. "They were late. Pissed me off, since I was already tired. You'd said they were coming at 9:00. They didn't strut in until, well, a lot later.

Speaking of strutting in, they looked like they were on their way to a Halloween party."

I chuckled, and Cal continued, "What else? Let's see, okay, they told a couple of corny jokes, and one of them, maybe it was Pete, started raising a ruckus about smoking. It's coming back to me now. Pete brought it up, remember, because of the one with the silly ascot. Wallace, the nutty one, started tag teaming me about smoking. Something about being funnier if the customers were puffin' on a cigarette, cigar, pipe, or funny weed. If they weren't staying with Theo, I'd have thrown the whole lot of them out the door. How am I doing?"

"Not bad." It wasn't what I was fishing for. "Do you recall one of them saying something about the death of the bookie?"

Cal rubbed his chin and tapped his fingers on the table. "Can't say that I do. Why?"

"At the time, little was known about Michael Hardin's death. Most folks didn't know who the victim was, fewer knew he was a bookie. One of the comics asked about the death and used the term bookie."

"Yeah, that was the first time I heard who he was. I think you're the one who told me. What's so important about that? Some people must've known."

"Yes, but Theo's houseguests weren't from here. They'd been on the island only a few days. Doesn't it seem unlikely that they would've known who or what Michael was?"

"I thought everyone knew that. Hasn't the nutty one confessed? I hear he was hauled off to jail. He would've been the one who knew the bookie was a bookie and said it that night. Mystery solved."

Cal made sense, but I didn't think it was Wallace. I said, "Could've been."

"There you go, that solves it."

I wasn't convinced. "Remember anything else they said?"

"Sure do. I didn't think they were that funny up there on the stage." He pointed at the microphone. "But when Sal referred to them wanting to perform in here as part of the Comedy Legends World Tour, that was danged hilarious. They should've saved that joke for their performance."

"They were serious."

Cal smiled. "That's what I thought when they said it. That's why I didn't laugh, even though it hurt my innards not to."

"Remember anything else?"

"Afraid not. Do the police think it's someone other than the one who needs to be in the looney bin?"

"They arrested Wallace because they found Michael's credit card in his room. That was the reason more than his confession."

"It seems to my withering brain that you don't buy into that."

"I'm not sure."

"You're playing detective?"

"Trying to wrap my hands around what's going on. Theo is a friend. I'd hate to see him caught up in something that isn't resolved. He's already hired an attorney for Wallace, he's putting up the group in his house, covering their expenses while they're there. It looks like they have no plans to leave."

"Except the nutty one."

"True."

"You'll figure it out."

"I wish I had your confidence."

Cal looked at Joy who appeared to have things under control and turned back to me. "Let me change gears. I learned something yesterday that I think you'd be interested in."

"About the comedians?"

"Nope, about Janice Raque. Remember, you, Chester, and I were confabbing about her? You said folks mentioned her ferocious temper?"

"Yes."

"Rumor is that Horace packed up his belongings and skipped out on her. Somebody told me that somebody told them that he found a young chickadee over in Mt. Pleasant that he'd rather spend time, dusk 'til dawn time with, than with his beloved spouse. Looks like he decided to extend that time to twenty-four-seven. To this old observer of heartbreaks, I'd say that's why she's been on such a tear. I feel sorry for her. She's not as bad as she's been made out to be."

That could explain her tantrums in the Dog, explain arguing with the bookie.

"That's too bad. What's she going to do?"

"Don't know. She doesn't work so, unless the creep Horace keeps paying on her condo in Mariner's Cay, she'll have to find somewhere else to live. Tell you what, I won't miss her bickering with hubby every time she's here."

Joy came to the table and said she was sorry to interrupt, but she needed Cal at the bar, something about the credit card machine had a mind of its own and wasn't charging enough.

Cal said he couldn't have that.

Janice wasn't high on my list of suspects since she would've been the least likely candidate to have put the credit card in Wallace's room. She had now all but fallen off the list after hearing what Cal had shared about Horace. Where did that leave me?

I listened to Freddy Fender sing "Before the Next Teardrop Falls" then headed home. I had learned a couple of things. My number one question still hadn't been answered.

Chapter Forty

Theo had been in Cal's during the comedians' visit to the bar, when they had asked its owner if they could perform, plus when the conversation turned to the identity of the body found at the beach. A morning walk to his house would give me some much-needed exercise, a chance to breathe the fresh morning air, and with luck, get the answer to the question that had been nagging me for the last twenty-four hours.

It was almost 9:00 in the morning and, according to Theo, the middle of the night for his houseguests, so I was surprised that the Lincoln wasn't in the drive. Theo's Mercedes was there, so I rang the doorbell. It took a long time for anyone to answer, and I was beginning to think that Theo had left with the comedians. I turned to leave when he opened the door.

He rubbed his eyes and was moving slower than his normal slow pace.

"Is this a bad time?" I asked.

"No, come on in. Had a late night. The guys are shook about Wallace."

I followed him to the kitchen and was quick to accept his offer of coffee.

We each got a cup, and he pointed at the table.

I sat, sipped coffee, and said, "Are they gone? Their car wasn't here."

"Sal was up early, early for the guys, and said he was so traumatized by Wallace's situation that he needed to go for a drive. He asked if I wanted to go. I declined. I couldn't see an upside to being stuck in a car with my upset brother."

"Where was he going?"

"I don't know. When I asked him, he said the same thing.

"Did Pete go with him?"

"He's upstairs sawing logs."

"Have you heard anything about Wallace?"

"Sal called the hospital, but they wouldn't tell him anything. They referred him to the Sheriff's Office. He didn't figure he could get anything out of them and decided to wait for the police, or Wallace's attorney to call."

"Think Sal went to the hospital to see Wallace?"

"No, the hospital told him yesterday that no one would be allowed in. It's nice that you stopped by, although something tells me it's not for coffee."

"I have a question. Remember the first night you brought your houseguests to Cal's?"

"When Wallace and Pete tried to snooker Cal into letting people smoke in his bar? The only smoke I saw was coming out of Cal's ears as he lambasted them for trying to change his rules."

I smiled. "That's the night."

"What's the question?"

I asked the same thing I asked Cal and got the same answer. Theo didn't remember who among his group said anything about the bookie. He did remember how shocked

Cal had been when I told him the identity of the body, but that was all.

I got a refill on my drink, then said, "You don't sound happy about your guests."

"Chris, I've been hospitable. I've given them room and board, paid for all sorts of stuff they claim to need, and listened to their jokes, banter, moaning and groaning." He held his thumb and forefinger three inches apart. "I'm about this close to telling them that they've overstayed their welcome. I hate to be rude, but I'm surprised that my brother thought he could bring his friends here and expect me to be their den mother and bank." He stood, walked to the window, and looked out before returning to the chair. "Am I being unfair?"

"You've been more than generous."

"The worse thing is their sniping. You'd think they can't stand each other." He hesitated. "Maybe they can't."

"What do you mean?"

"Remember when Ray stormed out of Cal's the first time they performed there?"

"When Wallace was joking about something Ray did when he was young?"

"Yeah, I thought that was what it was about, but the guys had been bitching at each other all night. Then Pete said something about the stupid joke, Ray nearly hit him and said something like, 'At least all he kills is the audience.' That's one example. Here's another, last night, after poor Wallace was hauled out, Sal said he got what he deserved. Gee, Chris, those guys are supposed to be friends."

"It sounds like they're getting on each other's nerves as much as they're bothering you."

"What can I do about it? I can't throw my brother out; the others don't have anywhere to go."

I heard someone clomping down the stairs. "What's all the racket down here?" Pete said as he came in the kitchen.

Theo glared at him. "If it's okay with you, my friend and I are having a peaceful conversation."

I had never heard Theo that sharp with anyone. He was right about his houseguests getting to him.

"Well excuse me, Mr. Touchy. Hi, Chris, sorry to interrupt."

Pete nodded my direction. "Did you hear that, after Theo's honeymoon, he said he felt like a new man? So did his wife."

Theo's wife had died six months after moving to Folly, so I wanted to tell Theo that I'd help him pack their stuff. Instead, I frowned as Pete laughed at his inappropriate, untimely joke.

Pete poured a cup of coffee and said, "If you guys can get along without me, I'll take this upstairs."

Neither of us responded.

"I rest my case." Theo said after Pete was gone.

———

Instead of heading home after leaving Theo's, I went to the Dog for a late breakfast. The restaurant was packed, with a handful of customers waiting around the front door for a table. I didn't want to hog too much real estate, so I told the hostess I'd be okay sitting at the bar, where there was a short wait before a seat became available. Zack, one of the managers, asked if I wanted coffee. I declined. Amber wasn't around to scold me, so I said French toast was all I needed. I was watching the cooks do their thing on the other side of the food pass-through, when I felt a tap on the shoulder.

I turned to see Chief LaMond grin before she said, "Thought that was the back of your bald head."

I returned her smile. "Why don't you go ahead and say fat, old, and ugly while you're at it?"

"Now Chris, don't be hard on yourself. You're not that ugly."

I realized that insults from my friends were ways they showed that they cared. I then wondered if it was true of Theo's houseguests.

Cindy inched closer and nudged the man sitting to my right. He scooted his plate over and offered her his seat. She thanked him for his act of chivalry, which I suspected was more because she was chief. Either way, it worked.

"Any update on Wallace?"

Zack asked if she wanted anything. She said she's already had seventy-three cups of coffee this morning and better not add any more.

She leaned closer to me. "Detective Callahan called to say that Wallace was worse last night than he'd been since we hauled him in. As you know, that was already bad."

"What's he doing?"

"Callahan said that, every time someone looks the poor guy's way, he cracks a joke." She hesitated, and continued, "Well, he cracks part of a joke. Either the punchline is unrelated to the first part, or doesn't make a whit of sense. Callahan said the hospital staff isn't in stitches."

Convenient, I thought. "Do they think he's faking?"

"Callahan said that the head docs will need time to come to a definitive diagnosis." She retrieved a notebook from her rear pocket and flipped through a few pages. "They were throwing out terms like dissociative identity disorder, schizophrenia, dissociative amnesia, and other psychobabble that to this lowly cop meant nutzoid. None of the docs have bandied about the word faker."

I was more confused than before. Even if one of those

diagnoses was accurate, whether he knew what he was doing or not, he could have killed Michael.

"Chris, I'd love to stay and carry on an intellectual conversation about various psychiatric nomenclatures and taxonomies. Instead, I've got a meeting with one of my nutty officers who'd rather hand out tickets to vacationers whose cars have their tires an inch on the pavement than stopping people driving thirty miles an hour over the speed limit on Arctic."

I smiled. "Nomenclatures and taxonomies?"

Cindy elbowed me and said, "And you thought I was just another pretty face."

She hopped up and was gone before I could tell her that I was impressed, impressed with her vocabulary as well as her pretty face.

Chapter Forty-One

I was at Bert's the next day, grabbing an early-morning cup of coffee and a cinnamon roll, when Charles called to ask if I was up for a walk. We often took strolls around the island, but my friend seldom called this early to suggest one. I agreed to meet him in front of City Hall.

Charles would've been hard to miss. He was standing in front of the salmon-colored seat of local government and wearing a gold long-sleeve T-shirt with *Grambling State University* in black letters on the chest, and orange shorts that went as well with the T-shirt as would a flute in a rap band. His head was covered with a more traditional canvas, Tilley, with his feet covered with green-trimmed tennis shoes.

I chose not to mention his fashion statement, or maybe his getting dressed in the dark. Instead, I asked, "What direction?"

He waved in the direction of the Folly Pier. "The Pier or bust."

The two-block walk didn't rate *or bust*. I was pleased with what appeared to be a good mood from the man who hadn't exhibited many lately. "Lead on."

We crossed Cooper and waited for the traffic light to turn red before crossing Ashley. After another block, we were standing at the steps leading up to the structure and Pier 101 restaurant. Charles hadn't said more than a dozen words during the walk. The only words out of his mouth were when he carried on a brief conversation with a Dalmatian that was escorting its owner past us on the sidewalk. If Charles ever failed to talk to a passing canine, I'd know he was close to being committed.

The walk was a wise, albeit silent, choice. The sky was cloudless, the temperature a perfect, seventy-two degrees. We were far from the only people taking advantage of the weather. The Pier was more crowded than I'd seen in months. Groups of vacationers, apparent from chalky-white skin and resort clothing, competed for space with fishermen who lined sections of the railings. A couple with a man in a wheelchair and the woman walking along beside him, maneuvered around groups. They appeared to be enjoying the view, as well as the Pier's level surface.

Charles suggested that we go to the two story, diamond-shaped structure at the end.

We found a vacant picnic table shaded by the second-story roof, where he gazed at the beach and the Tides. He didn't speak for a long time. There was something on his mind, and I didn't want to give him an excuse not to tell me. I remained silent.

Charles leaned toward me but continued to gaze at the shore. "Remember when we first met?"

"Of course."

He smiled but didn't turn from looking at the hotel. "I had to spend a lot of time teaching you everything Folly. You were like a lost puppy in the middle of I-26."

"I don't think—"

"This isn't the spot where you argue," he interrupted. "Hear me out."

I nodded.

"I don't know what I saw in you. You were a stiff, prim and proper bureaucrat, whose sense of adventure was ordering onion rings instead of French fries. Anyway, I suppose my superhuman wisdom saw potential to turn that old you into a true Folly person."

"I think you—"

He waved his Tilley in my face. "What part of 'hear me out' befuddled you?"

I didn't know whether to laugh or apologize, so I stared at him.

"The point is that you gave me purpose, a challenge, something to do that was bigger than thinking about myself. You stumbled on a murder and, without my help, I'd be sitting here today talking to your ghost."

That wasn't how I remembered it.

"You opened the photo gallery and hired me—never paid me but hired me—to help run it. That was another challenge that I, if I say so myself, met with flying colors. I don't need to mention the close scrapes we've found ourselves in. Some gave me purpose, some gave me ulcers. Along came Heather, who gave me a chance at love, something that I never thought would happen."

He hesitated and looked down at the wooden deck, shook his head, and looked at me for the first time. "Franklin Roosevelt said, 'Be sincere, be brief, be seated.'"

Too late, I thought.

"Bottom line is that I'm rudderless, and don't know what to do about it."

He seldom admitted shortcomings. I had to think before responding.

"Charles, you're a wonderful person. You're liked by everyone you meet. Those who know you best love you. You've helped countless people. You've saved lives. How many people can say that?"

"History," he interrupted. "That's all history, some ancient, some recent. Still history."

I didn't want to get in a philosophic discussion about everything that all of us have accomplished is history. "Charles, that's true of all of us. You've led, you're leading, a good life, you've meant much to so many, and the world, especially the small corner of it on Folly Beach, is a much better place because of it. What makes you think you will change and not continue to bring joy to others?"

"Nothing, but——"

"But nothing. You don't know what's going to happen tomorrow. That's true. Neither do I, nor does anyone. What happened with you and Heather was sad. I think you loved each other. For whatever reason, it didn't work. Was it your fault? Some. Was it her fault? Some. Does that mean you won't find happiness with someone else? Absolutely not. The one thing I've learned about you is that you are at your best and feel the best about yourself when you're helping others. Is there a reason to think that you won't continue to do that?"

"I suppose not. You're right about it making me feel good."

"So, you're not rudderless, you simply don't know what direction your helping will turn you toward."

Charles smiled for the second time since we'd arrived on the pier. "So your best pep talk is I'm lost, don't know what direction I'm going, and not to worry. I won't run aground?"

I returned his smile. "Something like that."

"That's honest to God stupid, but I think I understand. I still don't hurt any less about losing Heather."

"You won't for a long time."

He picked at the cuticle on his left hand, stood, and looked over the railing to the deck below before returning to the bench. "Okay, have you got this mess with Theo, the funny guys, the dead bookie, and the missing, unmissing frog figured out?"

That was the Charles I'd come to admire and make fun of at every opportunity. Getting involved in someone else's problems was the quickest way to bring him out of his funk. I was determined to help him along the way. I told him what I'd learned about Wallace and his current state, about Horace leaving Janice, plus the latest on Neil, including that he'd been in prison a decade ago. He listened without interrupting which told me he wasn't over feeling rudderless.

I finished summarizing, and he said, "What again did Theo tell you that Ray said to, umm, Pete I guess, before Ray charged out of Cal's during the comedians first appearance?"

"Something about Wallace killing the audience. I'm not sure of the exact words. Why?"

"Could that mean Ray was implying that Wallace killed something other than the audience?"

"I don't know. Theo wasn't clear about what he heard. He said all of them were down each other's throats the entire night, even before they got to Cal's."

"Don't suppose we can go right to the horse's mouth to find out since Ray bounced down the steps to the hereafter."

"I'll ask Pete."

"You do that." Charles hesitated before saying, "See, I'm already helping."

I put my arm around his shoulder. "Yes, you are."

"My rudder's on the mend. Why don't we mosey over to Theo's house and see if the sleeping beauties are awake yet, so we can ask Pete?"

It was still before 10:00. I told Charles that from what I had seen on previous visits, Theo may be awake, but the odds that Pete and Sal were vertical were near zero.

"If our p.m. is their a.m., I'll meet you outside Theo's at two. Don't be late."

I told him that was a plan, not one I would have preferred, although it was one that would keep Charles involved in something other than himself. Instead of talking to Pete, I'd rather talk to Theo first. I was unclear what he had said about what Ray told Pete about killing the audience. It may have been nothing, but the word killing still stuck with me.

———

I was standing at the bottom of Theo's steps at 1:30, looking around for my friend. Instead of seeing Charles, my phone rang. His name was on the screen.

"Guess what?" Charles said.

I smiled. "You got a pet aardvark."

"Guess again."

"Why don't you tell me?"

"You're still no fun. Okay, Dude has me delivering a wetsuit for some guy from London, the one in England, who's staying at a big ole mansion out West Ashley Avenue. Something about the guy doesn't have a car with him. He just absolutely has to surf this afternoon, *old chap*, and needs the *bloody* wetsuit."

I was surprised. "Dude, the master of the annihilated vocabulary, said it like that?"

"Course not. That's my interpretation of whatever he said."

"Are you saying you're not coming to Theo's?"

"No. I'll be a couple of minutes late. Must go, the Brit's awaitin' to catch a wave."

I told him that I'd wait for him in the vacant lot across the street.

He said, "Cheers."

I turned to cross the street, when the front door opened.

Pete stuck his head out and yelled, "You selling encyclopedias or wanting me to join the Mormons?"

I smiled. "Yeah, you buying or converting?"

He motioned me up the steps and said, "Got a question that's been bothering me since 1979. If everybody says you're not supposed to eat at night, why's there a lightbulb in the refrigerator?"

I humored him with a smile, thought, *Once a comedian, always a comedian,* and followed him into the house.

Before I could tell him that Charles was on his way, Pete patted me on the back and said, "Heard anything about Wallace or the dead bookie?"

Then it hit me. I was looking at the person who first asked about the dead bookie. I was looking at the man who wouldn't have had any reason to know the occupation of the man found murdered at the beach. Unless ….

How do I ease out of here or stall for Charles to arrive? *Stay calm,* I told myself. *Act natural.* I told him that I hadn't heard anything about the bookie or Wallace, and said, "Is Theo here?"

Pete pushed the front door closed. "Yep, Old ET's roaming around upstairs. Go on up."

I looked at the steps leading to the second floor. "I don't want to bother him. I'll come back later."

I turned and saw Pete several feet behind me. He looked like anything but a comedian. I saw nothing funny about the pistol in his right hand, the pistol pointed at my heart.

The same moment I noticed the gun, the front door flung open. Charles stepped in and saw me standing by the stairs. Pete had moved behind the door and out of Charles's line of sight.

Charles was breathing heavily, took a deep breath, and said, "Hope it's okay for me to barge in. I saw the door close, so I figured you'd be close."

Pete stepped out from behind the door and slammed Charles's head with the weapon. My friend's eyes rolled up in his head and he hit the floor like a sack of rocks. He didn't utter a sound on the way down.

I started to kneel to see how he was when Pete slammed the door, mumbled a string of profanities, and again, pointed the pistol at me.

Chapter Forty-Two

"Let me help my friend," I said, staring at the gun.

Pete motioned for me to go up the stairs. "He'll be fine. That's the least of your worries."

Charles still didn't make a sound. I was afraid he was dead but didn't get a chance to check.

Pete barked, "Upstairs. Now!"

He was four feet behind me, too far away for me to reach the firearm. I shook my head and started up the steps.

Pete said, "Know what Theo said about you?"

I walked up two more steps when he said, "Stop. Change of plans."

I stopped and waited for directions.

He appeared indecisive, looked up the stairs, and said, "We're going to the kitchen." He waved the handgun in that direction.

I descended the steps, glanced down at Charles's unmoving body, and headed toward the kitchen.

"What'd Theo say about me?"

"After you left the first time I met you, the old coot kept

going on, and on, and on, about how you singlehandedly caught more killers than all the cops in South Carolina combined. Sal and Wallace laughed like they thought he was joking. I figured he was exaggerating. Either way, I stuck that bit of trivia in here." He hesitated then, with his free hand, pointed to his head.

"You killed Michael Hardin," I said, to keep him talking.

"I've got the mic. You'll get your turn."

The only sound I heard was coming from Pete, so I assumed either Theo wasn't in the house or, if he was, he was unable to say anything, like my friend splayed out on the entry floor. I waited for him to continue.

"I wasn't worried. Poor Wallace was doing a bang-up job convincing everyone that he killed the guy. He was nearby when the bookie took his last breath but didn't get there soon enough to see what happened. He was so out of it, he couldn't tell if he saw what he saw, or if he imagined it." He hesitated and chuckled. "Saw, see, seesaw, there's a joke in there somewhere. I bet you don't think it's funny." His smile turned to a frown. "The poor guy's been losing it for years. The rest of us have been propping him up, pretending he's sane." He chucked again. "I would've loved to have seen his face when the cop showed him the credit card that magically appeared under his mattress. That would've been worth the price of admission."

"I didn't—"

He waved the gun in my face.

I closed my mouth.

We entered the kitchen, Pete looked around, then back at me. "I kept seeing you nosing around. You weren't buying Wallace's confession. You were looking at each of us like we were criminals, not hilarious Legends. It damned near hurt my feelings. I knew, as sure as I'm standing here, that you were going to be a thorn in my side. I don't know how, but you were going to figure it out. You understand why I couldn't have that, don't you? Know what my plan was?"

"What?"

Pete appeared distracted like he was trying to find something in the kitchen. I faced him and with my right hand, slipped the phone out of my back pocket. If I could tap 911, the dispatcher might hear our conversation and trace the call. I slid my finger over the screen to unlock it and glanced back to see the phone icon.

Two things happened. Pete looked at my hand holding the phone, and the phone rang. Pete lunged toward me as I saw Chief LaMond's name on the screen.

Before I hit the answer button, Pete smacked the phone out of my hand. He muttered a profanity as the device hit the floor. The screen cracked on impact. The rest of the phone met instant death when Pete stomped on it. His arm holding the gun bounced around like it had a mind of its own, but not for long.

Pete took a deep breath, moved the gun in its previous position pointing at my head, then grinned like nothing had happened. "I was going to get you and Wallace somewhere together and put a bullet in your meddling body. You'd be able to visit the bookie guy. Poor Wallace is so brain-rattled that I could convince him that he shot you, then sit back and watch him confess to a second murder. Poor, pitiful Wallace would spend the rest of his days in a nuthouse. I'd mourn the loss of one of Theo's friends, and be so sad about poor Wallace." He shook his head and made a clicking sound with his mouth.

Pete slammed the butt of the gun against the wall. I jumped. He laughed. "Wallace screwed my plan up when he went loony. He got the cops interested enough to find the credit card and haul him off before my perfect crime could commence. When Wallace was at his best, oh so many years ago, he had trouble with timing. Even you, one of the least funny people I know, could understand how that could mess up a joke." He looked down at the gun, then back at me. "A recent study found that women who carry a little extra weight live longer than men who mention it."

I sighed. How could I get the gun away without getting killed?

"See, knew you didn't have a sense of humor. That was funny."

"Why'd you kill the bookie?" I asked, to stall.

He laughed, again. "Who said I killed him. Think I'm stupid? If I said I did it, I'd be admitting to a crime. Now shut up and let me think about plan B, that being how to get rid of you and get away with it. I've almost got it, so chill." He chuckled. "That was funny, wasn't it?" He looked around the room.

I inched my way toward the patio door.

He twirled back to me. "My humorless friend, where do you think you're going?"

I stopped.

He smiled, not the kind he would use on stage, but one teemed with anger. He motioned with the gun for me to sit. "I'm getting long in the tooth, not as fast as I used to be, but bullets are swift."

I sat. He hadn't admitting to killing the bookie, so I tried another theory that had been rattling around in my head. "Why'd you push Ray down the stairs?"

His eyes narrowed, and he nodded. "Theo was right about you. Didn't you pay attention to the idiot cops? Poor drunken Ray got up in the middle of the night in a strange house. It was dark up there." He pointed the gun to the ceiling before returning it to my head. "Everyone knows he stumbled out in the hall in a drunken stupor and fell down the steps. A tragic accident."

I needed to keep him talking. "Did he know you killed Michael Hardin?"

Pete sighed. "There you go again. Did I say I killed the bookie, or anyone else for that matter?"

I didn't respond.

"Okay, let's pretend I'm not only a comedy legend but, in my spare time, I'm a genie. If you're stupid enough to make your last wish a question about a damned bookie, I'll answer. Yes, I killed him."

"Why?"

"Sal fed his brother some fantasy about us being successful, playing all over the country to sold-out crowds, rolling in dough. Fed him the story that the reason we showed up here was out of concern for Theo." He shrugged. "Suppose some of that's true. Sal was worried about Theo. When we got here, it took us seven minutes to figure out that Theo was in better shape than we were. There was nothing wrong with his mind. Years ago, we were hot stuff on the comedy tour. The key words being *years ago*." He looked over my head and shook his head. "I told you before, we're broke. That's a condition I'm not comfortable with."

"So, you killed him for money?"

"Duh."

I didn't know what I'd hoped would happen. What I knew was, the longer I kept him talking, the better chance something would happen—or so I prayed.

"How'd you meet Michael or learn he had money on him?"

"You know what, it's like hanging around in this house with two old farts who think everything they say is a joke, one son of a ... umm, son of one of the old farts who thinks the only jokes in the house are the rest of us, and took every opportunity to make fun of us or put us down?"

"No, I don't—"

He waved the gun in my face. "Then, there's the slowest moving human in history who tries to be nice to each of us, but grates on my nerves like a piece of sandpaper. That's a long way to say that I got out of here every chance I could. I walked around, would've liked to plant my ass on a barstool at one of your bars, but didn't have enough money to buy a used beer."

He hadn't answered my question but was helping me stall. "So?"

"I was out on that long pier, saw some well-dressed guy wearing a god-awful looking hat with, would you believe, a feather sticking out the top. He was scrunched up against another guy. He looked around like he was hawking meth. I figured he was a dope dealer. One thing those guys have in common, other than selling death in a plastic bag, is a roll of cash. I thought there goes my bank, walking down the beach. I jogged down the handicap ramp then followed him out past where people were sunning themselves in front of the hotel."

Still no sounds from Charles.

"A robbery gone bad."

"You make it sound so cold. I wanted a permanent loan, not to hurt him. He was a drug dealer. It would've been stupid for him to go to the cops about being robbed. I caught up with him and didn't think there was anyone nearby. I pulled this out of my pocket and said for him to give me his money. The damn dealer looked at the gun, up at my face, said something like he didn't want any trouble, then asked if he owed me money. That confused the hell out of me. Why would a drug dealer owe me money? I asked him why. He acted like I should know." Pete rolled his eyes. "The guy said he was a bookie."

"Because taking bets wasn't as big a crime as selling drugs, you thought that he might go to the police to report a robbery, and—"

"I couldn't have that, could I?"

"Shooting him would draw too much attention."

"Sure would. Your god of the sea, Neptune, left a piece of wood by the bookie's feet. Unfortunate for him, he lunged for it. It all happened before I could think. He was a lot younger than me, but not as quick." He shook his head. "I grabbed the wood, swung it at him before he got to me. He was deader than a doornail, as they say. I found a bundle of cash in his pocket, grabbed it, and casually strolled away." He hesitated and shook his head again. "Did you know there are more than 300 million people living in this country?"

I didn't think this was a time to show off. I stared at him and waited for his point.

"Out of all 300 million, what are the odds that the one person who happened to come by after I took the guys money was Wallace? Whatever the odds, it was lucky for me. Lucky because he didn't see me—lucky that he was so out of it he confessed just because he happened to see the body. Considering where he is now, it was unlucky for Wallace. If the bookie was still alive, he could have taken bets on what would happen next."

"Why'd you kill Ray?"

"Do you ever stop asking questions?"

"You told me about the bookie. We both know you don't plan to let me live to tell anyone, so you might as well tell me."

"Perceptive fellow, aren't you? You're right. Why'd I kill Ray? Good question. It could've been because he was one of the most obnoxious humans I've ever known. Believe me, I've known my share. I didn't think he knew anything until the day we went to Cal's to ask—beg—for a gig. Ray came up to me and in his self-righteous, cocky, demeaning way, said something like, 'I know what you did.' I played dumb, acted like I didn't know what he was talking about. He said killing the guy was the only way I could have come up with the money I started spending. Said he'd make me pay. At Cal's, he made that smartass comment about all Wallace killed was the audience. When we got back here, Ray was in his room. After everybody either went to sleep or were in an alcohol-induced coma, I went to his room to have it out."

"What'd he say?"

"He was so drunk, I had trouble figuring out what he was saying. He laughed and said I'd get mine. Then he made a mistake, turned out to be a deadly one. He stumbled to the hall and announced he was going for a beer. Let's just leave it at me helping him down the stairs." Pete gave me another sinister smile and tapped his non-gun toting hand on the granite island. "Got it?"

"Got what?"

"Plan B. Your grand finale."

Chapter Forty-Three

I had hoped to find a way to distract the gun-toting comedian before he came up with an alternative plan to kill me and, if he wasn't already dead, kill Charles. That was not to be.

He kept the gun trained on me, stepped back to the sink, and grabbed the purple dish-washing gloves from the top drawer. "Take baby steps to the great room. Don't try anything funny. Pretend like your and your friend's lives depend on it." He chuckled. "I suppose they do. For a few minutes."

He was still too far away for me to reach, so I followed his instructions. I was in the center of the room as he moved to look out the double doors leading to the deck.

"You're so nosy about everything, I think you'll be interested in hearing Plan B."

"Yes," I said, in hopes it may give me a way to thwart it.

"It's more painful than Plan A." He laughed. "More painful for me, no different for you." He waved the gun in front of his face. "You won't be around for most of the plan, so I'll give you a preview. First, we will drag your friend's body to the kitchen where he's going to be on the floor near the door. You're going to be lying on the floor about right where you are now. You'll be dead. If your friend isn't already, he will be shortly."

"You don't want to—"

"Shut up. I'm telling the story. Here's where my pain comes in. I'm going to shoot myself in the arm. A flesh wound, you know, the kind that'll bleed all over Theo's ritzy room." He chuckled. "Hell, I'll drip some on his expensive couch just to piss him off." He held the purple elbow-length gloves out for me to see. "Oh, yeah, in case you were wondering why I have these with me, I'm going to wear one on my gun hand. Want to hear more?"

I said yes, hoping for a miracle.

He moved the pistol to his other hand, pointed the forefinger on the hand that previously held the deadly weapon, and pointed it at his upper arm. "Bang, two shots, or three shots in case Charles ain't already visiting the bookie. See, no gunshot residue on my hand or arm. Look at me, Mr. Policeman, I couldn't have done it." He grinned. "Anyway, with my arm feeling like it'd been bit by an alligator, I'm going to walk out there, fill the gloves with sand and tie the ends together. It's such a lovely day, I'll stroll to the end of Theo's private pier, throw the gun and gloves in the river, never to be seen again.

"I'll come back in, call 911, and tell the cops about a masked intruder who slipped in the back door. You know, the door I'll leave unlocked after depositing the gun and gloves. The guy was in a rage and going to rob Theo. Everyone knows he has money. Instead of money, the intruder found you, Charles, and me. Wow, was the gunman surprised? That's why he hit Charles over the head and shot us. He must've panicked. He ran out instead of stealing anything. Such a terrible thing to have happen." He shook his head, and grinned. "There it is, Plan B."

"The police are good. What makes you think you'll get away with it?"

"You give them too much credit. What reason would I have for shooting you? What kind of fool would they think I was to shoot myself? Don't forget, poor old Wallace has already admitting to killing the bookie. Everyone knows that Wallace's evil sperm, Ray, got himself drunk and fell down the stairs. You see, everything is solved, except catching the bad guy who came in here, killed you, killed your buddy, and thought he'd done the same to me. Yep, the perfect crime. Sadly, I won't even get to hear an appreciative audience give me a standing ovation. *C'est la vie.*"

He was so proud of his plan that I thought he was going to take a bow, regardless if there was an audience or not.

He didn't get a chance. The front door swung open. Theo yelled, "I'm back!"

Things happened so quickly that I wasn't sure of the sequence of events. I think Pete jumped back and twisted his body, so it faced the open front door.

Theo stared at Charles on the floor then at Pete, and said, "What's going—"

His question was interrupted by a gunshot. Theo collapsed.

I took two steps to the table along the wall and grabbed the silver frog.

Pete jerked back around to me, and yelled, "Stop!"

I swung my arm, and the frog caught him on the side of the head.

He staggered and fell to one knee.

Before I could get away, he grabbed my other arm as he raised his gun hand.

I didn't have as much leverage. I yanked my arm as far as I could, managed to bring the frog back around, and caught his wrist with the silver amphibian.

The gun bounced on the floor.

Pete screamed, bared his teeth, and reached for the firearm with his good hand.

He may have been a weightlifter in years gone by, but most of Pete's muscles had turned to flab. I still couldn't afford to let him get a solid grip on me. I kicked the gun under the couch, then hit him one more time with the frog.

He went down for the count. I thanked Wallace, or whomever had taken the frog, for returning it.

Pete wasn't moving, so I rushed to Theo lying half in the doorway. I didn't see a bullet hole or blood on my friend. I gave a sigh of relief. I grabbed Theo's phone and punched in 911. The second-best thing I heard was the dispatcher saying that emergency vehicles were on their way. The best thing I heard was a moan coming from Charles as he slowly moved his arm to the back of his head. I breathed another sigh of relief when Theo started to sit up.

Charles slowly sat, closed his eyes, and said, "Sorry I was late to the party. What'd I miss?"

I alternated between catching my breath and laughing although, if pressed, I wouldn't be able to tell what was so funny. Being alive trumped funny.

Sirens came from all directions before Charles regained his composure. "What happened?"

Theo had moved to a seated position and leaned back against the doorframe. "I'll second that question."

I told them they'd have to wait to be part of my audience when I told the police.

Chapter Forty-Four

"How come 'you're a peach' is a complement but 'you're bananas' is an insult?" Sal asked the standing room only crowd at Cal's. "Why are we allowing fruit discrimination to tear society apart?"

The room was not torn apart with uproarious laughter, although a sizable number of patrons laughed, a handful applauded. I attributed most of it to the clusters of empty beer bottles sitting on many of the tables. I attributed the laughter coming from those sitting at the two tables I'd pulled together two hours ago to several things, none of which were the jokes Sal was sharing from the stage.

It'd been two weeks—two traumatic weeks—since my near-death experience at Theo's. Tonight, I would've laughed if Sal was reading the phone book. I was alive, something I wouldn't have put money on that fateful day.

Charles, who'd spent the first week after being assaulted in his apartment, complaining about headaches, finally ventured out to tonight's performance. He leaned my direction. "Think he really got someone to pay him real money for telling those jokes?"

Cindy and Larry LaMond were sitting beside Charles. "Hush," Larry said, "I'm trying to listen. That guy's funny."

Cindy put her arm around her husband. "Larry thinks a can of Drano's funny. He doesn't get out much." She kissed him on the cheek.

"Eww," Charles said as he rolled his eyes.

Despite a concussion and incessant complaining about headaches, he'd shown more life and enthusiasm the last two weeks than I had seen in months. As tragic as it may have been, he seemed to thrive when first, there was something bad happening, and second, when he could help be part of the solution, albeit a painful part. I was thrilled to see him back to being Charles.

Sal continued unfazed. "Don't know why those prospectors out west during the gold rush had so much trouble. All they had to do was dig where the gold was. Who knows, maybe they needed the exercise."

"Larry thinks that's funny?" Charles asked.

"So did one guy over there," I said tilting my head toward the table where I thought I heard laughter, or maybe someone belching.

Sal said, "Any married man should forget his mistakes. There's no use in two people remembering the same thing."

A spattering of laughter followed, along with a couple of groans.

Sal reached for a bottle of water on the floor.

Theo took advantage of the break in the hilarity. "Guys, thanks for coming out. This has been a rough time for Sal. He feels horrible about subjecting me and all of you to Wallace, Ray, and don't even get him started on Pete."

"Any news on Wallace?" Barb asked.

Over the last fourteen days, she heard more about the group of comedians than anyone should have been subjected to. I'd spent several hours in her bookstore, talking about the near-tragic events, then when we went to the Dog for breakfast, 5,000 of Folly's 2,000 locals had stopped by our table to ask about the comedians and to share their experiences with the funny men.

Theo looked at the stage where Sal was still sipping water. "Afraid he's going to be in the psychiatric ward for a long time. At least Pete's confession got him off the hook for killing the bookie."

"What about stealing your money?" she asked.

Theo glanced at Sal and turned to face Barb. "I'm not pressing charges. I told Cindy I might have misplaced the cash."

Barb grinned. "Did she believe you?"

"Can't imagine she did, but she let it slide. Poor Wallace will be going through enough misery without adding that to his plate. Besides, he brought the frog back. That little hunk of silver ended up making it possible for Chris and me to be here tonight."

Sal tapped on the mic to regain everyone's attention and smiled. "Two construction workers were building a wooden storage shed. One worker was surprised to see the other going through the box of nails and throwing out half of them and said, 'Why are you doing that?' The other worker said, 'Those nails have the heads on the wrong end.' The first worker said, 'You idiot. They're for the other side of the shed.'"

The joke received the best response of the evening, and even Sal laughed. I suspected it was more from relief than thinking what he'd said was that funny.

Cal joined us after helping Joy and Kristin deliver beers to his thirsty crowd. He looked toward the entry, waved at some-one, and said, "Neil, tomorrow, 5:00. See you then."

I turned and saw Neil leaving. "Cal, what's that about?"

He looked toward the door. "I figured, with all the new funny business I'll be bringing in, I'll need more help in the kitchen. Did you know Neil's a cook?"

I told him that I did.

"He's going to be using that talent working here."

"That's great."

Cal pulled his chair close to Charles, Barb, and me.

"Cal," Barb said, "I hear you're going to let Sal do comedy between your sets on the weekends."

Cal pushed his Stetson back. "He's spent a lot of time in here since the frog conking at Theo's. He's not a bad guy. According to Theo, the old broken-down comedian's going to become a permanent resident of our island." Cal leaned closer to Barb. "Tell him this, and I'll swear on a stack of Lenny Bruce albums that I never said it. I think we could become friends."

Charles, who apparently had been suffering withdrawal symptoms from not being the center of attention, tapped Cal on the arm. "Woodrow Wilson said, 'Friendship is the only cement that will ever hold the world together.'"

Sal must have been channeling Woodrow Wilson when he said, "Folks, it's been great being here with you tonight. I hope you come back Friday, when I'll be sharing the stage with my good friend, the legendary Country Cal. And, speaking of friends, let me finish with an observation. Friends wave red flags when you have a bad idea. Real friends pick up a camera."

About the Author

Bill Noel is the best-selling author of sixteen novels in the popular Folly Beach Mystery series. Besides being an award-winning novelist, Noel is a fine arts photographer and lives in Louisville, Kentucky, with his wife, Susan, and his off-kilter imagination. Learn more about the series, and the author by visiting www.billnoel.com.